BEST SF: 1973

BEST SF: 1973

Edited by

HARRY HARRISON

and

BRIAN W. ALDISS

G. P. Putnam's Sons, New York

INDEXED IN 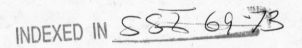 S82 69-73

Copyright Acknowledgments

Contents

Introduction

The river of science fiction rushes silently from the past into the future, widening steadily, growing in volume. We cannot dam it, nor would we want to, but we can, as we do in this annual anthology, dip in and sample its waters. Here is what we found in the year 1973.

Schools are teaching more and more courses in science fiction. No one dares guess how many high schools teach SF, but by the enthusiastic sales of the first text aimed directly at these readers *(A Science Fiction Reader,* Scribner Student Paperbacks), and the surge of similar texts now in production, the classes must number in the thousands. While last year there were about two hundred American colleges and universities with SF courses, this year there appear to be four hundred. The number has doubled. Does this mean eight hundred in 1974? If it keeps up there will be 102,400 classes by 1981 when SF takes over all higher education

A new science fiction magazine, *Vertex*, has appeared and as of this writing is well and flourishing. It is a handsome production with two color interiors and most glossy, large of size, and costing $1.50, and we wish it all health and prosperity. No SF magazines died during the year, though the bottom two still stagger under the burden of dropping sales and indifferent stories, and we wish them luck as well if only to see two old and treasured names spared from extinction. Sales are up on all the other magazines and that, too, is a healthy and happy sign.

And more original anthologies have been published and more appear to be on the way. These provide sound and remunerative markets for writers and we are happy to see them and read them all.

Six of the stories in *Best SF: 1973* are from original anthologies while only four stories come from the traditional science fiction magazines. This is a good trend, a sign that science fiction has emerged (is emerging?) from the ghetto at last. Perhaps an indication of the trend is the William Harrison story anthologized from *Esquire*, a magazine that never printed SF before and, so it is rumored, swore it never would. Perhaps they were waiting for the moment when a writer of stature from outside the SF field would write an SF story that they could, quite rightly, snap up.

The cinema still enjoys its love-hate affair with science fiction. They know SF makes money, but are afraid to hire anyone who knows anything about SF to be involved in films. Even when they purchase an SF novel they make sure that the author has nothing to do with the script. Despite this a bit of the original occasionally leaks through and *Soylent Green* appears to be the biggest grossing film that MGM had in 1973. Goodness knows the authors are waiting restlessly in the wings, waving their stories enthusiastically, and will be happy to rush forward if asked. We can only hope this will happen soon.

This was also the year that saw the publication of the first critical history of science fiction (*Billion Year Spree* by Brian W. Aldiss, Doubleday and Company). Though academic attention and writing have been focused on SF for many years now, there has been no single volume that attempted a survey of the entire field. SF fans who tried this exercise came closer in scale, but their attempts suffered from either personal biases or indifferent scholarship. Now our own Mr. Aldiss has done the complete job in a book that was acclaimed on both sides of the Atlantic and which is destined for continual success as the official text on the subject.

In the realm of the SF novel a new award was presented for the first time this year. This is the John W. Campbell Memorial Award for the best novel of the year. It carries with it a handsome trophy and the sum of six hundred dollars. The first award went to Barry Malzberg for his *Beyond Apollo* (Random House). Five judges —authors, critics, and professors of science fiction—read all of the novels and made their studied selection. That this is an award of literary as well as science fictional value cannot be denied, and we sincerely hope it will live forever and prosper. The award, under the guidance of Dr. Willis McNelly, is presented in the spring at California State University at Fullerton.

The annual world science fiction convention was held in Toronto, Canada, this year with a record membership. A convention "first" was an electronic tentacle belonging to the computer at the City of Toronto Finance Department data processing center wriggling into the convention hotel where it could be consulted. Two of its programmers (SF readers, obviously, when not on the job), John Fruhwirth and Craig Gregory, instructed the electronic beast to write SF stories by programming it with Gahan Wilson's "Science Fiction Horror Movie Pocket Computer." If that item sounds familiar it should—because it was published in *Best SF: 1971.* Using this program the computer created original stories by joining together a series of randomly selected phrases. (Can this be all that the writers have been doing through the years? The mind boggles.) To zip up the stories that it wrote—and undoubtedly to stir envy in the hearts of the authors—its memory contained the names of many SF writers. The computer used these as part of its raw material and wrote the authors into its stories as characters, no doubt a well-deserved fate. One of the stories it wrote is as follows:

THE EARTH IS ATTACKED BY GIANT VENUSIAN REPTILES WHO LOOK UPON US ONLY AS A SOURCE OF NOURISHMENT AND ARE HIGHLY RADIOACTIVE, AND WHO CANNOT BE KILLED BY HARRY HARRISON AND BRIAN ALDISS WHO SHOOT AT THEM WITH LASER CANNONS, BUT THEY PUT US UNDER A BENIGN DICTATORSHIP AND EVERYONE LIVES HAPPILY EVER AFTER.

Other than having a tendency to run-on sentences the computer seems a workmanlike writer in the older tradition, and if we won't be seeing any stories from it in the magazines I am sure that it has a great future in films.

As a climax to this survey of attention to SF from outside the field is a document I hold titled "Preaching and Worship Schedule," from a church that is not mentioned (presumably all who attend know it is there), which from internal evidence is not Jewish or Catholic. It says that "the sermon series in August and September will be based on some of the books and short stories of Ray Bradbury. The first one, titled 'The Voice of the Clock' uses both *The Martian Chronicles* and Mathew 6:25-34 for source material." Things *are* changing, aren't they? Remember the covers of *Planet Stories,* where many Bradbury stories appeared with the girl, in brass brassiere and celluloid spacesuit, being attacked by a space monster?

Despite the ever-widening impact of SF no one is still really sure just what the stuff is. In the introduction to last year's volume I attempted to deal with the definition of this slippery medium, and now I shall carry that attempt a step farther. I have never seen a definition of the term "science fiction" that completely pleased me. They all err to one extreme or the other, either being too narrow in definition ("stories about rocket ships and time machines") or so broad they bring in most of modern fiction ("the impact of science upon people" or "stories that might be true" as opposed to fantsasy which consists of stories that could not be true).

Not that there will be any wont of trying. Science fiction writers have often been approached to write definitions for dictionaries and encyclopedias and have rushed into the fray. I have heard many panel discussions at science fiction conventions about the meaning of this term. It is strange, but all of them reached similar conclusions. Either finding a definition so short that it did not work—or producing a page of qualifications that might work if you could wend your way through them.

Though I doubt if I shall lay this fascinating controversy to rest forever, I can at least make a try. First we must toss aside all of the pretenders to the name, including scientifiction which should be dead by now, pace its creator the noble Hugo Gernsback. Nor can we hide behind speculative fiction or science fantasy or any of the others. I rather like the Italian *fantascienza*; it rolls off the tongue so smoothly, but I am afraid it doesn't work in English. It is interesting to note that many other languages, after trying to create a term on their own, simply drop back to using the correct English one. Except the Germans, of course, who with their joyous love of organization have at least a dozen different terms for what they think are the different types of science fiction, a specie of Linnean camouflage for the fact that they simply don't have a single one that works. The Russians on the other hand—how our language reflects our culture—refuse to have even a single term for SF. Perhaps they will come to it someday, and simply lump the stuff under the general heading of fantasy and let it go at that.

In order to see if we can arrive at a simple definition let us begin by defining our subject. What exactly *is* science fiction? Getting answers is many times the art of answering the right question—and this is the right question. Let us go to the beginning and narrow down on our target.

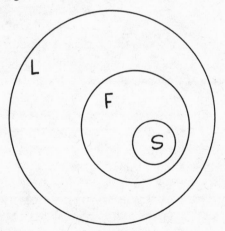

In the beginning there is literature, world literature, and, in this diagram, it will be seen as the large circle L which encloses everything. We shall attach specific definitions to terms used for the sake of this argument, so that literature here is defined as the totality of all written world literature that is fiction. Works of the imagination. Within this circle you will find the French antinovel, the English gothics, Russian, Japanese, and Basque fiction of all kinds. It is all here.

Within the larger circle L there is a smaller one which is F. This is fantasy. Part of the greater whole of fiction. And, within fantasy, we have the smaller circle that encloses the area known as science fiction, circle S.

I do not think that any of these statements can be contested. Science fiction is fantasy and fantasy is certainly fiction—so there we are.

Well, just where are we? Coming close to the promised definition, but not quite there yet. Before we reach it I would like you to consider an axiom. Not the axiom the dictionaries define as "a recognized truth," but the one with the mathematical definition. A proposition which is assumed without proof for the sake of studying the consequences that follow from it. So here is the axiom; let the consequences fall where they may.

$$SFQ = \frac{F + L + 6}{S}$$

SFQ is our Science Fiction Quotient which, leaving humility aside for the moment, I shall call Harrisons' Axiom, the measure of the science fiction content of a story. (The plural Harrison is explained by the fact that, while the theory is mine, the actual construction of the axiom owes a great deal to my son Todd, who is much more at home with mathematics.) S is science fiction, F fiction, and L literature as they apply in the diagram.

The reasoning behind this axiom, as can be seen in the diagram, is that science fiction is a new thing in the world, a construction of man just like his culture and his automobiles. New things define themselves by existing. We invent them, we know what they are, then apply a new term to a referent that has just come into existence.

The dictionary says that an automobile is "a vehicle, especially one for passengers, carrying its own power-generating and propelling mechanism for travel on ordinary roads." Oh, like a motorcy-

cle or a steamroller? Well, no, we'll have to define a bit more . . .
thereby falling into the same endless SF definition trap. The only
short SF definition that works, like the one for the automobile, is
"SF is what I am pointing at when I say this is SF." But this is too
subjective and we should have a definition that is a bit more
rigorous, one applicable by constant rules. Therefore this axiom
which attempts to determine the "science fictionness" of a story.

Let us determine how it works and begin with an unarguable
sample of hardcore, solid fuel SF. Any one of Van Vogt's stories
of the War against the Rull will fit, "Cooperate or Else" being a
fine example. No one would deny that all of this story falls within
the science fiction circle—there are no gnomes or elves and the
story would never be published in *Harper's*. If we say that any
story has six parts to be divided up and assigned to categories, this
story gets the full six in SF and emerges with an SFQ of 1. Unity,
the real thing.

Now let us venture away from the hardcore a bit and consider the
Aldiss story "Hothouse." This is at least half science fiction, for a
3 in that category, because this is a scientific prediction of the state
of the world in the far future when the sun gets a good bit warmer
and causes a large number of mutations. But cobwebs to the Moon
must be fantasy, as lovely as the concept is, and, since no part of
the story is out there in L, the mainstream, the other 3 parts go to
fantasy alone to produce an SFQ of 3.

Now take *Tarzan,* pride of the Burroughs bibliophiles. A slight
whif of SF with the Scientific gimmickry here and there, but worth
no more than a 1 in that category. And at least a 1 for the L
category, for it is really pure action fiction most of the time. And a
well-deserved 4 in F for talking apes (they don't), hidden cities,
total unreality of Africa, and such. The SFQ is 11.

Consider next *Arrowsmith*. I mention this novel because Robert
Heinlein once attempted to define science fiction in an essay. His
definition is one hundred and seventy words long and still doesn't
work. One reason it does not work, as has been pointed out, is that
Arrowsmith is an SF novel according to this definition. Let's see
how it shapes up by the SFQ. It certainly has no science fictional or

fantasy content and sits firmly in the realm of L as a mainstream novel about a hard-working doctor. Its SFQ is 0.

A pattern has been formed—as well as a recognition that there is hardcore science fiction, fringe and borderline SF, and a number of variations in between. One is science fiction, the pure quill. The science fictional content diminishes numericially up to 11, which is fringe SF that barely qualifies. All else is 0 and does not belong, for the answer falls into the null set and is beyond the realm of SF.

The SFQ is a very useful tool to work out whether those borderline cases have any SF content at all. In this way the Hobbit stories are pure fantasy and rate a 12, and have nothing to do with SF at all. If one cares to call them SF to any degree, assigning a meager one, the area that is SF must be clearly defined in order for it to creep into the outermost fringe SF category. A book like *On the Beach* must surely rate an S of 2 or 3 for its extrapolation of the affects of nuclear bomb warfare, so it has an SFQ of 5 or 3, thus reassuring our intuition that it is indeed SF.

Using the SFQ we begin to realize that the trouble with many earlier definitions of science fiction is that they attempted a *yes* or *no* description. It either is or is not science fiction. This does not work. The definition of SF is very firm at the center, but gets more and more ragged until it gets out to the very edge and ceases having any science fictional content at all.

The definition of science fiction is:
Science fiction is.

As always in this annual anthology we try to bring you the best, the most interesting, the most provocative of the science fiction stories published during the year. All the way from the sturdy 1 rating to the occasional 11 when the story is too good to pass up. I say *we* because, as always, I owe a great deal to the efforts of my English colleague, Brian W. Aldiss, who scours the British and world publishing scene for stories of interest. The *we* this year also includes Professor Bruce McAllister, who between teaching stints (classes in English and science fiction, of course) helps delve into the unlikely as well as the likely places. He is no stranger to this series for you will find his very first story anthologized in *Best SF: 1969*.

Their aid is not only appreciated but greatly needed since science fiction, no longer completely the child of scorn, is appearing in the most unlikely places. As always, the final choice of all the stories is completely my own.

Once again, I am happy to report, it has been a good year for science fiction.

Harry Harrison

Roller Ball Murder

WILLIAM HARRISON

William Harrison is well known for his short stories and novels —such as Lessons In Paradise *(1971)—that are not science fiction. He teaches creative writing at the University of Arkansas, though at the present he is in London enjoying the benefits of a Guggenheim Award. Here is his first SF story, a very chill look at the world and at the future of the spectator sports we so enjoy.*

The game, the game: here we go again. All glory to it, all things I am and own are because of Roller Ball Murder.

Our team stands in a row, twenty of us in salute as the corporation hymn is played by the band. We view the hardwood oval track which offers us the rewards of mayhem: fifty yards long, thirty yards across the ends, high-banked, and at the top of the walls the cannons which fire those frenzied twenty-pound balls—similar to bowling balls, made of ebonite—at velocities over three hundred miles an hour. The balls careen around the track, eventually slowing and falling with diminishing centrifugal force, and as they go to ground or strike a player, another volley fires. Here we are, our team: ten roller skaters, five motorbike riders, five runners (or clubbers). As the hymn plays, we stand erect and tough; eighty thousand sit watching in the stands and another two billion viewers around the world inspect the set of our jaws on multivision.

The runners, those bastards, slip into their heavy leather gloves and shoulder their lacrosselike paddles—with which they either catch the whizzing balls or bash the rest of us. The bikers ride high on the walls (beware, mates, that's where the cannon shots are too hot to handle) and swoop down to help the runners at opportune

1

times. The skaters, those of us with the juice for it, protest: we clog the way, try to keep the runners from passing us and scoring points, and become the fodder in the brawl. So two teams of us, forty in all, go skating and running and biking around the track while the big balls are fired in the same direction as we move— always coming in from behind to scatter and maim us—and the object of the game, as if you didn't know, is for the runners to pass all skaters on the opposing team, field a ball, and pass it to a biker for one point. Bikers, by the way, may give the runners a lift—in which case those of us on skates have our hands full overturning 175-cc. motorbikes.

No rest periods, no substitute players. If you lose a man, your team plays short.

Today I turn my best side to the cameras. I'm Jonathan E, none other, and nobody passes me on the track. I'm the core of the Houston team and for the two hours of play—no rules, no penalties once that first cannon fires—I'll level any bastard runner who raises a paddle at me.

We move: immediately there are pileups—bikes, skaters, referees, runners, all tangled and punching and scrambling when one of the balls zooms around the corner and belts us. I pick up momentum and heave an opposing skater into the infield at center ring; I'm brute speed today, driving, pushing up on the track, dodging a ball, hurtling downward beyond those bastard runners. Two runners do hand-to-hand combat and one gets his helmet knocked off in a blow which tears away half his face; the victor stands there too long admiring his work and gets wiped out by a biker who swoops down and flattens him. The crowd screams and I know the cameramen have it on an isolated shot and that viewers in Melbourne, Berlin, Rio, and L.A. are heaving with excitement in their easy chairs.

When an hour is gone I'm still wheeling along, though we have four team members out with broken parts, one rookie maybe dead, two bikes demolished. The other team, good old London, is worse off.

One of their motorbikes roars out of control, takes a hit from one of the balls, and bursts into flame. Wild cheering.

Cruising up next to their famous Jackie Magee, I time my punch. He turns in my direction, exposes the ugly snarl inside his helmet, and I take him out of action. In that tiniest instant, I feel his teeth and bone give way and the crowd screams approval. We have them now, we really have them, we do, and the score ends 7-2.

The years pass and the rules alter—always in favor of greater crowd-pleasing carnage. I've been at this more than fifteen years, amazing, with only broken arms and collarbones to slow me down, and I'm not as spry as ever, but meaner—and no rookie, no matter how much in shape, can learn this slaughter unless he comes out and takes me on in the real thing.

But the rules: I hear of games in Manila, now, or in Barcelona, with no time limits, men bashing each other until there are no runners left, no way of scoring points. That's the coming thing. I hear of Roller Ball Murder played with mixed teams, men and women, wearing tear-away jerseys which add a little tit to the action. Everything will happen. They'll change the rules till we skate on a slick of blood. We all know that.

Before this century began, before the Great Asian war of the 1990's, before the corporations replaced nationalism and the corporate police forces supplanted the world's armies, in the last days of American football and the World Cup in Europe, I was a tough young rookie who knew all the rewards of this game. Women: I had them all—even, pity, a good marriage once. I had so much money after my first trophies that I could buy houses and land and lakes beyond the huge cities where only the executive class were allowed. My photo, then, as now, was on the covers of magazines, so that my name and the name of the sport were one, and I was Jonathan E, no other, a survivor and much more in the bloodiest sport.

At the beginning I played for Oil Conglomerates. Then those

corporations became known as ENERGY. I've always played for the team here in Houston; they've given me everything.

"How're you feeling?" Mr. Bartholemew asks me. He's the head of ENERGY, one of the most powerful men in the world, and he talks to me like I'm his son.

"Feeling mean," I answer, so that he smiles.

He tells me they want to do a special on multivision about my career, lots of shots on the side screens showing my greatest plays, and the story of my life, how ENERGY takes in such orphans, gives them work and protection, and makes careers possible.

"Really feel mean, eh?" Mr. Bartholemew asks again, and I answer the same, not telling him all that's inside me because he would possibly misunderstand; not telling him that I'm tired of the long season, that I'm lonely and miss my wife, that I yearn for high, lost, important thoughts, and that maybe, just maybe, I've got a deep rupture in the soul.

An old buddy, Jim Cletus, comes by the ranch for the weekend. Mackie, my present girl, takes our dinners out of the freezer and turns the rays on them; not so domestic, that Mackie, but she has enormous breasts and a waist smaller than my thigh.

Cletus works as a judge now. At every game there are two referees—clowns, whose job it is to see nothing's amiss—and the judge who records the points scored. Cletus is also on the International Rules Committee and tells me they are still considering several changes.

"A penalty for being lapped by your own team, for one thing," he tells me. "A damned simple penalty, too: they'll take off your helmet."

Mackie, bless her bosom, makes an O with her lips.

Cletus, once a runner for Toronto, fills up my oversized furniture and rests his hands on his bad knees.

"What else?" I ask him. "Or can you tell me?"

"Oh, just financial things. More bonuses for superior attacks. Bigger bonuses for being named World All-Star—which ought to be good news for you again. And talk of reducing the two-month off-season. The viewers want more."

After dinner Cletus walks around the ranch with me. He asks if there's anything I want.

"Something, but I don't know what," I tell him truthfully.

"Something's on your mind," he says, watching my profile as we trudge up the path of a hillside. The Texas countryside stretches before us. Pavilions of clouds.

"Did you ever think about death in your playing days?" I ask, knowing I'm a bit pensive for old Clete.

"Never in the game itself," he answers proudly. "Off the track I never thought about anything else."

We pause and take a good long look at the horizon.

"There's another thing going in the Rules Committee," he finally admits. "They're considering dropping the time limit—at least, god help us, Johnny, the suggestion has come up officially."

I like a place with rolling hills. Another of my houses is near Lyon in France, the hills similar to these although more lush, and I take my evening strolls there over an ancient battleground. The cities are so uninhabitable one has to have a business passport to enter such immensities as New York.

"Naturally I'm holding out for the time limit," Cletus goes on. "I've played, so I know a man's limits. Sometimes in that committee, Johnny, I feel pretty clumsy, sitting there and insisting there should still be a few rules."

The statistical nuances of Roller Ball Murder entertain the multitudes as much as any other aspect of the game. The greatest number of points scored in a single game: 81. The highest velocity of a ball when actually caught by a runner: 176 m.p.h. Highest number of players put out of action in a single game by a single skater: 13, world's record by yours truly. Most deaths in a single contest: 9, Rome vs. Chicago, December 4, 2012.

The giant lighted boards circling above the track monitor our pace, record each fact of the slaughter, and we have millions of fans—strange, it always seemed to me—who never look directly at the action, but just study those statistics.

A multivision survey established this.

Before going to the stadium in Paris for our evening game, I stroll under the archways and along the Seine.

Some of the French fans call to me, waving and talking to my bodyguards as well, so I become oddly conscious of myself, conscious of my size and clothes and the way I walk. A curious moment.

I'm six foot three inches and weigh 255 pounds. My neck is eighteen and a half inches. Fingers like a pianist. I wear my conservative pinstriped jump suit and the famous flat Spanish hat. I am thirty-four years old now, and when I grow old, I think, I'll look a lot like the poet Robert Graves.

The most powerful men in the world are the executives. They run the major corporations which fix prices, wages, and the general economy, and we all know they're crooked, that they have almost unlimited power and money, but I have considerable power and money myself and I'm still anxious.

What can I possibly want, I ask myself, except, possibly, more knowledge?

I consider recent history—which is virtually all anyone remembers—and how the corporate wars ended, so that we settled into the Six Majors: ENERGY, TRANSPORT, FOOD, HOUSING, SERVICES, and LUXURY. Sometimes I forget who runs what—for instance, now that the universities are operated by the Majors (and provide the farm system for Roller Ball Murder), which Major runs the universities? SERVICES or LUXURY? Music is one of our biggest industries, but I can't remember who administers it. Narcotic research is now under FOOD, I know, though it used to be under LUXURY.

Anyway, I think I'll ask Mr. Bartholemew about knowledge. He's a man with a big view of the world, with values, with memory. My team flings itself into the void while his team harnesses the sun, taps the sea, finds new alloys, and is clearly just a hell of a lot more serious.

The Mexico City game has a new wrinkle: they've changed the shape of the ball on us.

Cletus didn't even warn me—perhaps he couldn't—but here we are playing with a ball not quite round, its center of gravity altered, so that it rumbles around the track in irregular patterns. This particular game is bad enough because the bikers down here are getting wise to me; for years, since my reputation was established, bikers have always tried to take me out of a game early. But early in the game I'm wary and strong and I'll always gladly take on a biker—even since they put shields on the motorbikes so that we can't grab the handlebars. Now though, these bastards know I'm getting older—still mean, but slowing down, as the sports pages say about me—so they let me bash it out with the skaters and runners for as long as possible before sending the bikers after me. Knock out Jonathan E, they say, and you've beaten Houston; and that's right enough, but they haven't done it yet.

The fans down here, all low-class FOOD workers mostly, boil over as I manage to keep my cool—and the oblong ball, zigzagging around at lurching speeds, hopping two feet off the track at times, knocks out virtually their whole team. Finally, some of us catch their last runner/clubber and beat him to a pulp, so that's it: no runners, no points. Those dumb FOOD workers file out of the stadium while we show off and rack up a few fancy and uncontested points. The score: 37-4. I feel wonderful, like brute speed, but, sure, the oblong ball is a worry.

Mackie is gone—her mouth no longer makes an O around my villa or ranch—and in her place is the new one, Daphne. My Daphne is tall and English and likes photos—always wants to pose for me. Sometimes we get out our boxes of old pictures (mine as a player, mostly, and hers as a model) and look at ourselves.

"Look at the muscles in your back!" Daphne says in amazement as she studies a shot of me at the California beach—and it's as though she never before noticed.

After the photos, I stroll out beyond the garden. The brown waving grass of the fields reminds me of Ella, my only wife, and of her soft long hair which made a tent over my face when we kissed.

I lecture to the ENERGY-sponsored rookie camp and tell them they can't possibly comprehend anything until they're out on the track getting belted.

My talk tonight concerns how to stop a biker who wants to run you down. "You can throw a shoulder right into the shield," I begin. "And that way it's you or him."

The boys look at me as though I'm crazy.

"Or you can hit the deck, cover yourself, tense up, and let the bastard flip over your body," I go on, counting on my fingers for them and doing my best not to laugh. "Or you can feint, sidestep uphill, and kick him off the track—which takes some practice and timing."

None of them know what to say. We're sitting in the infield grass, the track lighted, the stands empty, and their faces are filled with stupid awe. "Or if a biker comes at you with good speed and balance," I continue, "then let the bastard by—even if he carries a runner. That runner, remember, has to dismount and field one of the new odd balls, which isn't easy—and you can usually catch up."

The rookies get a studious look on their faces when a biker bears down on me in the demonstration period.

Brute speed. I jump to one side, dodge the shield, grab the arm and separate the bastard from his machine in one movement. The bike skids away. The biker's shoulder is out of socket.

"Oh yeah," I say, getting back to my feet. "I forgot about that move."

Toward mid-season when I see Mr. Bartholemew again, he has been deposed as the chief executive at ENERGY. He is still very important, but lacks some of the old certainty; his mood is reflective, so that I decide to take this opportunity to talk about what's bothering me.

We lunch in Houston Tower, and there's a nice Beef Wellington, a good Burgundy. Daphne sits there like a stone, probably imagining she's in a movie.

"Knowledge, ah, I see," Mr. Bartholemew replies in response to my topic. "What're you interested in, Jonathan? History? The arts?"

"Can I be personal with you?"

"Sure, naturally," he answers uneasily, and although Mr. Bartholemew isn't especially one to inspire confession, I decided to blunder along.

"I began in the university," I remind him. "That was—let's see—more than seventeen years ago. In those days we still had books and I read some, quite a few, because I thought I might make an executive."

"Jonathan, believe me, I can guess what you're going to say," Mr. Bartholemew sighs, sipping the Burgundy and glancing at Daphne. "I'm one of the few with real regrets about what happened to the books. Everything is still on tapes, but it just isn't the same, is it? Nowadays only the computer specialists read the tapes and we're right back in the Middle Ages when only the monks could read the Latin script."

"Exactly," I answer, letting my beef go cold.

"Would you like me to assign you a specialist?"

"No, that's not exactly it."

"We have the great film libraries: you could get a permit to see anything you want. The Renaissance. Greek philosophers. I saw a nice summary film on the life and thought of Plato once."

"All I know," I say with hesitation, "is Roller Ball Murder."

"You don't want out of the game?" he asks warily.

"No, not at all. It's just that I want—god, Mr. Bartholemew, I don't know how to say it: I want *more*."

He offers a blank look.

"But not things in the world," I add. "More for *me*."

He heaves a great sigh, leans back, and allows the steward to refill his glass. I know that he understands; he is a man of sixty, enormously wealthy, powerful in our most powerful executive class, and behind his eyes is the deep, weary, undeniable comprehension of the life he has lived.

"Knowledge," he tells me, "either converts to power or it converts to melancholy. Which could you possibly want, Jonathan? You *have* power. You have status and skill and the whole masculine dream many of us would like to have. And in Roller Ball Murder there's no room for melancholy, is there? In the game the mind exists for the body, to make a harmony of havoc, right? Do you want to change that? Do you want the mind to exist for itself alone? I don't think you actually want that, do you?"

"I really don't know," I admit.

"I'll get you some permits, Jonathan. You can see video films, learn something about reading tapes, if you want."

"I don't think I really *have* any power," I say, still groping.

"Oh, come on. What do *you* say about that?" he asks, turning to Daphne.

"He definitely has power," she answers with a smile.

Somehow the conversation drifts away from me; Daphne, on cue, like the good spy for the corporation she probably is, begins feeding Mr. Bartholemew lines and soon, oddly enough, we're discussing my upcoming game with Stockholm.

A hollow space begins to grow inside me, as though fire is eating out a hole. The conversation concerns the end of the season, the All-Star Game, records being set this year, but my disappointment—in what, exactly, I don't even know—begins to sicken me.

Mr. Bartholemew eventually asks what's wrong.

"The food," I answer. "Usually I have great digestion, but maybe not today."

In the locker room the dreary late-season pall takes us. We hardly speak among ourselves, now, and, like soldiers or gladiators sensing what lies ahead, we move around in the surgical odors assuring ourselves we'll survive.

Our last training and instruction this year concerns the delivery of death blows to opposing players; no time now for the tolerant shoving and bumping of yesteryear. I consider that I possess two good weapons: because of my unusually good balance on skates, I can often shatter my opponent's knee with a kick; also, I have a fine backhand blow to the ribs and heart, when wheeling side by side with some bastard who raises an arm against me. If the new rules change removes a player's helmet, of course, that's death; as it is right now (there are rumors, rumors every day about what new version of RBM we'll have next) you go for the windpipe, the ribs or heart, the diaphragm, or anyplace you don't break your hand.

Our instructors are a pair of giddy Oriental gentlemen who have all sorts of anatomical solutions for us and show drawings of the human figure with nerve centers painted in pink.

"What you do is this," says Moonpie, in parody of these two. Moonpie is a fine skater, in his fourth season, and fancies himself an old-fashioned drawing Texan. "What you do is hit 'em on the jawbone and drive it up into their ganglia."

"Their *what?*" I ask, giving Moonpie a grin.

"Their goddamned *ganglia*. Bunch of nerves right here underneath the ear. Drive their jawbones into that mess of nerves and it'll ring their bells sure."

Daphne is gone now, too, and in this interim before another companion arrives, courtesy of all my friends and employers at ENERGY, Ella floats back into my dreams and daylight fantasies.

I was a corporation child, some executive's bastard boy, I always preferred to think, brought up in the Galveston section of the city. A big kid, naturally, athletic and strong—and this, according to my theory, gave me healthy mental genes, too, because I take it now that strong in body is strong in mind: a man with brute speed surely also has the capacity to mull over his life. Anyway, I married at age fifteen while I worked on the docks for Oil Conglomerates. Ella was a secretary, slim, with long brown hair, and we managed to get permits both to marry and enter the university together. Her fellowship was in General Electronics—she was clever, give her that—and mine was in some pre-executive courses and Roller Ball Murder. She fed me well that first year, so I put on thirty hard pounds and at night she soothed my bruises (was she a spy, too, I've sometimes wondered, whose job it was to groom the killer?) and perhaps it was because she was my first woman ever, eighteen years old, lovely, that I've never properly forgotten.

She left me for an executive, just packed up and went to Europe with him. Six years ago I saw them at a sports banquet where I was presented an award: there they were, smiling and being nice, and I asked them only one question, just one, "You two ever had children?"

Ella, love: one does consider: did you beef me up and break my heart in some great design of corporate society?

There I was, whatever, angry and hurt. Beyond repair, I thought at the time. But the hand that stroked Ella soon dropped all the foes of Houston.

I take sad stock of myself in this quiet period before another woman arrives; I'm smart enough, I know that: I had to be to survive. Yet, I seem to know nothing—and can feel the hollow spaces in my own heart. Like one of those computer specialists, I have my know-how; I know what today means, what tomorrow likely holds, but maybe it's because the books are gone—Mr. Bartholemew was right, it's a shame they're transformed—that I feel so vacant. If I didn't remember my Ella—this I realize—I wouldn't even *want* to remember because it's love I'm recollecting.

Recollect, sure: I read quite a few books that year with Ella and afterward, too, before turning professional in the game. Apart from all the volumes about how to get along in business, I read the history of the kings of England, that pillars of wisdom book by T. E. Lawrence, all the forlorn novels, some Rousseau, a bio of Thomas Jefferson, and other odd bits. On tapes now, all that, whirring away in a cool basement someplace.

The rules crumble once more.

At the Tokyo game, we discover there will be three oblong balls in play at all times.

Some of our most experienced players are afraid to go out on the track. Then, after they're coaxed and threatened and finally consent to join the flow, they fake injury whenever they can and sprawl in the infield like rabbits. As for me, I play with greater abandon than ever and give the crowd its money's worth. The Tokyo skaters are either peering over their shoulders looking for approaching balls when I smash them, or, poor devils, they're looking for me when a ball takes them out of action.

One little bastard with a broken back flaps around for a moment like a fish, then shudders and dies.

Balls jump at us as though they have brains.

But fate carries me, as I somehow know it will; I'm a force field, a destroyer. I kick a biker into the path of a ball going at least two hundred miles an hour. I swerve around a pileup of bikes and skaters, ride high on the track, zoom down, and find a runner/clubber who panics and misses with a roundhouse swing of his paddle; without much ado, I belt him out of play with the certain knowledge—I've felt it before—that he's dead before he hits the infield.

One ball flips out of play soon after being fired from the cannon, jumps the railing, sails high, and plows into the spectators. Beautiful!

I take a hit from a ball, one of the three or four times I've ever been belted. The ball is riding low on the track when it catches me and strikes my calf and skate boot, so it's not too tough although I tumble like a baby. One bastard runner comes after me, but one of our bikers chases him off. Then one of their skaters glides by and takes a shot at me, but I dig him in the groin and discourage him, too.

Down and hurting, I see Moonpie killed. They take off his helmet, working slowly—it's like slow motion and I'm writhing and cursing and unable to help—and open his mouth on the toe of some bastard skater's boot. Then they kick the back of his head and knock out all his teeth—which rattle downhill on the track. Then

kick again and stomp: his brains this time. He drawls a last
groaning good-bye while the cameras record it.

And later I'm up, pushing along once more, feeling bad, but
knowing everyone else feels the same; I have that last surge of
energy, the one I always get when I'm going good, and near the
closing gun I manage a nice move: grabbing one of their runners
with a headlock, I skate him off to limbo, bashing his face with my
free fist, picking up speed until he drags behind like a dropped
flag, and disposing of him in front of a ball which carries him off in
a comic flop. Oh, god, god.

Before the All-Star Game, Cletus comes to me with the news I
expect: this one will be a no-time-limit extravaganza in New York,
every multivision set in the world tuned in. The bikes will be more
high-powered, four oblong balls will be in play simultaneously,
and the referees will blow the whistle on any sluggish player and
remove his helmet as a penalty.

"With those rules, no worry," I tell him. "It'll go no more than
an hour and we'll all be dead."

We're at the Houston ranch on a Saturday afternoon, riding
around in my electro-cart viewing the Santa Gertrudis stock. This
is probably the ultimate spectacle of my wealth: my own beef cattle
in a day when only a few special members of the executive class
have any meat to eat with the exception of mass-produced fish.

"You owe me a favor, Clete," I tell him.

"Anything," he answers, not looking me in the eyes.

I turn the cart up a lane beside my rustic rail fence, an archway of
oak trees overhead and the early spring bluebonnets and daffodils
sending up fragrances from the nearby fields. Far back in my
thoughts is the awareness that I can't possibly last and that I'd like
to be scattered out here—burial is seldom allowed anymore—to
become the mulch of flowers.

"I want you to bring Ella to me," I tell him. "After all these
years, yeah: that's what I want. You arrange it and don't give me
any excuses, okay?"

We meet at the villa near Lyon in early June, only a week before the All-Star Game in New York, and I think she immediately reads something in my eyes which helps her to love me again. Of course I love her: I realize, seeing her, that I have only a vague recollection of being alive at all, and that was a long time ago, in another century of the heart when I had no identity except my name, when I was a simple dock worker, before I ever saw all the world's places or moved in the rumbling nightmares of Roller Ball Murder.

She kisses my fingers. "Oh," she says softly, and her face is filled with true wonder, "what's happened to you, Johnny?"

A few soft days. When our bodies aren't entwined, we try to remember and tell each other everything: the way we used to hold hands, how we fretted about receiving a marriage permit, how the books looked on our shelves in the old apartment in River Oaks. We strain, at times, trying to recall the impossible; it's true that history is really gone, that we have no families or touchstones, that our short personal lives alone judge us, and I want to hear about her husband, the places they've lived, the furniture in her house, anything. I tell her, in turn, about all the women, about Mr. Bartholemew and Jim Cletus, about the ranch in the hills outside Houston.

It would be nice, I think, once, to imagine that she was taken away from me by some malevolent force in this awful age, but I know the truth of that: she went away, simply, because I wasn't enough back then, because those were the days before I yearned for anything, when I was beginning to live to play the game. But no matter. For a few days she sits on my bed and I touch her skin like a blind man.

Our last morning together she comes out in her traveling suit with her hair pulled up underneath a fur cap. The softness has left her voice and she smiles with efficiency. She plays like a biker, I decide; she rides up there high above the turmoil, decides when to swoop down, and makes a clean kill.

"Good-bye, Ella," I say, and she turns her head slightly away from my kiss so that I touch her fur cap with my lips.

"I'm glad I came," she says politely. "Good luck, Johnny."

New York is frenzied with what is about to happen.

The crowds throng into Energy Plaza, swarm the ticket offices at the stadium, and wherever I go people are reaching for my hands, pushing my bodyguards away, trying to touch my sleeve as though I'm some ancient religious figure, a seer or prophet.

Before the game begins I stand with my team as the corporation hymns are played. I'm brute speed today, I tell myself, trying to rev myself up; yet, adream in my thoughts, I'm a bit unconvinced.

A chorus of voices joins the band now as the music swells.

The game, the game, all glory to it, the music rings, and I can feel my lips move with the words, singing.

Mason's Life

KINGSLEY AMIS

Kingsley Amis is a friend of science fiction, author of New Maps of
Hell—*the first major volume of SF criticism—a few SF stories,
exceedingly fine mainstream novels and editor of a number of SF
anthologies. We welcome, with happy smiles, this all-too-rare
contribution.*

"May I join you?"

The medium-sized man with the undistinguished clothes and the
blank, anonymous face looked up at Pettigrew, who, glass of beer
in hand, stood facing him across the small corner table. Pettigrew,
tall, handsome and of fully-molded features, had about him an
intent, almost excited air that, in different circumstances, might
have brought an unfavorable response, but the other said amiably,
"By all means. Do sit down."

"Can I get you something?"

"No, I'm fine, thank you," said the medium-sized man, gestur-
ing at the almost-full glass in front of him. In the background was
the ordinary ambience of bar, barman, drinkers in ones and twos,
nothing to catch the eye.

"We've never met, have we?"

"Not as far as I recall."

"Good, good. My name's Pettigrew, Daniel R. Pettigrew.
What's yours?"

"Mason. George Herbert Mason, if you want it in full."

"Well, I think that's best, don't you? George . . . Herbert . . .
Mason." Pettigrew spoke as if committing the three short words to
memory. "Now let's have your telephone number."

Again Mason might have reacted against Pettigrew's demanding manner, but he said no more than, "You can find me in the book easily enough."

"No, there might be several . . . We mustn't waste time. Please."

"Oh, very well; it's public information, after all. Two-three-two, five——"

"Hold on, you're going too fast for me. Two . . . three . . . two . . ."

"Five-four-five-four."

"What a stroke of luck. I ought to be able to remember that."

"Why don't you write it down if it's so important to you?"

At this, Pettigrew gave a knowing grin that faded into a look of disappointment. "Don't you know that's no use? Anyway: two-three-two, five-four-five-four. I might as well give you my number too. Seven——"

"I don't want your number, Mr. Pettigrew," said Mason, sounding a little impatient, "and I must say I rather regret giving you mine."

"But you must take my number."

"Nonsense; you can't make me."

"A phrase, then—let's agree on a phrase to exchange in the morning."

"Would you mind telling me what this is all about?"

"Please, our time's running out."

"You keep saying that. Our time for what?"

"Any moment everything might change and I might find myself somewhere completely different, and so might you, I suppose, though I can't help feeling it's doubtful whether——"

"Mr. Pettigrew, either you explain yourself at once or I'll have you removed."

"All right," said Pettigrew, whose disappointed look had deepened, "but I'm afraid it won't do any good. You see, when we started talking I thought you must be a real person, because of the way you——"

"Spare me your infantile catchphrases, for heaven's sake. So I'm not a real person," cooed Mason offensively.

"I don't mean it like that, I mean it in the most literal way possible."

"Oh, god. Are you mad or drunk or what?"

"Nothing like that. I'm asleep."

"Asleep?" Mason's nondescript face showed total incredulity.

"Yes. As I was saying, at first I took you for another real person in the same situation as myself: sound asleep, dreaming, aware of the fact, and anxious to exchange names and telephone numbers and so forth with the object of getting in touch the next day and confirming the shared experience. That would prove something remarkable about the mind, wouldn't it—people communicating via their dreams. It's a pity one so seldom realizes one's dreaming: I've only been able to try the experiment four or five times in the last twenty years, and I've never had any success. Either I forget the details or I find there's no such person, as in this case. But I'll go on——"

"You're sick."

"Oh, no. Of course it's conceivable there is such a person as you. Unlikely, though, or you'd have recognized the true situation at once, I feel, instead of arguing against it like this. As I say, I may be wrong."

"It's hopeful that you say that." Mason had calmed down, and lit a cigarette with deliberation. "I don't know much about these things, but you can't be too far gone if you admit you could be in error. Now let me just assure you that I didn't come into existence five minutes ago inside your head. My name, as I told you, is George Herbert Mason. I'm forty-six years old, married, three children, job in the furniture business. . . . Oh, hell, giving you no more than an outline of my life so far would take all night, as it would in the case of anybody with an average memory. Let's finish our drinks and go along to my house, and then we can——"

"You're just a man in my dream saying that," said Pettigrew loudly. "Two-three-two, five-four-five-four. I'll call the number if it exists, but it won't be you at the other end. Two-three-two—"

"Why are you so agitated, Mr. Pettigrew?"

"Because of what's going to happen to you at any moment."

"What can happen to me? Is this a threat?"

Pettigrew was breathing fast. His finely drawn face began to coarsen, the pattern of his jacket to become blurred. "The telephone!" he shouted. "It must be later than I thought!"

"Telephone?" repeated Mason, blinking and screwing up his eyes as Pettigrew's form continued to change.

"The one at my bedside! I'm waking up!"

Mason grabbed the other by the arm, but that arm had lost the greater part of its outline, had become a vague patch of light already fading, and when Mason looked at the hand that had done the grabbing, his own hand, he saw with difficulty it likewise no longer had fingers, or front or back, or skin, or anything.

Welcome to the
Standard Nightmare

ROBERT SHECKLEY

The nice thing about modern science fiction, when handled by writers of the caliber of Robert Sheckley, is that it can reexamine itself with fascinating results. The invasion-of-Earth theme has been around since H. G. Wells wrote his War of the Worlds. *That was the definitive first one; here is the definitive last.*

Johnny Bezique was a spaceship driver for SBC Explorations, Inc. He was surveying a fringe of the Seergon Cluster, which at that time was *terra incognita*. The first four planets showed nothing interesting. Bezique went to the vicinity of the fifth. The standard nightmare began then.

His ship's loudspeaker came on, apparently activated by remote control. A deep voice said, "You are approaching the planet Loris. We presume that you intend to put down here."

"That's right," Johnny said. "How come you speak English?"

"One of our computers deduced the language from inferential evidence available during your approach to our planet."

"That's pretty good going," Johnny said.

"It was nothing," the voice said. "We will now speak directly to your ship's computer, feeding it landing orbit, speed, and other pertinent data. Is that agreeable to you?"

"Sure, go ahead," Johnny said. He had just made Earth's first contact with alien life. That was how the standard nightmare always began.

John Charles Bezique was a bandy-legged little man with

ginger-colored hair and an irascible disposition. He was mechanically competent at his job. He was also conceited, disputatious, ignorant, fearless, and profane. In short, he was perfectly suited for deep-space exploration. It takes a particular kind of man to endure the shattering immensities of space and the paranoid-inducing stresses of threats from the unknown. It takes a man with a large and impervious ego and a consistently high degree of aggressive self-confidence. It takes a kind of a nut. So exploring spaceships are piloted by men like Bezique, whose self-complacency is firmly based upon unconquerable self-conceit and supported by impenetrable ignorance. The Conquistadores had possessed that psychic makeup. Cortez and his handful of cut-throats conquered the Aztec empire by not realizing that the thing was impossible.

Johnny sat back and watched as the control panel registered an immediate change in course and velocity. The planet Loris appeared in his viewplate, blue and green and brown. Johnny Bezique was about to meet the folks next door.

It's nice to have intelligent neighbors, speaking intergalactically, but it's not nice if those neighbors are a great deal smarter than you are, and maybe quicker and stronger and more aggressive, too. Neighbors like that might want to do things for us or to us or about us. It wouldn't necessarily have to go that way, but let's face it, it's a tough universe, and the primordial question is always, who's on top?

Expeditions were sent out from Earth on the theory that, if there is anything out there, it would be better for us to find them, rather than to have them come dropping by on us some quiet Sunday morning. Earth's standard nightmare scenario always began with contact with a formidable alien civilization. After that, there were variations. Sometimes the aliens were mechanically advanced, sometimes they had incredible mental powers, sometimes they were stupid but nearly invincible—walking plant people, swarming insect people, and the like. Usually they were ruthlessly amoral, unlike the good guys on Earth.

But those were minor details. The main sequence of the nightmare was always the same: *Earth contacts a powerful alien civilization, and they take us over.*

Bezique was about to learn the answer to the only question that seriously concerned Earth: Can they lick us or can we lick them?

So far, he wouldn't care to make book on the outcome.

On Loris you could breathe the air and drink the water. And the people were humanoid. This, despite the fact that the Nobel-prizewinner Serge Von Blut had stated that the likeliness of this was contraindicated to the tune of 10^{93} to one.

The Lorians gave Bezique a hypnopaedic knowledge of their language and a guided tour around their major city of Athisse, and the more Johnny saw the gloomier he got, because these people really had an impressive setup.

The Lorians were a pleasant, comely, stable, inventive and progressive people. They had had no wars, rebellions, insurrections or the like for the last five hundred years, and none seemed imminent. Birth and death rates were nicely stabilized: there were plenty of people, but enough room and opportunity for everyone. There were several races, but no racial problems. The Lorians had a highly developed technology, but also maintained a beautiful ecological balance. All individual work was creative and freely chosen, since all brute labor had been given over to self-regulating machines.

The capital city of Athisse was a cyclopean place of enormous and fantastically beautiful buildings, castles, palaces and the like, all public of course, and all visually exciting in their bold asymmetry. And this city had everything—bazaars, restaurants, parks, majestic statues, houses, graveyards, funparks, hot-dog stands, playgrounds, even a limpid river—you name it, they had it. And everything was free, including all food, clothing, housing, and entertainment. You took what you wanted and gave what you wanted, and it all balanced out somehow. Because of this there was no need for money on Loris, and without money you don't need banks, treasuries, vaults, or safe-deposit boxes. In fact, you don't even need locks: on Loris all doors were opened and closed by simple mental command.

Politically, the government mirrored the near-unanimous collective mind of the Lorian people. And that collective mind was calm, thoughtful, *good*. Between public desire and government action there was no discernible distortion, gap, or lag.

In fact, the more Johnny looked into it, the more it seemed that Loris had just about no government at all, and what little it did have governed mostly by not governing. The closest thing to a ruler was Veerhe, Chief of the Office of Future Projections. And Veerhe never gave any orders—he just issued economic, social, and scientific forecasts from time to time.

Bezique learned all of this in a few days. He was helped along by a specially assigned guide named Helmis, a Lorian of Johnny's age whose wit, forbearance, sagacity, gentleness, irrepressible humor, keen insights, and self-deprecatory manner caused Johnny to detest him immeasurably.

Thinking it all over in his beautifully appointed suite, Johnny realized that the Lorians came about as close to human ideals of perfection as you could expect to find. They seemed to be really fine people, and paragons of all the virtues. But that didn't change Earth's standard nightmare. Humans, in their perversity, simply do not want to be governed by aliens, not even wonderfully good aliens, not even if it is for Earth's own good.

Bezique could see that the Lorians were a pretty unaggressive stay-at-home people with no desire for territory, conquest, spreading their civilization, and other ego-trips. But on the other hand, they seemed smart enough to realize that unless they did something about Earth, Earth was sure as hell going to do something about them, or kick up a lot of dust trying.

Of course, maybe it would be no contest; maybe a people as wise and trusting and peaceful as the Lorians would have no armament to speak of. But he learned that that was an incorrect assumption on the following day, when Helmis took him to look at the Ancient Dynasty Spacefleet.

This was the last heavy armament ever built on Loris. The fleet was a thousand years old and all seventy ships worked as if they had been built yesterday.

"Tormish II, last ruler of the Ancient Dynasty, intended to conquer all civilized planets," Helmis said. "Luckily, our people matured before he could launch his project."

"But you've still got the ships around," Johnny said.

Helmis shrugged. "They're a monument to our past irrationality. And practically speaking, if someone *did* try to invade us . . . we could perhaps cope."

"You just might be able to at that," Johnny said. He figured that one of those ships could handle anything Earth might put into space for the next two hundred years or so. No doubt about it, the Lorians had a lot going for them.

So that was life on Loris, just like the standard nightmare scenario said it would be. Too good to be true. Perfect, dismayingly, disgustingly perfect.

But was it really so perfect? Bezique had the Earthman's abiding belief in the doctrine that every virtue had its corresponding vice. This he usually expresses as: "There's gotta be a loophole in this thing somewhere." Not even God's own heaven could run that well.

He looked at everything with a critical eye. Loris *did* have policemen. They were referred to as monitors, and were excruciatingly polite. But they were cops. That implied the existence of criminals.

Helmis set him straight on that. "We have occasional genetic deviants, of course, but no criminal class. The monitors represent a branch of education rather than of law enforcement. Any citizen may ask a monitor for the ruling on a pertinent question of personal conduct. Should he break a law inadvertently, the monitor will point this out."

"And then arrest him?"

"Certainly not. The citizen will apologize, and the incident will be forgotten."

"But what if a citizen breaks the law over and over again? What do the monitors do then?"

"Such a circumstance never arises."

"But if it did?"

"The monitors are programmed to take care of such problems, if they should ever arise."

"They don't look so tough to me," Johnny said. Something didn't quite convince him. Maybe he couldn't afford to be convinced. Still . . . Loris worked. It worked damned well. The only thing in it that didn't work right was John Charles Bezique. This was because he was an Earthman—which is to say, an unbalanced primitive. Also, it was because Johnny was getting increasingly morose, depressed, and savage.

The days went by, and everything went along beautifully. The monitors moved around like gentle maiden aunts. Traffic flowed evenly without the tieups or frayed nerves. The million automatic systems brought in vital products and took away wastes. The people strolled along, delighting in each other's company, and pursuing various art forms. Every last mother's son of them seemed to be an artist of some sort, and all of them seemed to be good at it.

No one worked at a paying job, no one felt guilty about it. Work was for machines, not people.

And they were all so reasonable about everything! And so accommodating! And so sweet-natured! And so highly intelligent and attractive.

Yes, it was paradise all right. Even Johnny Bezique had to admit that. And that made his increasingly bad mood even more difficult to understand, unless you happen to be an Earth person yourself.

Put a man like Johnny in a place like Loris and you have to get trouble. Johnny behaved himself for nearly two weeks. Then one day he was out for a drive. He had the car on manual control, and he made a left turn without signaling.

A car behind him and on his left had just moved up to pass. Johnny's abrupt turn almost beat the other vehicle's automatic reflexes. Not quite, but it was a near thing. The cars slewed around and ended up nose to nose. Johnny and the other driver both got out.

The other driver said mildly, "Well, old man, it seems we have had a mix-up here."

"Mix-up, hell," Johnny said, "you cut me off."

The other driver laughed a gentle laugh. "I think not," he said. "Though, of course, I'm aware of the possibility that . . ."

"Look," Johnny said, "you cut me off and you could have killed us both."

"But surely you can see that since you were ahead of me, and since you began to make an unauthorized left turn. . . ."

Johnny put his face within an inch of the other driver's face. In a low, unpleasant snarl, he said, "Look, mac, you were in the wrong. How many times I gotta tell you that?"

The other driver laughed again, a little shakily now.

"Suppose we leave the matter of guilt to the judgment of the witnesses," he said. "I'm sure that these good people standing here. . . ."

Johnny shook his head. "I don't need no witnesses," he said. "I *know* what happened. I *know* you were in the wrong."

"You seem very sure about that."

"Sure I'm sure," Johnny said. "I'm sure because I know."

"Well, in that case, I. . . ."

"Yeah?" Johnny said.

"Well," the man said, "in that case, I guess there's nothing for me to do but apologize."

"I think it's the least you could do," Johnny said, and stalked to his car and drove away at an illegal speed.

After that, Bezique felt a little better, but more stubborn and recalcitrant than ever. He was sick of the superiority of the Lorians, sick of their reasonableness, sick of their virtues.

He went back to his room with two bottles of Lorian medicinal brandy. He drank and brooded for several hours. A social adjustment counselor came to call on him and pointed out that Johnny's behavior concerning the near-accident had been provocative, impolite, dominating, and barbaric. The counselor said all of that in a very nice way.

Johnny told him to get lost. He was not being especially unreasonable—for a Terran. Left alone, he would probably have apologized in a few days.

The counselor continued to remonstrate. He advised social-adjustment therapy. In fact, he insisted upon it: Johnny was too subject to angry and aggressive moods; he was a risk to citizens at large.

Johnny told the counselor to leave. The counselor refused to leave with the situation still unresolved. Johnny resolved the situation by punching him out.

Violence offered to a citizen is serious; violence actually performed is grave indeed. The shocked counselor picked himself off the floor and told Johnny that he would have to accept restraint until the case was cleared.

"Nobody's going to restrain me," Johnny said.

"Make it easy on yourself," the counselor said. "The restraint will not be unpleasant or of long duration. We are aware of the cultural discrepancies between your ways and ours. But we cannot permit unchecked and unmotivated violence."

"If people don't bug me I won't pop off again," Johnny said. "In the meantime, make it easy on yourself and don't try to lock me up."

"Our rules are clear on this," the counselor said. "A monitor will be here soon. I advise you to go along quietly with him."

"You really do want trouble," Johnny said. "Okay, baby, you do what you have to do and I'll do what I have to do."

The counselor left. Johnny brooded and drank. A monitor came. As an official of the law, the monitor expected Johnny to go along voluntarily, as requested. He was baffled when Johnny refused. No one refuses! He went away for new orders.

Johnny continued drinking. The monitor returned in an hour and said he was now empowered to take Johnny by force, if necessary.

"Is that a fact?" Johnny said.

"Yes, it is. So please don't force me to——" Johnny punched him out, thus sparing the monitor from being forced to do anything.

Bezique left his room a little unsteadily. He knew that assault on a monitor was probably very bad stuff indeed. There was no easy way of getting out of this one. He thought he had better get to his ship and get out. True, they could prevent his takeoff, or blow him out of the sky. But perhaps, once he was actually aboard, they wouldn't bother. They'd probably be glad to get rid of him.

Bezique was able to reach his ship without incident. He found about twenty workmen swarming over it. He told their foreman that he wanted to take off at once. The foreman was desolated by his inability to oblige. The ship's main drive had been removed and was being cleaned and modernized—a gift of friendship from the Lorian people.

"Give us five more days and you'll have the fastest ship west of Orion," the foreman told him.

"A hell of a lot of good that does me now," Johnny snarled. "Look, I'm in a hurry. What's the quickest you can give me some sort of propulsion?"

"Working around the clock and going without meals, we can have the job done in three and a half days."

"That's just great," Bezique snarled. "Who told you to touch my ship, anyhow?"

The foreman apologized. That got Bezique even angrier. Another act of senseless violence was averted by the arrival of four monitors.

Bezique shook off the monitors in a maze of winding streets, got lost himself, and came out in a covered arcade. The monitors appeared behind him. Bezique ran down narrow stone corridors and found his way blocked by a closed door.

He ordered it to open. The door remained closed—presumably ordered so by the monitors. In a fury, Bezique demanded again. His mental command was so strong that the door burst open, as did all doors in the immediate vicinity. Johnny outran the monitors, and finally stopped to catch his breath in a mossy piazza.

He couldn't keep on rushing around like this. He had to have some plan. But what plan could possibly work for one Earthman pursued by a planetful of Lorians? The odds were too high, even for a conquistador type like Johnny.

Then, all on his own, Johnny came up with an idea that Cortez had used, and that had saved Pizarro's bacon. He decided to find the ruler of this place and threaten to kill him unless people were willing to calm down and listen to reason.

There was only one flaw in the plan: these people didn't have any ruler. It was the most inhuman thing about them.

However, they did have one or two important officials. A man like Veerhe, Chief of the Future Projections Bureau, seemed to be the nearest thing the Lorians had to an important man. A big shot like that ought to be guarded, of course; but on a crazy place like Loris, they just might not have bothered.

A friendly native supplied him with the address. Johnny was able to get within four blocks of the Future Projections Bureau before he was stopped by a posse of twenty monitors.

They demanded that he give himself up. But they seemed unsure of themselves. It occurred to Bezique that even though arresting people was their job, this was probably the first time they had actually had to perform it. They were reasonable, peaceful citizens, and cops only secondarily.

"Who did you want to arrest?" he asked.

"An alien named Johnny Bezique," the leading monitor said.

"I'm glad to hear it," Johnny said. "He's been causing me considerable embarrassment."

"But aren't you——"

Johnny laughed. "Aren't I the dangerous alien? Sorry to disappoint you, but I am not. The resemblance *is* close, I know."

The monitors discussed the situation. Johnny said, "Look, fellows, I was born in that house right over there. I can get twenty people to identify me, including my wife and four children. What more proof do you want?"

The monitors conferred again.

"Furthermore," Johnny said, "can you honestly believe that I really am this dangerous and uncontrolled alien? I mean, common sense ought to tell you——"

The monitor apologized. Johnny went on, got within a block of his destination, and was stopped by another group of monitors. His former guide, Helmis, was with them.

They called on him to surrender.

"There's no time for that now," Bezique said. "Those orders have been countermanded. I am now authorized to reveal my true identity."

"We know your true identity," Helmis said.

"If you did, I wouldn't have to reveal it now, would I? Listen closely. I am a Lorian of Planner Classification. I received special aggression-training years ago to fit me for my mission. It is now accomplished. I returned—as planned—and performed a few simple tests to see if everything on Loris was as I had left it, psychologically. You know the results, which, from a galactic survival standpoint, are not good. I must now report on this and various other high matters to the Chief Planner at the Future Projections Bureau. I can tell you, informally, that our situation is grave and there is no time to spare."

The monitors were confused. They asked for confirmation of Johnny's statements.

"I told you that the matter is urgent," Bezique said. "Nothing would please me better than to give you confirmation—if there were only time."

Another conference. "Sir, without orders, we can't let you go."

"In that case, the probable destruction of our planet rests on your own heads."

A high monitor officer asked, "Sir, what rank do you hold?"

"It is higher than yours," Johnny said promptly.

The officer reached a decision. "In that case, what are your orders, sir?"

Johnny smiled. "Keep the peace. Calm the worried citizens. More detailed orders will be forthcoming."

Bezique went on confidently. He reached the door of the Planning Office and ordered it to open. It opened. He was about to walk through . . .

"Put up your hands and step away from that door!" a hard voice behind him said.

Bezique turned and saw a group of monitors. There were ten of them, they were dressed in black, and they were holding weapons.

"We are empowered to shoot to kill if need be," one of them said. "You needn't try any of your lies on us. Our orders are to ignore anything you say and take you in."

"No sense in my trying to reason with you, huh?"

"No chance at all. Come along."

"Where?"

"We've put one of the ancient prisons into service just for you. You will be held there and given every amenity. A judge will hear your case. Your alienness and low level of civilization will be taken into consideration. Beyond doubt you will get off with a warning and a request to leave Loris."

"That doesn't sound so bad. Do you really think it'll go like that?"

"I've been assured of it," the monitor said. "We are a reasonable and compassionate people. Your gallant resistance to us was, indeed, exemplary."

"Thank you."

"But it is all over now. Will you come along peacefully?"

"No," Johnny said.

"I'm afraid I don't understand."

"There's a lot you don't understand about me or about Terrans. I'm going through that door."

"If you try, we will shoot."

There is an infallible way of telling the true conquistador type, the genuine berserker, the pure and unadulterated kamikaze or crusader, from ordinary people. Ordinary people faced with an impossible situation tend to compromise, to wait for a better day to fight. But not your Pizarros or Godfreys of Bouillon or Harold Hardradas or Johnny Beziques. They are gifted with great stupidity, or great courage, or both.

"All right," Bezique said. "So shoot, and the hell with you."

Johnny walked through the door. The special monitors did not shoot. He could hear them arguing as he went down the corridors of the Future Projections Bureau.

Soon he came face to face with Veerhe, the Chief Planner. Veerhe was a calm little man with an aging pixy face.

"Hello," the Chief Planner said. "Take a seat. I've completed the projection on Earth vis-a-vis Loris."

"Save it," Johnny said. "I've got one or two simple requests to make, which I'm sure you won't mind doing. But if you do——"

"I think you'll be interested in this forecast," Veerhe said. "We've extrapolated your racial characteristics and matched them against ours. It looks like there's sure to be a conflict between our peoples over preeminence. Not on our part, but definitely on yours. You Earth people simply won't rest until you rule us or we rule you. The situation is inevitable, given your level of civilization."

"I didn't need any office or fancy title to figure out that one," Johnny said. "Now look ——"

"I'm not finished," Veerhe said. "Now, from a purely technological standpoint, you Terrans haven't got a chance. We could blow up anything you sent against us."

"So you haven't anything to worry about."

"Technology doesn't count for as much as psychology. You Terrans are advanced enough not to simply throw yourselves against us. There will be discussions, treaties, violations, more discussions, aggressions, explanations, encroachments, clashes and all of that. We can't act as if you don't exist, and we can't refuse to cooperate with you in a search for reasonable and even-handed solutions. That would be impossible for us, just as it would be impossible for you simply to leave us alone. We are a straightforward, stable, reasonable and trusting people. You are an aggressive, unbalanced race, and capable of amazing deviousness. You are unlikely to present us with clear-cut and sufficient reasons for us to destroy you. Failing that, and all factors remaining constant, you are sure to take us over, and we are sure to be psychologically unable to do anything about it. In your terms, it is what happens when an extreme Apollonian culture meets an extreme Dionysian culture."

"Well, hell," Johnny said. "That's a hell of a thing to lay on me. I feel sort of stupid offering you advice—but look, if you know all that, why not adapt yourselves to the situation? Make yourselves become what you have to become?''

"As you did?'' Veerhe asked.

"Well, okay, I didn't adapt. But I'm not as smart as you Lorians.''

"Intelligence has nothing to do with it,'' the Chief Planner said. "One doesn't change one's culture by an act of will. Besides, suppose we could change ourselves? We would have to become like you. Frankly, we wouldn't like that.''

"I don't blame you,'' Johnny said truthfully.

"And even if we did bring off this miracle and made ourselves more aggressive, we could never reach in a few years the level you have reached after tens of thousands of years of aggressive development. Despite our advantages in armament, we would probably lose if we tried to play your game by your rules.''

Johnny blinked. He had been thinking along the same lines. The Lorians were simply too trusting, too gullible. It wouldn't be difficult to work up some kind of a peace parlay, and then take over one of their ships by surprise. Maybe two or three ships. Then. . . .

"I see that you've reached the same conclusion,'' Veerhe said.

"I'm afraid you're right,'' Johnny said. "The fact is, we want to win much harder than you do. When you get right down to it, you Lorians won't go all out: You're nice people and you play everything by rules, even life and death games. But we Terrans aren't very nice, and we'll stop at nothing to win.''

"That is our extrapolation,'' Veerhe said. "So we thought it would only be reasonable to save a lot of time and trouble and put you in charge of us now.''

"How was that?''

"We want you to rule us.''

"Me personally?''

"Yes. You personally.''

"You gotta be kidding,'' Johnny said.

"There is nothing here to joke about,'' Veerhe said. "And we Lorians do not lie. I've told you my extrapolation of the situation. It is only reasonable that we should save ourselves a great deal of unnecessary pain and hardship by accepting the inevitable immediately. Will you rule us?''

"It's one hell of a nice offer," Bezique said. "I'm really not qualified. . . . But what the hell, no one else is, either. Sure, I'll take over this planet. And I'll do a good job for you people because I really do like you.''

"Thank you," Veerhe said. "You will find us easy to manage, as long as your orders are within our psychological capabilities.''

"Don't worry about that," Johnny said. "Everything's going to continue just as before. Frankly, I can't improve on this setup. I'm going to do a good job for you people, just as long as you cooperate.''

"We will cooperate," Veerhe said. "But your own people may not prove so amenable. They may not accept the situation.''

"That's the understatement of the century," Johnny said. "This'll give the governments of Earth the biggest psychic bellyache in recorded history. They'll do their damnedest to pull me down and put in one of their own boys. But you Lorians will back me, right?''

"You know what we are like. We will not fight for you, since we will not fight for ourselves. We will obey whoever actually has the power.''

"I guess I can't expect anything more," said Bezique. "But I see I'm going to have some problems bringing this off. I guess I'll bring in a few buddies to help me, set up an organization, do some lobbying, play off one group against the other. . . .''

Johnny paused. Veerhe waited. After a while Johnny said, "I'm leaving something out. I'm not being logical. There's more to this than I thought. I haven't gone all the way in my reasoning.''

"I cannot help you," the Chief Planner said. "Frankly, I am out of my depth.''

Johnny frowned and rubbed his eyes. He scratched his head. Then he said, "Yeah. Well, it's clear enough what I gotta do. You see it, don't you?''

"I suppose there are many promising avenues of application.''

"There's only one," Johnny said. "Sooner or later, I gotta

conquer Earth. Either that, or they're going to conquer me. Us, I mean. Can you see that?''

"It seems a highly probable hypothesis.''

"It's God's own truth. Me or them. There's room for just one Number One.''

The Planner didn't comment. Johnny said, "I never dreamed of anything like this. From spaceship driver to emperor of an advanced alien planet in less than two weeks. And now I gotta take over Earth, and that's a weird feeling. Still, it'll be the best thing for them. We'll bring some civilization to those monkeys, teach them how things should really be done. Someday they'll thank us for it.''

"Do you have any orders for me?'' Veerhe asked.

"I'll want to review all the data about the Ancient Dynasty fleet. But first I think a coronation would be in order. No, first a referendum electing me emperor, then a coronation. Can you arrange all that?''

"I shall begin at once,'' the Chief Planner said.

For Earth, the standard nightmare had finally taken place. An advanced alien civilization was about to impose its culture upon Earth. For Loris, the situation was different. The Lorians, previously defenseless, had suddenly acquired an aggressive alien general, and soon would have a group of mercenaries to operate their spacefleet. All of which was not so good for Earth, but not bad at all for Loris.

It was inevitable, of course. For the Lorians were a really advanced and intelligent people. And what is the purpose of being really intelligent if not to have the substance of what you want without mistaking it for the shadow?

Serpent Burning on an Altar

BRIAN W. ALDISS

If you have read the Aldiss novels Barefoot in the Head *and* Report on Probability A *you will know that he is the foremost practitioner of what might be called stretching the bounds of science fiction writing. He experiments—and he succeeds—and opens up new areas for the rest of us to colonize. Here he stretches very nicely indeed.*

The cranes flying south at window level were a splendid omen for the getting and giving of amatory gifts. Accordingly, after the morning's rehearsal, my friend Lambant decided he would order a nuptial present for his sister, whose marriage date had been announced. This chanced to be on the first day of the autumn fair or mop.

Lambant and I visited a glass-engraver's studio to order some glass goblets as a gift befitting the great family occasion. The studio stood beyond the city wall. The paint on its orange door flaked and fell like frost-nicked leaves as we heaved it open. The entrance was narrow and the stairs as crooked as any in Malacia, leading to Master Giovanni Bledlore's studio.

He came out on the landing to us, an ague-ridden old figure, closing his creaking workshop door behind him.

"You young fellows are a nuisance to an honest craftsman," he said. "You disturb the dust, and dust will spoil my colors. What do you want of me? I shall have to go back and sit still for a quarter hour before the dust settles and I can open my palettes again!"

"Then you should keep cleaner premises, Master Bledlore," I

said. "Open up the windows—even your bluebottles are crying for escape."

"I need you to make me a dozen goblets with local scenes on them, such as you designed for Thiepol of Tera a twelve-month ago," Lambant told him.

The old man threw up his hands and wagged his beard in our faces. "Spare me your needs! Every one of those designs aged me by a lifetime. Nor has Thiepol paid me yet. My eyesight's too bad for any more of that sort of order. My hand shakes too much. Besides, my wife is ill and I must care for her. My foreman has deserted me and gone over to that rogue Dapertuto. . . . No, no, I could not possibly attempt. . . . Besides, when would you require them?"

He took much persuading. Before we had signed our bond on the deal and paid him a token in advance, the old craftsman had shown us the treasures of his workshop, and the beautiful miniatures on which he had worked with so much pain and skill, their tiny figures incised on glass and glowing with color.

"Ah, what accomplishment!—It's nothing short of alchemy," Lambant said, as we passed through the narrow doorway and strolled, hands on each other's shoulders, across the green to where the pedlars were putting up the frail stalls of their autumn fair. "You saw his azure vase with its vignette? You saw those two children sporting by the whale's skeleton, with the hurdy-gurdy man playing in the background? What could be more beautiful in such small compass?"

"Indeed, it was beautiful. And isn't perfection greater for being so small? He confirms what I have heard rumored, that he studies everything from life. The broomstick is copied from one in his niece's yard, the hurdy-gurdy belongs to an old man living over by the flea market, and no doubt the two urchins are running ragged-assed about the gates even now!"

"What a decadent age we live in! Giovanni Bledlore is the last of the grand masters, and he scarcely recognized except by a few cognoscenti!"

"Such as ourselves, Lambant!"

"Such as ourselves, Prian! People are so blind in these last years of the century—the lees of time!—that they only appreciate merit on a grand pretentious scale. Write a history of the universe and it will be applauded, however lousy and steeped in errors factual and grammatical; yet paint a tiny perfect landscape on your thumb and nobody will cheer."

A pleasant warbling filled the air. A flute seller was moving toward us, bearing his tray full of flutes and playing one as he came. As we circled him, I snatched a flute and played a quick echo to his own charming tune, "When the Still Air Hath Waked."

"Flutes would be no better if they could be heard half a dozen valleys off—you're not suggesting that Bledlore should take to monstrous frescos in his old age, to make his name?"

"I'm condemning the general taste, not Bledlore's. He has found perfection because he has first found his correct scale. I'm regretting that he does not receive the just acclamation due to him. Thirty kopits per glass!—He should demand and get ten times that!"

We had stopped by the marionette stall, to watch both puppets and their childish audience. "I feel as you do on that score. Better paid, he could fight his dust obsession with a vacuum cleaner. But in that we are perhaps merely children of our admittedly decadent age. Should not the real reward of a true artist be his ability, and not the applause it merits him?"

"Real . . . true . . . your adjectives baffle me, Prian! Who was it said that Reality and Truth are weapons in the dialectical armory of all schools of thought?"

The school of thought whose activities we were now negligently observing was a primitive one, designed to elicit immediate and uproarious pleasure from its unreflecting spectators. Robber Man came on with red-masked eyes and tried to break into Banker Man's big safe. Banker Man, fat and hairy and crafty, appeared and caught him at it. Robber Man socked him with his sack, to the plaudits of the children. Banker Man pretended genial, asked to see how much money Robber Man could get into sack. Robber

Man, despite warning cries of children in front, climbs obligingly into safe. Banker Man slams safe shut, laughs, goes for Police Man. Meets Allosaur Man instead. Children roar with merriment, open and honest, as Allosaur Man gets multitudinous teeth round Banker Man's nose. Space Man descends, traps Allosaur Man in helmet. During fracas, Banker's Lady, togged to nines, enters to take some cash from safe. Releases and is walloped by Robber Man. And so on. Continuous entertainment.

Two cool girls near us in frocks that hover between innocence and indecency comment to each other. She to her: "Disastrous lowbrow hokum! I can't think how we laughed at it last year!"

She to her: "Hokum maybe, Chloe, but brilliant Theater!"

I had propped myself against the stones of a fallen arch. Lambant had hoisted himself up and now sprawled on them. He said in my ear, "Be warned by that exchange!—Thus, enjoyment in youth gives way to criticism in old age!"

His casual words were caught by the girls, who failed to join in the general laughter then prevailing as Judy, the Law Man's Daughter, tried to kiss Allosaur Man—mistaking him, still trapped in the helmet, for Space Man. They turned to us, and one turned rosy and one pale at Lambant's affront, so that I was vexed to think which coloring effect took me most.

"We also overheard *your* conversation, cavaliers, but less insultingly, since our overhearing was involuntary, and caused purely by the loudness and coarseness of your voices," one of these delicate creatures indited. "We found your remarks as amusing as you appear to have found ours!"

She it was whose sister had addressed her as Chloe. She was the smaller and the more rounded of the two, with pretty chestnut hair and soft brown eyes—though they attempted to pierce both Lambant and me at that moment. She it was who had turned to so fair a shade of rose, her sister who bore cheeks that temporarily resembled ivory.

Her sister, whose name we soon discovered to be Lise, was no less ferocious, but of a more willowy physique, slender and dark, with hair as black and shining as midnight reflected down a well, and eyes as blue-gray as the flower of speedwell. Neither of them could have been much more than halfway through their second decade, and neither was empty of words; for Lise, following swift on her sister's jibe, cried, with stormy brows—but I saw the moon shine through the storm—"To hear brainless gallants like you discussing the just rewards of artists! I'd as lief go to my maid for instruction in the True Religion!"

Lambant slid from his stone to his feet, saying, "Your maid should instruct me in anything she liked, miss, if she were one half as fair as you!"

"She should instruct me in nothing, were either of you princesses present to teach the lesson!" I said, looking from one to the other to decide which one of them had my heart more firmly in sway, and perceiving that the dark and willowy Lise had its chief custody.

"Your compliments are as feeble as your insults!" Chloe said.

She spoke among the general applause of the little audience, for the show had now ended, the Banker's Lady had gone off with the Space Man, the Banker had rewarded the Police Man, the Joker had had his way with Bettini, the Banker's Daughter, and the Allosaur Man had devoured the Robber Man. Now the puppet master came round with his wooden plate, thrusting it hopefully among the dissolving auditory. As he leveled it at us, I tossed in a kopetto, and said, "Here's one true artist at least believes his reward should be neither ability nor applause alone."

"Faith, master," he quoth, rolling his eyes, "I need fuel as well as flattery for my performance. So do my missus and our six children!"

"Six children!" said Lambant. "Then you also need a *lettro* for your performance!"

Our two young beauties looked abashed at this pleasant crudity and, perhaps to hide their embarrassment, Chloe said, "These carnival men deserve money possibly, but not the title of artist."

Boldly, I took her sister's arm and said, "Since the subject of artistry interests you, let's stroll awhile and see whether you have an equivalent knowledge of it. Our main topic—of which the theme of artistic reward was merely a subtopic—was whether this was not a decadent age.''

"How very strange, sirs,'' said Chloe, smiling, "for we had been saying to each other how *creative* this age was, although our seniors little realized the fact.''

"Stabbed to the heart!'' I cried, clutching at my chest and falling against Lambant. ''You hear that, brother? 'Our seniors' . . . that's for us, at least six years the senior of these two old maids. Poor croaking graybeards, they must think us!''

Taking the cue, Lambant began to gobble before us, clutching one knee and limping like an old man.

"Quick, quick, Prian, my embrocation! My rheumatics are killing me!''

'' 'Tis your wit rather that will be the death of us!'' exclaimed Lise, but she and Chloe were laughing prettily, making their youthful bosoms shake like fresh-boiled dumplings. So pleasant was the sight that Lambant redoubled the vigor of his parody of senility, somewhat spoiling the effect.

"Hokum, Lambant, maybe, but brilliant Theater!'' I said. "Now take your bows before we take these ladies somewhere where we may have out our argument in peace. Let's stroll to the river.''

The girls were looking doubtfully at one another when we saw, distantly, one of the winged women take off gracefully from the city walls and come flying in our direction. As was often the fashion of her kind, she wore long ribbons in her hair which trailed out behind her in the tranquil air. She was both young and naked and the sight of her overhead was in sunlight very pleasing; as she passed behind the Big Cornet to alight, we heard the solemn flutter of her wings, like some transvestite Jove seeking an hermaphrodite Leda.

No doubt the sight inspired Lise. "We'll come with you if we can fly,'' she said, resting a pretty hand upon my sleeve.

"Done,'' said Lambant and I together. "Let's go and find the carpet man!'' And we swept them along, whistling "When the Still Air Hath Waked'' in march-time, Lambant taking the melody and I the counterpoint, past the booths of chance and cheiromancy.

Since it was by now growing late in the afternoon, the crowds at the fair were thickening. The most crowded and the gayest time would come after dusk, when flares were lit and masks were donned, and the Eastern dancers started their contortions on the open stage. We soon found our way to the nearest carpet man. His carpets were of plastic and too brilliantly colored for our liking; but they carried a six-hour guarantee, and we were in no mood to be particular. We paid the man's fee and a deposit besides, mounting his rickety little scaffold with a good deal of jesting.

As the meter showed, our carpet had a twelve-foot ceiling, but it bore us swiftly enough, flapping above the motley heads of the people and avoiding other fliers. The girls squealed and laughed prettily, so that Lambant and I looked at each other behind their delicious backs, nodding in silent agreement that we were lucky in finding—and so soon—the two prettiest and most intelligent girls in the autumn fair.

We left the stalls behind and threaded our way through a grove of slender birches. Ahead lay the river and, beyond, the foothills of the Vokoban Mountains. Lambant pointed to them.

"Let's go to a nest I know, safe from interruption!"

"No, take us no further than the river!" cried the girls. Perhaps they recalled the old legends about what happens when one flies over water on a fine day.

Lambant would not hear argument, and we sailed across to a mossy ledge high up a slope on which wild autumn crocus grew, pink on pink. So high were we that we could still clearly see the tiny bright booths of the fair, and the fortifications of the town, and even hear, now and again, the strepitation of a tinsel trumpet. Above us, to one side, we could see the jagged grey slates of a mountain village—Heist was its name—and peasants toiling with their man-lizards among the vines below its walls.

"This is supposed to be an evil mountain," Chloe said. "My father tells me that the Exiles are imprisoned within the entrails of these peaks!"

"Are you girls apprenticed to sorcerers that you believe such tales!'' I asked. ''If there are indeed Exiles, then they are imprisoned in each one of us, and not in mere rocks.''

''Mere rocks!'' said Lise. ''Mere rocks throw out stranger things than men, since men themselves were thrown from rock. Only last year, on the coasts of Lystra, a new sort of crab was born from the earth which climbs trees and signals to its friends and enemies with a claw especially enlarged for the purpose.''

Lambant laughed. ''That sounds a very old sort of crab to me! What we require by way of newness in crabs is a species that will crow like a cockerel, yield milk every Monday in the month, and raise its carapace when requested to reveal beautiful doll's-house jewelry underneath. Or a really big tame land crab the size of that boulder but with a better turn of speed, which we could train to gallop like a stallion.''

''Marvelous! And it would be amphibious and carry us across the seas to lands of legend!''

''And not only across the seas but under them, for we could creep inside its carapace and be secure from the waters outside.''

''Then we should see the lairs of the ancient sea monsters, where they are still supposed to hide, growing as civilized as men and conveying sea lore to one another.''

''I'd grow ivy and bright creepers and ferns all over my crab, until it looked like a fantastic itinerant garden.''

''Mine would have musical claws that played as it ran!''

''Girls, girls, you take up the silly game so violently, you'll batter your brains out on your imaginations!''

We laughed again, and sat together beneath a plaque let into the rock, on which was written a legend in the Old Language. They asked me to translate it and with some effort I did so.

''This sculptured stone has a melancholy voice. It bears an inscription to a friend who appears, from the dating, to have passed over into shade at least eleven centuries ago. It's sort of verse. It says. . . .''

I hesitated, and then spoke firmly.

*　　*　　*

"Shall I forget Phalanda? I shall,
For Death is a forgetting which contains
Forgetfulness for mourned and mourner; so
My tear but not its prompting yet remains;
The thought of Death dies in a youthful heart
Or, living, seems but savor to Life's art.
Now to my autumn, Death's remembered lot
Brings more forgetting than my spring forgot."

Chloe laughed politely, hand halfway to her pretty mouth.

"Well, it is certainly elegaic, even if it doesn't make sense. Of course, such verses don't rely too strongly on sense for their impact."

"Nothing about Death makes sense," said Lambant, striking a pose. "For Death is the negative of sense; we know it not until it bears us hence—and then 'tis positive we know it not. . . ."

". . . . for it and we are both a load of rot!" completed Lise, and we hugged each other and laughed. Meanwhile, Lambant had swung the old plaque open and drawn from behind it a piping and highly spiced dish for our lunch, the saffr grains amply punctuated with dates and sultanas and little fish, their gaping mouths stuffed with bunny-cloves, in the Phrustian fashion. We cried with pleasure to the gods and, feeling deeper into the rock, brought out wine in clay bottles and a cream-colored cloth.

"All we need is some of Master Bledlore's glasses, and we have here a feast for a king—or a prince, at the least. After all, even princes have to slim on some occasions. Now, Prian, while we eat, we must talk of more serious matters than Death, whose very existence is suspect on such days as this—besides which, there are spells against him, which is why I wear this serpent's fang tied by a thread of scarlet cotton at my buttonhole. . . . So, let's begin our debate."

"Maybe the girls don't want to talk about decadence," I said, helping myself to a handful of rice, as the others were doing. "And I for my part would rather talk about the girls."

"That's real decadence for you!" said Chloe. With her ravishing mouth full, she added, "But the fish are delectable!"

Addressing myself to her sister, I said, "I notice that your sister is the bolder of you in speech. In action, which is the bolder?"

"Pooh, Chloe is not my sister! Does she look like me? Does she speak like me? Do you suppose she thinks like me?"

"You are alike in beauty and wit, but perhaps, on reflection, both your sentences and your skirts are a bit shorter. And you eat faster!"

"We should have guessed they aren't sisters, Prian! How could one matriarchal womb manage to coin two such masterpieces?"

"Thank you, Master Lambant, we will leave wombs on one side."

"Such asymmetry would spoil the look of you ladies."

"This decadent conversation proves it a decadent age;" I said, tipping the wine bottle. "How can there be further argument? Girls, concede it cannot be a creative age and we'll say no more on the subject."

"No, no, Prian!" cried Lambant. "I must side with the girls, for was not our decadent conversation about wombs, and what is more creative than a womb? Therefore it is proved a creative age!"

I gestured largely, spilling yellow grains over them all. "No, I won't allow it. You don't follow your own argument deeply enough, Lambant! For how is a womb made to be creative? To give you not too anatomical an answer and spare dear Chloe's blushes and dear Lise's divine pallors, it is made creative by the male's search for ever newer and more intense sensations. And what is the search for ever newer and more intense sensations but the essence of decadence? Thus, in this climax my conception is proved to the hilt."

"But you cannot conceive what a mistake you make," said Lise. "Your argument is abortive, for you are merely chopping logic."

"Yes, following your own private meaning," added Chloe.

"No, for you are privy to it, too. Do you think I want to conceal my movements? My droppings of wisdom all mount to the same thing—that this age is a decadent one. I for one rejoice in it. One is comfortable in a decadent age. There are no wars, no major questions to be answered, no cold winds blowing from a religious north."

I had steered the conversation to a less facetious turn, having almost wrecked it in the whirlpools of wit. Lise answered me seriously, "But you are not correct. This is what Chloe and I were talking about indirectly before we visited the marionettes. There are always wars—if not between nations, between households, between classes, between ages, between sexes, between one side of a person's nature and the other. And there are always major questions to be answered, and will be as long as life is staged in our outrageous universe. Even the marionette show raised questions in my breast I could not answer. Why was I moved by those trumpery wooden dolls? They did not seek to imitate or satirize or even parody people. They were just wooden dolls. Yet I found a part of myself cheering first for Banker Man and then for Robber Man. Was that artistry at work? And if so, then whose artistry? The puppeteer's or mine, that I used imagination despite myself? Why do I weep over characters in a book, who have no more flesh and blood than the thirty characters of the printed language? As for your absurd religious winds blowing from the north, Prian, are we not all the time in a storm of beliefs? What has all our talk been but different kinds of belief and disbelief?"

We heard music far off of a tinkling and involved kind, ignoring it as Lambant took over the discourse.

"You are admittedly right, Lise, yet right in such a small way that you must let me enlarge the argument on your behalf. It is true that even in a decadent age mankind is assailed by major questions—mysteries, I would prefer to call them. In a decadent age, of course, men simply turn their silken backs on such mysteries, or use them as stage settings. But there are mysteries much bigger than those you list. Look—I'll name one. Before we met you two angels, my devilish friend and I had been to visit an artist, a miniaturist who engraves his masterpieces on glass, Giovanni Bledlore. He works obsessively for a pittance. Why? My theory is that he feels Time is against him, and so he builds monuments to himself in the only way he knows how, almost like a coral insect whose anonymous life creates islands. Time makes Master Bled-lore create Art. Suppose he had all the time in the world! Suppose he could live forever! I'll wager he would not raise his hand to cut one single goblet! Time is one of those big mysteries which drives all before it with its lash.''

The music was nearer now, coming and going about the mountainside as intricately as its own measure. And its effect on me was measureless.

''Whoever the rogue is who plays, he has Time where he wants it,'' I said, rising to my feet. ''I've eaten enough. Lise, though it be the devil himself at his music, I must dance with you!''

She came into my arms, that beautiful willowy girl, and we danced, so that I felt for the first time the warmth of her vulnerable front against my body, and knew the delicate perfume of her in my nostrils. Her movements against me were so light, so taunting and in tune, that a special spring primed my step, powered by more than music. With a cry, Lambant and Chloe also jumped up and moved into each other's embrace.

So we were stepping lightly before the musician came into sight. When he rounded the rock, we scarcely heeded him, so rapt were we in our art, so much a part of our company he had become. I only saw that he was old and small and stocky, playing very gaily on his hurdy-gurdy, and that a man-lizard accompanied him.

As long as the music went, so went we. It seemed we could not stop, or had no need of stopping. It was more than dance we made; it was courtship, as the music told us, as our own closeness, our own movements, our own looks told us. When we fell apart gasping, and the music died, we were together more intimately than before.

We took up the bottles of wine and passed some to the gallant old musician and his friend. The hurdy-gurdy player was small and densely built, so that he seemed in his fustian clothes as thick as the city wall. His complexion was swarthy and we saw how old he was, his eyes sunken and his mouth receding, though there were black locks yet on the fringes of his white head. My friend and I recognized him at once. We had seen his likeness that very day.

"Do you not live by the flea market, O tuneful one?" asked Lambant.

"It's undeniable, sir." His thin, used voice had none of the brilliance of his music. "I have a poor shack there, if it's all the same to you."

"We saw you portrayed on one of Master Bledlore's glasses."

The old musician nodded. He came forward, holding out his instrument. It was painted all over yellow and bore a picture on its casing. We looked and saw there two children, chasing each other with arms outstretched. They were laughing. We knew the workmanship at once—and the children.

"This must be Bledlore's art! These children—they are the same ones on the azure vase in his studio?"

"As you so rightly say, sirs! The very same, bless their lovely hearts. Since Giovanni used me as his model to paint, he painted these other models here as his fee. They are my little grandchildren—or at least I should say they were, and the apple of my eye, until the thrice-cursed chills of last winter carried them both off. They would dance all day to my music if you let them, pretty little things. But the magicians at the North Gate put a spell on them and now they are no more than compost, alas!" He began to weep. "I have nothing left of them but their little picture here," and he cuddled his hurdy-gurdy to his cadaverous cheek.

"How fortunate you are to have that consolation," said Chloe pertly. "Now give us another tune, for we can't dance so nimbly to your tears as to your music."

"I must make for Heist, to earn myself a few kopettos," he said. "For it will soon be winter, however hard you young people dance." He shuffled on, and the lizard-man followed, upright on his two sturdy legs and giving us the smile of tight-lipped kindness which belongs to his kind. As for Lambant and me, we fell to kissing and petting our pretty dears when the others were scarcely out of sight.

"Poor old man, his music pleased us but not himself," said Lise's beautiful lips, close to mine.

I laughed. "The object of art is not always consolation!" I pulled her dark hair about my face.

"I don't really know what the object of art is—but then, I still don't know what the object of life is, either. Fancy, Prian, those little children dead, and yet their images living on after them, engraved on something as fragile as glass!" She sighed. "The shadow so eclipsing the substance. . . ."

"Well, art should be enduring, shouldn't it?"

"Yes, but you might say the same about life."

"You girls are so morbid! You talk so, when what you are enduring is only my hand groping up your silken underclothes. . . . Ah, you delightful creature!"

"Oh, dearest Prian, when you do that . . . no art can ever. . . ."

"Ah, sweet bird, now if only . . . yes. . . ."

But there is little merit in reporting on a conversation as incoherent as ours became for, of all the arts, none translates into words less readily than that we then pursued. Suffice it merely to say that I—in the words of my most favorite poet—" 'twixt solemn and joke, enjoyed the lady."

So much for us. As for the meteorological phenomena, the beautiful anticyclonic weather brought down a sunset of ancient armorial gold, so that the world glowed like an old polished shield before night sank in upon it, and scarcely a wind stirred meanwhile. The six-hour spell on our flying carpet was allowed to run out, until it lay there limp and useless, incapable of further transports—and, at last, the same condition held for lucky Lambant and me, relaxed in the arms of our still loving ladies.

We slept there in a huddle, the lamps of the distant fair our night lights, with kisses for prayers.

A cold predawn stirring woke us. One by one, we sat up and laughed at our negligence. The girls attended to their hair. In one corner of the sky the cloud cover had opened like a reluctant jaw, showing light in its gullet, but the light was as chill as the breeze that moved about our temples. We rose and made our way down the mountainside, following the path among the goosefoot, the amaranthus, and the gaudy spikes of broom. No movement or illumination showed from the city; up near the gray walls of Heist, however, where the mountain dialect was still spoken, dull-gleaming lanterns showed that peasants were already astir, going to a well or making for their slanting fields. Birds were beginning to call, without breaking the mountain hush.

We came down to the riverside and headed for a wooden bridge. An old wooden wizard still stood guarding it, leaning and well weathered as an ancient goat—but I saw that flowers had been laid fresh in his wormy hand, even this early in the day, and the symbolism was cheering. Taking Lise about the waist, I said, "However early you wake, someone is awake before you. However light you sleep, someone sleeps lighter. Whatever your mission, someone goes forth on an earlier one."

Lambant took it up, and then the dear girls, improvising, starting to chant and sing their words as we crossed over the creaking slats of the bridge.

"However light your sleep, the day is lighter. However bright your smile, the sun is brighter."

"However overdue the dawn, no dues delay it. . . . And what it owes the morn, in dew 'twill pay it." My clever little puss!

"However frail the blossoms that you bring, year after year, they still go blossoming."

"The water runs below our feet, ever-changing, ever-sweet, the birdlings burble and the brittle beetles beat!"

"However long night breezes last, day overthrows them, though day's overcast."

"And what a world of never-never lies in that little word, However. . . ."

We skirted the closed booths of the fair, which looked tawdry in the dregs of night, and moved toward the portal of the city. A first watery ray of sun, piercing over the chilly meadows, lit the huddle of buildings beyond the wall. Its beam was thrown back by a window. Looking up, I perceived it was Master Bledlore's casement, tight-closed. He would be sleeping still, obsessed and stuffy, his lungs scarcely moving for fear of stirring dust in his studio.

As I breathed deep of the air, an ancient musty odor came to me as of something being singed. Lise clutched my arm tighter, and I saw Chloe snuggle nearer to Lambant. We were moving toward two magicians and would have to pass them by to enter the portal.

The day favored them in their cloaks and tall hats, directing one of its first rays onto them, so that they were lit almost as artificially as characters in some old painting, appearing dramatically from the bitumen of night. On two huge and ungainly blocks of stone, fallen from some long-forgotten variant of the city's geometry, they had built a smouldering fire; beside it, they proceeded on their arcana, their eyes squint as a cat's, their faces square and malign. I turned away my head abruptly, not to see the serpent burning on the altar. It gave off a blue smoke which hung at heart level. None of us said a word.

The magicians moved their archaic bodies stiffly. Beyond the first arcades, daylight was still scarce, but people were moving in the shadows. We passed in under the gate of the city, the four of us, where torchlight was.

We Are Very Happy Here

JOE W. HALDEMAN

In Best SF: 1972 *there appeared the story "Hero" by Joe Halde-
man. It was a fine and realistic look at the future—and the future of
the military in particular. This new story is a sequel—though it
stands complete and separate—and reveals the keen eye of a
complete science fiction author who looks at the future as a
different place with different configurations, not just today with
more chrome.*

Scared? Oh yes, I was scared—and who wouldn't be? Only a
fool or a suicide or a robot. Or a line officer.

Submajor Stott paced back and forth behind the small podium in
the assembly-room/chop-hall/gymnasium of the *Anniversary*.
We'd just made our final collapsar jump, from Tet-thirty-eight to
Yod-Four. We were decelerating at one and a half gravities and our
velocity relative to that collapsar was a respectable nine-tenths c.
We were being chased.

"I wish you people would relax for a while and just trust the
ship's computer. The Tauran vessel at any rate will not be within
strike range for another two weeks and if you keep moping around
for two weeks neither you nor your men will be in any condition to
fight when the time comes. Fear is a contagious disease. Mandella!"

He was always careful to call me "Sergeant" Mandella in front
of the company. But everybody at this briefing was a squad leader
or more; not a private in the bunch. So he dropped the honorifics.

"Yes, sir."

"Mandella, you are responsible for the psychological as well as

53

the physical efficiency of the men and women in your squad. Assuming that you are aware of the morale problem building aboard this vessel *and* assuming that your squad is not immune . . . what have you done about it?''

"With my squad, sir?''

He looked at me for a long moment. "Of course.''

"We talk it out, sir.''

"And have you arrived at any dramatic conclusion?''

"Meaning no disrespect, sir, I think the major problem is obvious. My people have been cooped up in this ship, hell, everybody has, for fourteen—''

"Ridiculous. Every one of us has been adequately conditioned against the pressures of living in close quarters *and* the enlisted men have the privilege of confraternity.'' That was a delicate way of putting it. "Officers must remain celibate yet *we* have no morale problem.''

If he thought his officers were celibate, he should sit down and have a long talk with Lieutenant Harmony. Maybe he just meant line officers, though: himself and Cortez. Fifty-percent right, probably. Cortez was rather friendly with Corporal Kamehameha.

"The therapists reinforced your conditioning in this regard,'' he continued, "while they were working to erase the hate-conditioning—everybody knows how I feel about that—and they may be misguided but they are skilled.''

In our first battle with the Taurans, we had been so saturated with blind hatred that we'd massacred every last one of them, even though the object of the raid had been to take prisoners. Stott had stayed on the ship.

"Corporal Potter.'' He had to call her by rank to remind everybody why she hadn't been promoted along with the rest of us. Too soft. "Have you 'talked it out' with your people, too?''

"We've discussed it, sir.''

The submajor could "glare mildly'' at people. He glared mildly at Marygay until she continued.

"I don't think Sergeant Mandella was finding fault with the condi——''

"Sergeant Mandella can speak for himself. I want your opinion. Your observations." He said it in a way that indicated he didn't want them much.

"Well, I don't think it's the fault of the conditioning either, sir. We don't have any trouble living together. Everybody is just impatient, tired of doing the same thing week after week."

"They're anxious for combat, then?" No sarcasm in his voice.

"They want to get off the ship, sir; out of the routine."

"They *will* get off the ship," he said, allowing himself a small mechanical smile. "And then they'll be just as impatient to get back on."

It went back and forth like that for a long time. Nobody wanted to put words to the basic fact that our men and women had had over a year to brood on the upcoming battle; they could only become more and more apprehensive. And now a Tauran cruiser closing on us—we'd have to take our chances with it before we were within a month of the ground assault.

The prospect of hitting that portal planet and playing soldier was bad enough. But at least you have a chance, fighting on the ground, to influence your own fate. This bullshit of sitting in a pod, just part of the target, while the *Anniversary* played mathematical games with the Tauran ship . . . to be alive one nanosecond and dead the next, because of an error in somebody's thirtieth decimal place, *that's* what was giving me trouble. But try to tell that to Stott. I'd finally had to admit to myself that he wasn't putting on a grisly little act. He actually couldn't understand the difference between fear and cowardice. Whether he'd been purposefully conditioned into that viewpoint—which I doubted—or was just plain crazy, it no longer mattered.

He was raking Ching over the coals, the same old song and dance. I fingered the fresh Table of Organization they had given us.

I knew most of the people from the Aleph massacre. The only new ones in my platoon were Demy, Luthuli, and Heyrovsky. In the company (excuse me, the "strike force") as a whole, we had twenty replacements for the nineteen people we lost during

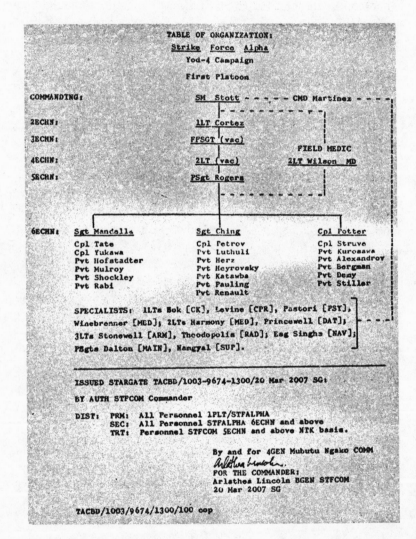

TABLE OF ORGANIZATION:

Strike Force Alpha

Yod-4 Campaign

First Platoon

COMMANDING: SM Stott ~ ~ ~ ~ ~ CMD Martinez ~ ~ ~ ~

2ECHN: 1LT Cortez

3ECHN: FPSGT (vac)

                                              FIELD MEDIC
4ECHN: 2LT (vac)   2LT Wilson MD

5ECHN: PSgt Rogers

6ECHN: Sgt Mandalla   Sgt Ching   Cpl Potter
          Cpl Tate   Cpl Petrov   Cpl Struve
          Cpl Yukawa   Pvt Luthuli   Pvt Kurosawa
          Pvt Hofstadter   Pvt Herz   Pvt Alexandrov
          Pvt Mulroy   Pvt Heyrovsky   Pvt Bergman
          Pvt Shockley   Pvt Katawba   Pvt Demy
          Pvt Rabi   Pvt Pauling   Pvt Stiller
                               Pvt Renault

SPECIALISTS: 1LTs Bok [CK], Levine [CPR], Pastori [PSY],
Winebrenner [MED]; 2LTs Harmony [MED], Princewell [DAT];
3LTs Stonewell [ARM], Theodopolis [RAD]; Esg Singhs [NAV];
PSgts Dalton [MAIN], Namgyal [SUP].

ISSUED STARGATE TACBD/1003-9674-1300/20 Mar 2007 SG:

BY AUTH STFCOM Commander

DIST: PRM: All Personnel 1PLT/STFALPHA
       SEC: All Personnel STFALPHA 6ECHN and above
       TRT: Personnel STFCOM 5ECHN and above NTK basis.

                        By and for 4GEN Mubutu Ngako COMM
                        FOR THE COMMANDER;
                        Arlethea Lincoln BGEN STFCOM
                        20 Mar 2007 SG

TACBD/1003/9674/1300/100 cop

the Aleph raid. One amputation, four deaders, and fourteen psychotics; casualties of overzealous hate-conditioning.

I couldn't get over the "20 Mar 2007" at the bottom of the T/O. I'd been in the Army ten years, though it felt like less than two. Time dilation, of course. Even with the collapsar jumps, traveling from star to star eats up the calendar.

After this raid, I would probably be eligible for retirement, with full pay. If I lived through the raid, and if they didn't change the rules on us. Me a twenty-year man, and only twenty-five years old.

Stott was summing up when there was a knock on the door, a single loud rap. "Enter," he said.

An ensign I knew vaguely walked in casually and handed Stott a slip of paper, without saying a word. He stood there while Stott read it, slumping with just the right degree of insolence. Technically, Stott was out of his chain of command; everybody in the Navy disliked him anyhow.

Stott handed the paper back to the ensign and looked through him.

"You will alert your squads that preliminary evasive maneuvers will commence at 2010, fifty-eight minutes from now." He hadn't looked at his watch. "All personnel will be in acceleration shells by 2000. Tench . . . hut!"

We rose and, without enthusiasm, chorused, "Hump you, sir." Idiotic.

Stott strode out of the room and the ensign followed, smirking.

I turned my ring to position four, my assistant squad leader's channel, and talked into it: "Tate, this is Mandella." Everyone else in the room was doing the same.

A tinny voice came out of the ring. "Tate here. What's up?"

"Get hold of the men and tell them we have to be in the shells by 2000. Evasive maneuvers."

"Crap. They told us it'd be days."

"I guess something new came up. Maybe the commodore has a bright idea."

"The commodore can stuff it. You up in the lounge?"

"Yeah."

"Bring me back a cup when you come, okay? Little bit of sugar?"

"Okay. Be down in half an hour."

"Thanks. I'll round 'em up."

There was a general movement toward the soya machine. I got in line behind Corporal Potter.

"What do you think, Marygay?"

"I'm just a corporal, Sarge. I'm not paid to——"

"Sure, sure. Seriously."

"Well, it doesn't have to be very complicated. Maybe the commodore just wants us to try out the shells again."

"Once more before the real thing."

"Mm-hm. Maybe." She picked up a cup and blew into it. She looked worried, a tiny line bisecting the space between her eyebrows. "Or maybe the Taurans had a ship 'way out, waiting for us. I've wondered why they don't do it, like we do at Stargate."

I shrugged. "Stargate's a different thing. It takes seven or eight cruisers, moving all the time, to cover the most probable exit angles. We can't afford to do it for more than one collapsar, and neither can they."

"I don't know." She didn't say anything while she filled her cup. "Maybe we've stumbled on their version of Stargate. Or maybe they have ten times as many ships. A hundred times. Who knows?"

I filled and sugared two cups, sealed one. "No way to tell." We walked back to a table, careful with the rapid sloshing of the soya in the high gravity.

"Maybe Singhe knows something," she said.

"Maybe he does. But I'd have to get to him through Rogers and Cortez. Cortez would jump down my throat if I tried to bother him now."

"Oh, I can get to Singhe directly. We. . . ." She looked at me very seriously and then dimpled a little bit. "We've been friends."

I sipped some scalding soya and tried to sound nonchalant. "That's where you disappeared to Wednesday night?"

"I'd have to check my roster," she said and smiled. "I think it's

Mondays, Wednesdays, and Fridays during months with an 'r' in them. Why? You disapprove?''

''Well . . . damn it, no, of course not. But—but he's an officer! A *Navy* officer!''

''He's attached to us and that makes him part Army.'' She twisted her ring and said, ''Directory.'' To me: ''What about you and cuddly little Miss Harmony?''

''That's not the same thing.'' She was whispering a directory code into the ring.

''Yes, it is. You just wanted to do it with an officer. Pervert.'' The ring bleated twice. Busy. ''How was she?''

''Adequate.'' I was recovering.

''Besides, Ensign Singhe is a perfect gentleman. And not the least bit jealous.''

''Neither am I,'' I said. ''If he ever hurts you, tell me and I'll break his ass.''

She smiled at me across her cup. ''If Lieutenant Harmony ever hurts you, tell me and I'll break *her* ass.''

''It's a deal.'' We shook on it solemnly.

II

The acceleration shells were something new, installed while we rested and resupplied at Stargate. They enabled us to use the ship at closer to its theoretical efficiency, the tachyon drive boosting it to over twenty-five G's acceleration.

Tate was waiting for me in the shell area. The rest of the squad was milling around, talking. I gave him his soya.

''Thanks. Find out anything?''

''Afraid not. Except that the swabbies don't seem to be scared, and it's their show. Probably just another practice run.''

He slurped some soya. ''What the hell. It's all the same to us, anyhow. Just sit there and get squeezed half to death. God, I hate those things.''

"Oh, I don't know. They might make the infantry obsolete. Then we can all go home."

"Sure thing." The medic came by and gave me my shot.

I waited until 1950 and hollered to the squad: "Let's go. Strip down and zip up."

The shell is like a flexible spacesuit; at least the fittings on the inside are pretty similar. But instead of a life-support package, there's a hose going into the top of the helmet and two coming out of the heels, as well as two relief tubes per suit. They're crammed in shoulder-to-shoulder on light acceleration couches; getting to your shell is like picking your way through a giant plate of olive-drab spaghetti.

When the lights in my helmet showed that everybody was suited up, I pushed the button that flooded the room. No way to see, of course, but I could imagine the pale-blue solution—ethylene glycol and something else—foaming up around and over us. The suit material, cool and dry, collapsed in to touch my skin at every point. I knew that my internal body pressure was increasing rapidly to match the increasing fluid pressure outside. That's what the shot was for: to keep your cells from getting squished between the devil and the pale-blue sea. You could still feel it, though. By the time my meter said "two" (external pressure equivalent to a column of water two nautical miles deep), I felt that I was at the same time being crushed and bloated. By 2005 it was at two point seven, and holding steady. When the maneuvers began at 2010, you couldn't feel the difference. I thought I saw the needle fluctuate a tiny bit, though, and wondered how much acceleration it took to make that barely visible wobble.

The major drawback of the system is that, of course, anybody caught outside of his shell when the *Anniversary* hits twenty-five G's would be just so much strawberry jam. So the guiding and the fighting have to be done by the ship's tactical computer—which does most of it anyway, but it's nice to have a human overseer.

Another small problem is that if the ship gets damaged and the pressure drops, you'll explode like a dropped melon. If it's the internal pressure, you get crushed to death in a microsecond.

And it takes ten minutes, more or less, to get depressurized and another two or three to get untangled and dressed. Not exactly something you can hop out of and come up fighting. Only four people have any mobility while the rest of us are trapped in our shells; that's the Navy maintenance crew. They essentially carry the whole acceleration chamber apparatus around with them, their suit becoming a twenty-ton vehicle. And even they have to remain in one place while the ship is maneuvering.

The accelerating was over at 2038. A green light went on and I chinned the button to depressurize.

Marygay and I were getting dressed outside. The residual fumes from the pressurizing fluid made me unpleasantly giddy and a little nauseous.

"How'd that happen?" I pointed to an angry purple welt that ran from beneath her right breast to the opposite hipbone.

"That's the second time," she said, pinching the skin angrily. "The first one was on my rear—I think that shell doesn't fit right, gets creases."

"Maybe you've lost weight."

"Wise guy." Our caloric intake and exercise had been rigorously monitored and controlled since suit-fitting at Stargate. You can't use a fighting suit unless the sensor-skin inside fits you like a film of oil.

A wall speaker drowned out the rest of her comment. "Attention all personnel. Attention. All Army personnel echelon six and above and all Naval personnel echelon four and above will report to the briefing room at 2130. Attention——"

It repeated the message twice. I went off to lie down for a few minutes while Marygay showed her bruise—and all the rest of herself—to the medic and the armorer. For the record, I didn't feel a bit jealous.

The commodore began the briefing. "There's not much to tell, and what there is, is not good news.

"Six days ago, the Tauran vessel that is pursuing us released a drone missile. Its initial acceleration was on the order of eighty gravities.

"After blasting for approximately a day, its acceleration suddenly jumped to a hundred and forty-eight gravities." Collective gasp.

"Yesterday, it jumped again. Two hundred and three gravities. I shouldn't need to tell you that this is twice the accelerability of the enemy's drones in our last encounter.

"We launched a salvo of drones, four of them, intersecting what the computer predicted to be the four most probable future trajectories of the enemy drone. One of them paid off, very near, while we were doing evasive maneuvers. We contacted and destroyed the Tauran weapon about ten million kilometers from here."

That was practically next door. "The only encouraging thing we learned from the encounter was from spectral analysis of the blast. It was no more powerful than ones we have observed in the past; so we might infer that at least their progress in explosives has not matched their progress in propulsion. Or perhaps they just didn't feel a more powerful blast was necessary.

"This is the first manifestation of a very important effect that has heretofore been of interest only to theorists. Tell me, soldier," he pointed at Negulesco, "how long has it been since we first fought the Taurans, at Aleph?"

"That depends on your frame of reference," she answered dutifully. "To me, it's been about eight months, Commodore."

"Exactly. You've lost about nine years, though, to time dilation, while we maneuvered between collapsar jumps. In an engineering sense, as we haven't done any important research and development during that period . . . that enemy vessel comes from our future!" He stopped to let that sink in.

"As the war progresses, this can only become more and more pronounced. The Taurans don't have any cure for relativity, though, so it will be to our benefit as often as to theirs.

"For the present, though, it is *we* who are operating with a handicap. As the Tauran pursuit vessel draws closer, this handicap will become more severe. They can simply outshoot us.

"We're going to have to do some fancy dodging. When we get within five hundred million kilometers of the enemy ship, everybody gets in his shell and we just have to trust the logistic computer. It will put us through a rapid series of random changes in direction and velocity.

"I'll be blunt. As long as they have one more drone than we, they can finish us off. They haven't launched any more since that first one. Perhaps they are holding their fire"—he mopped his forehead nervously—"or maybe they only *had* one. In that case, it's we who have them.

"At any rate, all personnel will be required to be in their shells with no more then ten minutes' notice. When we get within a thousand million kilometers of the enemy, you are to stand *by* your shells. By the time we are within five hundred million kilometers, you will be in them, and all shell compounds will be flooded and pressurized. We cannot wait for anyone.

"That's all I have to say. Submajor?"

"I'll speak to my people later, Commodore. Thank you."

"Dismissed." And none of this "Hump you, sir" nonsense. The Navy thought that was just a little beneath their dignity. We stood at attention—all except Stott—until he had left the room. Then some other swabbie said "Dismissed" again, and we left. I went up to the NCO room for some soya, company, and maybe a little information.

There wasn't much happening but idle speculation, so I took Rogers and went off to bed. Marygay had disappeared again, hopefully trying to wheedle something out of Singhe.

III

We had our promised get-to-gether with the submajor the next morning, where he more or less repeated what the commodore had said, in infantry terms and in his staccato monotone. He emphasized the fact that all we knew about the Tauran ground forces was that if their naval capability was improved, it was likely they would be able to handle us better than last time.

But that brings up an interesting point. In the only previous face-to face contact between humans and Taurans, we'd had a tremendous advantage: they had seemed not to quite understand what was going on. As belligerent as they had been in space, we'd expected them to be real Huns on the ground. Instead, they practically lined themselves up for slaughter. One escaped, and presumably described the idea of old-fashioned infighting to his fellows.

But that, of course, didn't mean that the word had necessarily gotten to this particular bunch, the Taurans guarding Yod-Four. The only way we know of to communicate faster than the speed of light is to physically carry a message through successive collapsar jumps. And there was no way of telling how many jumps there were between Yod-Four and the Tauran home base—so these might be just as passive as the last bunch, or they might have been practicing infantry tactics for a decade. We would find out when we got there.

The armorer and I were helping my squad pull maintenance on their fighting suits when we passed the thousand million kilometer mark and had to go up to the shells.

We had about five hours to kill before we had to get into our cocoons. I played a game of chess with Rabi and lost. Then Rogers led the platoon in some vigorous calisthenics, probably for no other reason than to get their minds off the prospect of having to lie halfcrushed in the shells for at least four hours. The longest we'd gone before was half that.

Ten minutes before the five hundred million kilometer mark, we squad leaders took over and supervised buttoning everybody up. In eight minutes we were zipped and flooded and at the mercy of—or safe in the arms of—the logistic computer.

While I was lying there being squeezed, a silly thought took hold of my brain and went round and round like a charge in a super-conducter; according to military formalism, the conduct of war divides neatly into two categories, tactics and logistics. Logistics has to do with moving troops and feeding them and just about everything except the actual fighting, which is tactics. And now we're fighting, but we don't have a *tactical* computer to guide us through attack and defense, just a huge, super-efficient pacifistic cybernetic grocery clerk of a logistic, mark that word, logistic computer.

And the other side of my brain, perhaps not quite as pinched, would argue that it doesn't matter what name you give to a computer; it's just a pile of memory crystals, logic banks, nuts and bolts . . . if you program it to be Genghis Khan, it *is* a tactical computer, even if its usual function is to monitor the Stock Market or control sewage conversion.

But the other side was obdurate and said that by that kind of reasoning, a man is only a hank of hair and a piece of bone and some stringy meat; and, no matter what kind of a man he is, if you teach him well you can take a Zen monk and turn him into a slavering bloodthirsty warrior.

Then what the hell are you/we—am I—answered the other side. A peace-loving vacuum-wielding specialist *cum* physics teacher snatched up by the Elite Conscription Act and reprogrammed to be a killing machine. You/I have killed and liked it.

But that was hypnotism, motivational conditioning, I argued back. They don't do that any more.

And the only reason, I said, they don't do it is because they think you'll kill better without it. That's logic.

Speaking of logic, the original question was, why do they send a logistic computer to do a man's job? or something like that . . . and we were off again.

The light blinked green and I chinned the switch automatically. The pressure was down to one point three before I realized that it meant we were alive, we had won the first skirmish.

I was only part right.

IV

I was belting on my tunic when my ring tingled and I held it up to listen. It was Rogers.

"Mandella, check squad bay three. Something went wrong; Dalton had to depressurize it from Control."

Bay three—that was Marygay's squad! I rushed down the corridor in bare feet and got there just as they opened the door from inside the pressure chamber and began straggling out.

The first one out was Bergman. I grabbed his arm. "What the hell is going on, Bergman?"

"Huh?" He peered at me, still dazed, as everyone is when they come out of the chamber. "Oh, s'you. Mandella. I dunno. Whad'ya mean?"

I squinted in through the door, still holding on to him. "You were late, man, you depressurized late. What happened?"

He shook his head, trying to clear it. "Late? Late. Uh, how late?"

I looked at my watch for the first time. "Not too—" Jesus Christ. "Uh, we zipped in at 0520, didn't we?"

"Yeah, I think that's it."

Still no Marygay among the dim figures picking their way through the ranked couches and jumbled tubing. "Um, you were only a couple of minutes late . . . but we were only supposed to be under four hours, maybe less. It's 1050."

"Hm-m-m." He shook his head again. I let go of him and stood back to let Stiller and Demy through the door.

"Everybody's late, then," Bergman said. "So we aren't in any trouble."

"Uh—" *Non sequiturs.* "Right, right—hey, Stiller! You seen——"

From inside: "Medic! MEDIC!"

Somebody who wasn't Marygay was coming out. I pushed her roughly out of my way and dove through the door landed on somebody else and clambered over to where Struve, Marygay's assistant, was standing by a pod, talking into his ring very loud and fast.

"—God, yes, we need blood——"

Where Marygay had gotten a welt the last time we were in the pods, now she had a deep laceration, nearly a meter long, diagonally across her body. She was covered with a bright sheen of blood and it was still oozing out of the cut, filling the pod.

Clear air passages/stop the bleeding/protect the wound/treat for shock—I worried the first-aid kit off my belt while I checked her mouth; she was breathing all right. Cracked the seal on the bandage and unrolled it. It was a few centimeters short but would have to do, so I laid it gently down the length of the wound. It was saturated with blood by the time I fumbled out the ampoule of No-shock, laid it against her arm, and pushed the button.

Then there was nothing else I could do and it hit me: Marygay was dying. I felt hollow and helpless, clamped my jaws and swallowed against sudden nausea.

"Mandella!" Struve had been talking to me.

"Yes?"

"I said, anything else you can do?"

"No." I stirred my finger through the ointments and ampoules in the kit. "Can you think of anything?"

"I'm no more of a medic than you are." Looking up at the door, he kneaded a fist, biceps straining. "Where the hell are they? You have morph-plex in that kit?"

"Yeah. You don't use it when you have internal——"

"There!" Doc Wilson crowded through the door, followed by two medics with a stretcher. They worked fast, saying nothing to us or to each other. One medic verified Marygay's blood type, rubbing the blood off the tattoo on her hip. He nodded to the other, who ran a needle into her thigh and started giving whole blood from a plastic bag.

Doc Wilson pulled on a pair of transparent gloves and gently lifted the soaked bandage off, dropped it to the floor, inspected the wound while he unrolled a new bandage. It was the same length as mine had been; he unrolled another and overlapped them, then fixed them in place with transparent tape. He measured her temperature, pulse and blood pressure.

"Surgery A," he said to the medics. "I'll be up in a half hour." He turned to Struve. "Anybody give her any medication?"

"No-shock," I said.

"Okay." He turned to go.

"Doc! Will she——"

"No time." He strode through the door.

"No *time?*" But he was gone.

"Haven't you heard, man?" One of the medics was fiddling with the stretcher, unfolding a vertical extension that would hold the bloodbag. "Don't you know the ship was hit?"

"Hit!" Then how could any of us be alive?

"That's right. Four squad bays. Also the armor bay. At least we won't be landing on Aleph—not a fighting suit left on the ship, we can't fight in our——"

"What—which squad bays, what happened to the people?"

"No survivors."

Thirty people. "Who was it?"

"All of the third platoon. First squad of the second."

Al-Sadat, Busia, Maxwell, Negulesco. "My God."

"Thirty-one deaders and they don't have the slightest idea of what caused it. Don't know but what it might happen again any minute." He looked up at the other medic. "Ready?"

"Yeah." He had removed all of the support tubes while we were talking. He held the blood-bag in his teeth to keep it higher than Marygay and the two of them lifted her slowly out of the pod.

"It wasn't a drone—they say we got all of the drones. Got the enemy vessel, too. Nothing on the sensors, just *blam!* and a third of the ship torn to hell. Lucky it wasn't the drive or the life-support system."

I was hardly hearing him. Penworth, LaBatt, Smithers. Christine and Frida. All dead. Marygay dying, that was even worse. I was numb.

"Let's go." They carried her out and I started to follow. In the corridor they told me to stay; it was too crowded upstairs.

I felt suddenly weak and sat down in the corridor. Sat for a long time with my head between my knees, trying not to think, shutting everything out, trying to relax myself back into shape.

The squawk-box crackled. "All personnel. Attention, all personnel echelon six and above. Report immediately to the assembly area unless you are directly involved in medical or maintenance emergencies."

After it had repeated the order three times I stood up and headed in that general direction.

V

Halfway to the assembly area I realized what a mess I was, and ducked into the head by the NCO lounge. Corporal Kamehameha was hurriedly brushing her hair.

"William! What happened to you?"

"Nothing." I turned on a tap and looked at myself in the mirror. Dried blood smeared all over my face and tunic. "It was Marygay—Corporal Potter—her suit . . . well, evidently it got a crease, uh. . . ."

"Dead?"

"No, just badly, uh, she's going into surgery——"

"Don't use hot water. You'll just set the stain."

"Oh. Right." I used the hot to wash my face and hands; dabbed at the tunic with cold. "Your squad's just two bays down from Al's, isn't it?"

"Yes."

"Did you see what happened?"

"No. Yes. Not *when* it happened." For the first time I noticed that she way crying, big tears rolling down her cheeks and off her chin. Her voice was even, controlled. She pulled at her hair savagely. "It's a mess."

I stepped over and put my hand on her shoulder. *"Don't touch me!"* she flared and knocked my hand off with the brush. "Sorry. Let's go."

At the door to the head she touched me lightly on the arm. "William. . . ." She looked at me defiantly. "I'm just glad it wasn't me. You understand? That's the only way you can look at it."

I understood, but I didn't know that I believed her.

"I can sum it up very briefly," the commodore said in a tight voice, "if only because we know so little.

"Some ten seconds after we destroyed the enemy vessel, two objects, very small objects, struck the *Anniversary* amidships. By inference, since they were not detected and we know the limits of our detection apparatus, we know that they were moving in excess of nine tenths the speed of light. That is to say, more precisely, their velocity vector *normal* to the axis of the *Anniversary* was greater than nine tenths the speed of light. They slipped in behind the repeller fields."

When the *Anniversary* is moving at relativistic speeds, it is designed to generate two powerful electromagnetic fields, one centered about five thousand kilometers from the ship and the other about ten thousand klicks away, both in line with the direction of motion of the ship. These fields are maintained by a "ramjet" effect, energy picked up from interstellar gas as we mosey along.

Anything big enough to worry about hitting (that is, anything big enough to see with a strong magnifying glass) goes through the first field and comes out with a very strong negative charge all over its surface. As it enters the second field, it's repelled from the path of the ship. If the object is too big to be pushed around this way, we can sense it at a greater distance and maneuver out of its way.

"I shouldn't have to emphasize how formidable a weapon this is. When the *Anniversary* was struck, our rate of speed with respect to the enemy was such that we traveled our own length every ten-thousandth of a second. Further, we were jerking around erratically with a constantly changing and purely random lateral acceleration. Thus the objects that struck us must have been guided, not aimed. And the guidance system was selfcontained, since there were no Taurans alive at the time they struck us. All of this in a package no larger than a small pebble.

"Most of you are too young to remember the term, *future shock*. Back in the seventies, some people felt that technological progress was so rapid that people, normal people, just couldn't cope with it; that they wouldn't have time to get used to the present, before the future was upon them. A man named Toffler coined the term, *future shock,* to describe this situation." The commodore could get pretty academic.

"We're caught up in a physical situation that resembles this scholarly concept. The result has been disaster. Tragedy. And, as we discussed in our last meeting, there is no way to counter it. Relativity traps us in the enemy's past; relativity brings them from our future. We can only hope that next time, the situation will be reversed. And all we can do to help bring that about is try to get back to Stargate, and then to Earth, where specialists may be able to deduce something, some sort of counterweapon, from the nature of the damage.

"Now we could attack the Taurans' portal planet from space, and perhaps destroy the base without using you infantry. But I think there would be a very great risk involved. We might be . . . shot down by whatever hit us today. And never return to Stargate with what I consider to be vital information. We could send a drone with a message detailing our assumptions about this new enemy weapon . . . but that might be inadequate. And the Force would be that much further behind, technologically.

"Accordingly, we have set a course that will take us around Yod-Four, keeping the collapsar as much as possible between us and the Tauran base. We will avoid contact with the enemy and return to Stargate as quickly as possible."

Incredibly, the commodore sat down and kneaded his temples. "All of you are at least squad or section leaders. Most of you have good combat records. And I hope that some of you will be rejoining the Force after your two years are up. Those of you who do will probably be made lieutenants, and face your first real command.

"It is to these people I would like to speak for a few moments; not as your . . . as one of your commanders, but just as a senior officer and adviser.

"One cannot make command decisions simply by assessing the tactical situation and going ahead with whatever course of action will do the most harm to the enemy with a minimum of death and damage to your own men and materiel. Modern warfare has become very complex, especially during the last century. Wars are not won by a simple series of battles, but by a complex interrelationship between military victory, economic pressures, logistic maneuvering, access to the enemy's information, political postures—dozens, literally dozens of factors."

I was hearing this, but the only thing that was getting through to my brain was that a third of our friends' lives had been snuffed out less than an hour before, and the woman I loved was dying upstairs, and he was sitting up there giving us a lecture on military theory.

"So sometimes you have to throw away a battle in order to help win the war. This is exactly what we are going to do.

"This was not an easy decision. In fact, it was probably the hardest decision of my military career. Because, on the surface at least, it may look like cowardice.

"The logistic computer calculates that we have about a sixty-two percent chance of success, should we attempt to destroy the enemy base. Unfortunately, we would only have a thirty percent chance of survival—as some of the scenarios leading to success involve ramming the portal planet with the *Anniversary* at light-speed." Jesus Christ.

"I hope none of you ever have to face such a decision. When we get back to Stargate I will in all probability be court-martialed for cowardice under fire. But I honestly believe that the information that may be gained from analysis of the damage to the *Anniversary* is more important than the destruction of this one Tauran base." He sat up straight. "More important than one soldier's career."

I had to stifle an impulse to laugh. Surely "cowardice" had nothing to do with his decision. Surely he had nothing so primitive and unmilitary as a will to live.

The maintenance crew managed to patch up the huge rip in the side of the *Anniversary* and repressurize that section. We spent the rest of the day cleaning up the area; without, of course, disturbing any of the precious evidence for which the commodore was willing to sacrifice his career.

The hardest part was jettisoning the bodies. It wasn't so bad except for the ones whose suits had burst.

Marygay came out of the operation alive but in pretty bad shape. Her intestine had ruptured under pressure and she'd developed peritonitis. Under these conditions, Doc Wilson said, her condition was very grave; he could keep her alive indefinitely in normal gravity or less, but he didn't know whether she would survive the period of acceleration before collapsar jump.

The week that followed was slow hell. I screwed up the most routine chores and snapped at everybody and couldn't sleep for worry and gathering grief. Marygay's condition got no better, no worse. I was allowed to see her a few times but she was so doped up I think she hardly recognized me.

Two days before collapsar jump, I was supervising routine maintenance on the pods and an idea that had been forming all along suddenly crystallized. I put Tate in charge and ran up to the infirmary. The nurse on duty calmed me down with a cup of soya and I had an hour to think over the plan while Doc Wilson worked on somebody's arm. Finally I got to see him.

"We're giving her a fifty-fifty chance, but that's pretty arbitrary. None of the published data on this sort of thing really fit."

He drew a cup of soya and sat down, sighing. "So you've got an idea."

"Well . . . look, Doctor, I don't know much about medicine,

but I *do* know physics. Now, isn't it safe to say that her chances are better, the less acceleration she has to endure?''

''Certainly. For what it's worth. The commodore's going to take it as gently as possible, but that'll still be four or five G's. Even three might be too much; we won't know until it's over.''

I nodded impatiently. ''Yes, but I think there's a way to expose her to less acceleration than the rest of us.''

''If you've developed an acceleration shield,'' he said, smiling, ''you better hurry and file a patent. You could sell it to Star Fleet for a considerable——''

''No, Doc, it wouldn't be worth much under normal conditions; our shells work better and they evolved from the same principles.''

''Explain away.''

''We put Marygay into a shell and flood——''

''Wait, wait. Absolutely not. A poorly-fitting shell was what caused this in the first place. And this time, she'd have to use somebody else's.''

''I know, Doc, let me explain. It doesn't have to fit her exactly, just so long as the life support hookups can function. The shell won't be pressurized on the inside; it won't have to be because she won't be subjected to all those thousands of kilograms per square centimeter pressure from the fluid outside.''

''I'm not sure I follow.''

''It's just an adaptation of—you've studied physics, haven't you?''

''A little bit, in medical school. My worst courses, after Latin.''

''Do you remember the principle of equivalence?''

''I remember there was something by that name. Something to do with relativity, right?''

''Uh-huh. It just means that . . . there's no difference being in a gravitational field and being in an equivalent accelerated frame of—it means that when the *Anniversary* is blasting five G's, the effect on us is the same as if it were sitting on its tail on a big planet, one with five G's surface gravity.''

''Seems obvious.''

''Maybe it is. It means that there's no experiment you could perform on the ship that could tell you whether you were blasting or just sitting on a big planet.''

"Sure there is. You could turn off the engines, and if——''

"Or you could look outside, sure; I mean isolated, physics-lab type experiments.''

"All right. I'll accept that. So?''

"You know Archimedes's Law?''

"Sure, the fake crown—that's what always got me about physics, they make a big to-do about obvious things and when it gets to the rough parts——''

"Archimedes's Law says that when you immerse something in a fluid, it's buoyed up by a force equal to the weight of the fluid it displaces.''

"That's reasonable.''

"And that holds no matter what kind of gravitation or acceleration you're in—in a ship blasting at five G's, the water displaced, if it's water, weighs five times as much as regular water, at one G.''

"Sure.''

"So if you float somebody in the middle of a tank of water, so that she's weightless, she'll still be weightless when the ship is doing five G's.''

"Hold on, son. You had me going there for a minute, but it won't work.''

"Why not?'' I was tempted to tell him to stick to his pills and stethoscopes and let me handle the physics, but it was a good thing I didn't.

"What happens when you drop a wrench in a submarine?''

"Submarine?''

"That's right. They work by Archimedes's principle——''

"Ouch! You're right.'' Jesus. Hadn't thought it through.

"That wrench falls right to the floor just as if the submarine weren't 'weightless'.'' He looked off into space, tapping a pencil on the desk. "What you describe is similar to the way we treat patients with severe skin damage, like burns, on Earth. But it doesn't give any support to the internal organs, the way the acceleration shells do, so it wouldn't do Marygay any good. . . .''

I stood up to go. "Sorry I wasted——"

"Hold on there, though, just a minute. We might be able to use your idea partway."

"How do you mean?"

"I wasn't thinking it through, either. The way we normally use the shells is out of the question for Marygay, of course." I didn't like to think about it. Takes a lot of hypno-conditioning to lie there and have oxygenated fluorocarbon forced into every natural body orifice and one artificial one. I fingered the valve fitting embedded above my hipbone.

"Yeah, that's obvious, it'd tear her—say . . . you mean, low pressure——"

"That's right. We wouldn't need thousands of atmospheres to protect her against five G's straightline acceleration; that's only for all the swerving and dodging—I'm going to call Maintenance. Get down to your squad bay, that's the one we'll use. Dalton'll meet you there."

It was five minutes before injection into the collapsar field and I started the flooding sequence. Marygay and I were the only ones in shells; my presence wasn't really vital since the flooding and emptying could be done by Control. But it was safer to have redundancy in the system and besides, I wanted to be there.

It wasn't nearly as bad as the normal routine; none of the crushing-bloating sensation. You were just suddenly filled with the plastic-smelling stuff (you never perceived the first moments, when it rushed in to replace the air in your lungs) and then there was a slight acceleration, and then you were breathing air again, waiting for the shell to pop; then unplugging and unzipping and climbing out——

Marygay's shell was empty. I walked over to it and saw blood.

"She hemorrhaged." Doc Wilson's voice echoed sepulchrally. I turned, eyes stinging, and saw him leaning in the door to the locker alcove. He was unaccountably horribly smiling.

"Which was expected. Doctor Harmony's taking care of it. She'll be just fine."

VI

Marygay was walking in another week, "confraternizing" in two, and pronounced completely healed in six.

Ten long months in space and it was Army, Army, Army all the way. Calisthenics, meaningless work details, compulsory lectures—there was even talk that they were going to reinstate the sleeping roster we'd had in Basic, but they never did, probably out of fear of mutiny. A random partner every night wouldn't have set too well with those of us who'd established more-or-less permanent pairs.

All this crap, this insistence on military discipline, mainly bothered me because I was afraid it meant they weren't going to let us out. Marygay said I was being paranoid; they only did it because there was no other way to maintain order for ten months.

Most of the talk, besides the usual bitching about the Army, was speculation about how much Earth would have changed, and what we were going to do once we got out. We'd be fairly rich: twenty-six years' salary all at once. Compound interest, too; the five hundred dollars we'd been paid for our first month in the Army had grown to over fifteen hundred dollars.

We arrived at Stargate in early 2023, Greenwich date.

The base had grown astonishingly in the nearly seventeen years we had been on the Yod-Four campaign. It was one building the size of Tycho City, housing nearly ten thousand. There were seventy-eight cruisers, the size of the *Anniversary* or larger, involved in raids on Tauran-held portal planets. Another ten guarded Stargate itself, and two were in orbit waiting for their infantry and crew to be out-processed. One other ship, the *Earth's Hope II,* had returned from fighting and had been waiting at Stargate for another cruiser.

They had lost two-thirds of their men and it was just not economical to send a cruiser back to Earth with only thirty-nine people aboard. Thirty-nine confirmed civilians.

We went planetside in two scoutships.

General Botsford (who had only been a major when we'd first met him, when Stargate was two huts and twenty-four graves) received us in an elegantly appointed seminar room. He was pacing back and forth at the end of the room, in front of a huge holographic operations cube. I could just make out the labels and was astonished to see how far away Yod-Four had been—but of course distance isn't important with the collapsar jump. It'd take us ten times as long to get to Alpha Centauri, which was practically next door but, of course, isn't a collapsar.

"You know——" he said, too loudly, and then more conversationally, "you know that we could disperse you into other strike forces and send you right out again. The Elite Conscription Act has been changed now, extended, five years' subjective service instead of two.

"We aren't doing that, but—damn it!—I don't see why some of you don't *want* to stay in! Another couple of years and compound interest would make you wealthy for life. Sure, you took heavy losses . . . but that was inevitable; you were the first. Things are going to be easier now. The fighting suits have been improved, we know more about Taurans' tactics, our weapons are more effective . . . there's no need to be afraid."

He sat down at the head of our table and looked down the long axis of it, seeing nobody. "My own memories of combat are over a half century old. To me it was exhilarating, strengthening. I must be a different kind of person from all of you."

Or have a very selective memory, I thought.

"But that's neither here nor there. I have an alternative to offer you, one that doesn't involve direct combat.

"We're very short of qualified instructors. You might even say we don't *have* any—because, ideally, the Army would like for all of its instructors in the combat arts to have been combat veterans.

"You people were taught by veterans of Vietnam and Sinai, the youngest of whom were in their forties when you left Earth. Twenty-six years ago. So we need you and are willing to pay.

"The Force will offer any one of you a lieutenancy if you will accept a training position. It can be on Earth; on the Moon at double pay; on Charon at triple pay; or here at Stargate for quadruple pay. Furthermore, you don't have to make up your mind now. You're all getting a free trip back to Earth—I envy you, I haven't been back in twenty years, will probably never get back—and you can get the feel of being a civilian again. If you don't like it, just walk into any UNEF installation and you'll walk out an officer. Your choice of assignment.

"Some of you are smiling. I think you ought to reserve judgment. Earth is not the same place you left."

He pulled a little card out of his tunic and looked at it, half-smiling. "Most of you have on the order of four hundred thousand dollars coming to you, accumulated pay and interest. But Earth is on a war footing and, of course, it is the citizens of Earth who are supporting the war with their tax dollars. Your income puts you in a ninety-two percent income tax bracket. Thirty-two thousand dollars could last you about three years if you're very careful.

"Eventually you're going to have to get a job, and this is one job for which you are uniquely trained. There aren't that many others available—the population of Earth is over nine billion, with five or six billion unemployed. And all of your training is twenty-six years out of date.

"Also keep in mind that your friends and sweethearts of two years ago are now going to be twenty-six years older than you. Many of your relatives will have passed away. I think you'll find it a very lonely world.

"But to tell you more about this world, I'm going to turn you over to Sergeant Siri, who just arrived from Earth. Sergeant?"

"Thank you, General." It looked as if there was something wrong with his skin, his face; and then I realized he was wearing face powder and lipstick. His nails were smooth white almonds.

"I don't know where to begin." He sucked in his upper lip and looked at us, frowning. "Things have changed so very much since I was a boy.

"I'm twenty-three, so I wasn't even born when you people left for Aleph . . . well, for starts, how many of you are homosexual?" Nobody. "That doesn't really surprise me. I am, though"—no kidding—"and I guess about a third of everybody in Europe and North America is. Even more in India and the Middle East. Less in South America and China.

"Most governments encourage homosexuality—the United Nations is officially neutral—they encourage it mainly because homolife is the one sure method of birth control."

That sounded specious to me. In the Army they freeze-dry and file a sperm sample and then vasectomize you. Pretty foolproof.

When I was going to school, a lot of the homosexuals on campus were using that argument. And maybe it was working, after a fashion. I'd expected Earth to have a lot more than nine billion people.

"When they told me, back on Earth, I was going to be talking to some of you codgers, I did some research—mainly reading old faxes and magazines.

"A lot of the things you were afraid were going to happen, didn't. Hunger, for instance. Even without using all of our arable land and sea, we manage to feed everybody and could handle twice as many. Food technology and impartial distribution of calories —when you left Earth there were millions of people slowly starving to death. Now there are none.

"You were concerned about crime. I read that you couldn't walk the streets of New York City or London or Hong Kong without a bodyguard. But with everybody better educated and better cared for, with psychometry so advanced that we can spot a potential criminal at the age of six—and give him corrective therapy that works—well, serious crime has been on the decline for twenty years. We probably have fewer serious crimes in the whole world than you used to have——"

"This is all well and good," the general broke in gruffly, making clear that it was neither, "but it doesn't completely mesh with what I've heard. What about the rest?"

"Oh, murder, assault, rape; all the serious crimes against one's person, all are down. Crimes against property—petty theft, vandalism, illegal residence—these are still——"

"What the hell is 'illegal residence'?"

Sergeant Siri hesitated and then said primly: "One certainly shouldn't deprive others of living space by illegally acquiring property."

Alexandrov raised his hand. "You mean there's no such thing as private ownership of property?"

"Of course there is. I . . . I owned my own rooms before I was drafted." For some reason the topic seemed to embarrass him. New taboos? "But there are limits."

Luthuli: "What do you do to criminals? Serious ones, I mean. Do you still brainwipe murderers?"

He was visibly relieved to change the subject. "Oh, no. That's considered very primitive. Barbaric. We imprint a new, healthy personality on them; then they are repatterned and society absorbs them without prejudice. It works very well."

"Are there jails, prisons?" Yukawa asked.

"I suppose you could call a correction center a jail. Until they have therapy and are released, people are held there against their will. But you could say it was a malfunction of the will which led them there in the first place."

I didn't have any plans for a life of crime, so I asked him about the thing that bothered me most. "The general said that over half your population is on the dole; that we wouldn't be able to get jobs either. Well?"

"I don't know this word 'dole'. Of course you mean the government-subsidized unemployed. That's true, the government takes care of over half of us—I'd never had a job until I was drafted. I was a composer.

"Don't you see that there are two sides to this business of chronic unemployment? The world and the war could be run smoothly by a billion, certainly two billion people. This doesn't mean that the rest of us sit around idle.

"Every citizen has the opportunity for up to eighteen years' free education—fourteen years are compulsory. This and the *freedom* from necessity of employment have caused a burgeoning of scholarly and creative activity on a scale unmatched in all of human history—there are more artists and writers working today than lived in the first two thousand years of the Christian era! And their works go to a wider and more educated audience than has ever before existed."

That was something to think about. Rabi raised his hand. "Have you produced a Shakespeare yet? A Michelangelo? Numbers aren't everything."

Siri brushed hair out of his eyes with a thoroughly feminine gesture. "That's not a fair question. It's up to posterity to make comparisons like that."

"Sergeant, when we were talking earlier," the general said, "didn't you say that you lived in a huge beehive of a building, that nobody could live in the country?"

"Well, sir, it's true that nobody can live on potential farmland. And where I live, *lived*, Atlanta Complex, I had seven million neighbors in what you could technically call one building—but it's not as if we ever felt crowded. And you can go down the elevator any time, walk in the fields, walk all the way to the sea if you want. . . .

"That's something you should be prepared for. A lot of cities don't bear any resemblance to the random agglomerations of buildings they used to be. Most of the big cities were burned to the ground in the food riots in 2004, just before the United Nations took over the production and distribution of food. The city planners usually rebuilt along modern, functional lines.

"Paris and London, for instance, had to be rebuilt completely. Most world capitals did, though Washington survived. It's just a bunch of monuments and offices, though; almost everybody lives in the surrounding complexes: Reston, Frederick, Columbia."

Then Siri got into specific towns and cities—everybody wanted to know about his hometown—and, in general, things sounded a lot better than we had expected.

In response to a rude question, Siri said that he didn't wear cosmetics just because he was a homosexual; everybody did. I decided I'd be a maverick and just wear my face.

We consolidated with the survivors from *Earth's Hope II* and took that cruiser back to Earth while analysts assessed the *Anniversary's* damage. The commodore was scheduled for a hearing, but, as far as we knew, was not going to be court-martialed.

Discipline was fairly relaxed on the way back. In seven months I read thirty books, learned how to play *Go,* taught an informal class in elementary physics, and grew ever closer to Marygay.

VII

I hadn't given it much thought, but of course we were celebrities on Earth. At Kennedy the Sec-Gen greeted each of us personally—he was a very old, tiny, black man named Yakubu Ojukwu—and there were hundreds of thousands, maybe millions, of spectators crowded as close as they could get to the landing field.

The Sec-Gen gave a speech to the crowd and the newsmen, then the ranking officers of *Earth's Hope II* babbled some predictable stuff while the rest of us stood more-or-less patiently in the tropical heat.

We took a big chopper to Jacksonville, where the nearest international airport was. The city itself had been rebuilt along the lines Siri had described. You had to be impressed.

We first saw it as a solitary gray mountain, a slightly irregular cone, slipping up over the horizon and growing slowly larger. It was sitting in the middle of a seemingly endless patchwork quilt of cultivated fields, dozens of roads and rails converging on it. The eye saw these roads, fine white threads with infinitesimal bugs crawling on them, but the brain refused to integrate the information into an estimate of the size of the thing. It couldn't be that big.

We came closer and closer—updrafts making the ride a little bumpy—until finally the building seemed to be just a light gray wall taking up our entire field of vision on one side. We moved closer and could barely see dots of people; one dot was on a balcony and might have been waving.

"This is as close as we can come," the pilot said over an

intercom, "without locking into the city's guidance system and landing on top. Airport's to the north." We banked away, through the shadow of the city.

The airport was no great marvel; larger than any I'd ever seen before but conventional in design: a central terminal like the hub of a wheel, with monorails leading out a kilometer or so to smaller terminals where airplanes loaded and unloaded. We skipped the terminals completely, just landed near a Swissair stratospheric liner and walked from the chopper to the plane. Our pathway was cordoned off and we were surrounded by a cheering mob. With six billion on relief, I didn't suppose they had any trouble rounding up a crowd for any such occasion.

I was afraid we were going to have to sit through some more speeches, but we just filed straight into the plane. Stewards and stewardesses brought us sandwiches and drinks while the crowd was being dispersed. And there are no words to describe a chicken-salad sandwich and a cold beer, after two years of synthetics.

Mr. Ojukwu explained that we were going to Geneva, to the United Nations building, where tonight we'd be honored by the General Assembly. Or put on display, I thought. He said most of us had relatives waiting in Geneva.

As we climbed over the Atlantic, the water seemed unnaturally green. I was curious, made a mental note to ask the stewardess; but then the reason was apparent. It was a farm. Four large rafts (they must have been huge but I had no idea how high up we were) moved in slow tandem across the green surface, each raft leaving a blue-black swath that slowly faded. Before we landed I found out that it was a kind of tropical algea, raised for livestock feed.

Geneva was a single building similar to Jacksonville, but seemed smaller, perhaps dwarfed by the natural mountains surrounding it. It was covered with snow, softly beautiful.

We walked for a minute through swirling snow—how great not to be exactly at "room temperature" all the time!—to a chopper that took us to the top of the building; then down an elevator, across a slidewalk, down another elevator, another slidewalk, down a broad stationary corridor to Thantstrasse 281B, room 45, matching the address on the directions they'd given me. My finger poised over the doorbell button; I was almost afraid.

I had gotten fairly well adjusted to the fact that my father was dead—the Army had had such facts waiting for us at Stargate —and that didn't bother me as much as the prospect of seeing my mother, suddenly eighty-four. I almost ducked out, to find a bar and desensitize, but went ahead and pushed the button.

The door opened quickly and she was older but not that much different, a few more lines and hair white instead of gray. We stared at each other for a second and then embraced and I was surprised and relieved at how happy I was to see her, hold her.

She took my cape and hustled me into the living room of the suite, where I got a real shock: my father was standing there; smiling but serious, inevitable pipe in his hand.

I felt a flash of anger at the Army for having misled me—then realized he couldn't be my father, looking as he did, the way I remembered him from childhood.

"Michael? Mike?"

He laughed. "Who else, Willy?" My kid brother, quite middle-aged. I hadn't seen him since '93, when I went off to college. He'd been sixteen then; two years later he was on the Moon with UNEF.

"Get tired of the Moon?" I asked, handshaking.

"Huh? Oh . . . no, Willy, I spend a month or two every year, back on *terra firma*. It's not like it used to be." When they were first recruiting for the Moon, it was with the understanding that you only got one trip back. Fuel cost too much for commuting.

The three of us sat down around a marble coffeetable and Mother passed around joints.

"Everything has changed so much," I said, before they could start asking about the war. "Tell me everything."

My brother fluttered his hands and laughed. "That's a tall enough order. Have a couple of weeks?" He was obviously having trouble figuring out how to act toward me. Was I his nephew, or what? Certainly not his older brother any more.

"You shouldn't ask Michael, anyhow," Mother said. "Loonies talk about Earth the way virgins talk about sex."

"Now, Mother. . . ."

"With enthusiasm and ignorance."

I lit up the joint and inhaled deeply. It was oddly sweet.

"Loonies live a few weeks out of the year on Earth and spend half that time telling us how we ought to be running things."

"Possibly. But the other half of the time we're observing. Objectively."

"Here comes my Michael's 'objective' number." She leaned back and smiled at him.

"Mom, you *know* . . . oh hell, let's drop it. Willy's got the rest of his life to sort it out." He took a puff on the joint and I noticed he wasn't inhaling. "Tell us about the war, man. Heard you were on the strike force that actually fought the Taurans. Face to face."

"Yeah. It wasn't much."

"That's right," Mike said. "I heard they were cowards."

"Not so much . . . that." I shook my head to clear it. The marijuana was making me drowsy and light-headed. "It was more like they just didn't get the idea. Like a shooting gallery. They lined up and we shot 'em down."

"How could that be?" Mom said. "On the news they said you lost nineteen people."

"Did they say nineteen were killed? That's not true."

"I don't remember exactly."

"Well, we did *lose* nineteen people, but only four of them were killed. That was in the early part of the battle, before we had their defenses figured out." I decided not to say anything about the way Chu died. That would get too complicated. "Of the other fifteen, one was shot by one of our own lasers. He lost an arm but lived. All of the others . . . lost their minds."

"What—some kind of Tauran weapon?" Mike asked.

"The Taurans didn't have anything to do with it! It was the Army. They conditioned us to kill anything that *moved*, once the sergeant triggered the conditioning with a few key words. When people came out of it, they couldn't handle the memory. Being a butcher." I shook my head violently a couple of times. The dope was really getting to me.

"Look, I'm sorry," I got to my feet with some effort. "I've been up some twenty——"

"Of course, William." Mother took my elbow and steered me to a bedroom and promised to wake me in plenty of time for the evening's festivities. The bed was indecently comfortable but I could've slept leaning up against a lumpy tree.

Fatigue and dope and too full a day: Mother had to wake me up by trickling cold water on my face. She steered me to a closet and identified two outfits as being formal enough for the occasion. I chose a brick-red one—the powder blue seeming a little foppish—showered and shaved, refused cosmetics (Mike was all dolled up and offered to help me), armed myself with the half page of instructions telling how to get to the General Assembly, and was off.

I got lost twice along the way, but they have these little computers at every corridor intersection that will give you directions to anyplace, in fourteen languages.

Men's clothing, as far as I was concerned, had really taken a step backward. From the waist up it wasn't so bad, tight high-necked blouse with a short cap; but then there was a wide shiny functionless belt, from which dangled a little jeweled dagger, perhaps adequate for opening mail; and then pantaloons that flounced out in great pleats and were tucked into shiny snythetic high-heeled boots that came almost to your knees. Give me a plumed hat and Shakespeare would've hired me on the spot.

The women fared better. I met Marygay outside the General Assembly hall.

"I feel absolutely naked, William."

"Looks good, though. Anyhow, it's the style." Most of the young women I'd passed had been wearing a similar outfit: a simple shift with large rectangular windows cut in both sides, from armpit to hem. The hem ended where your imagination began. For modesty, the outfit required very conservative movements and a great faith in static electricity.

"Have you seen this place?" she said, taking my arm. "Let's go on in, Conquistador."

We walked in through the automatic doors and I stopped short. The hall was so large that going into it, you felt as if you'd stepped outdoors.

The floor was circular, more than a hundred meters in diameter. The walls rose a good sixty or seventy meters to a transparent dome—I remembered having seen it when we landed—on which gray drifts of snow danced and blew swirling away. The walls were done in a muted ceramic mosaic, thousands of figures representing a chronology of human achievement. I don't know how long I stared.

Across the hall, we joined the other hardy veterans for coffee. It was synthetic, but better than soya. To my dismay, I learned that tobacco was rarely grown on Earth and even, through local option, was outlawed in some areas in order to conserve arable land. What you could get was expensive and usually wretched, having been grown by amateurs on tiny backyard or balcony plots. The only good tobacco was Lunar and its price was, well, astronomical.

Marijuana was plentiful and cheap. In some countries, like the United States, it was free; produced and distributed by the government.

I offered Marygay a joint and she declined. "I've got to get used to them slowly. I had one earlier and it almost knocked me out."

"Me too."

An old man in uniform walked into the lounge, his breast a riotous fruit salad of ribbons, his shoulders weighed down with five stars apiece. He smiled benignly when half the people jumped to their feet. I was too much a civilian already, and remained seated.

"Good evening, good evening," he said, making a patting sit-down motion with his hand. "It's good to see you here. Good to see so many of you." Many? A little more than half the number we started out with.

"I'm General Gary Manker, UNEF Chief of Staff. In a few minutes we're going over there"—he nodded in the direction of the General Assembly hall—"for a short ceremony. Then you'll be free for a well-deserved rest; put your feet up for a few months, see the world, whatever you want. So long as you can keep the reporters away.

"Before you go over, though, I'd like to say a few words about what you'll want to do *after* those months, when you get tired of being on vacation, when the money starts to run low. . . ." Predictably, the same spiel General Botsford had given us at Stargate: you're going to need a job and this is the one job you can be sure of getting.

The general left after saying that an aide would be by in a few minutes to herd us over to the rostrum. We amused ourselves for several minutes, discussing the merits of reenlistment.

The aide turned out to be a good-looking young woman who had no trouble jollying us into alphabetical order (she didn't seem to have any higher opinion of the military than did we) and leading us over to the hall.

The first couple of rows of delegates had abandoned their desks to us. I sat in the "Gambia" place and listened uncomfortably to tales of heroism and sacrifice. General Manker had most of the facts right, but used slightly wrong words.

Then they called us up one by one and Dr. Ojukwu gave each of us a gold medal that must have weighed a kilogram. Then he gave a little speech about mankind united in common cause while discreet holo cameras scanned us one by one. Inspiring fare for the folks back home. Then we filed out under waves of applause that were somehow oppressive.

I had asked Marygay, who had no living relatives, to come on up and sack with me. There was a crowd milling around the formal entrance to the hall, so we hustled the other way, took the first escalator up several stories and got totally lost on a succession of slidewalks and lifts. Then we used the little corner boxes to find our way home.

I'd told Mother about Marygay and that I'd probably be bringing her back. They greeted each other warmly and Mother settled us in the living room with a couple of drinks and went off to start dinner. Mike joined us.

"You're going to find Earth awfully boring," he said after amenities.

"I don't know," I said. "Army life isn't exactly stimulating. Any change has got to be——"

"You can't get a job."

"Not in physics, I know; twenty-six years is like a geologic——"

"You can't get *any* job."

"Well, I'd planned to go back and take my Master's degree over, maybe go on. . . ." Mike was shaking his head.

"Let him finish, William." Marygay shifted restlessly. "I think he knows something we don't."

He finished his drink and swirled the ice around in the bottom of the glass, staring at it. "That's right. You know, the Moon is all UNEF, civilians and military, and we amuse ourselves by passing rumors back and forth."

"Old military pastime."

"Uh-huh. Well, I heard a rumor about you"—he made a sweeping gesture—"you veterans and went to the trouble to check it out. It was true."

"Glad to hear it."

"Yeah, you will be." He set down his drink, took out a joint, looked at it, put it back. "UNEF is going to do anything short of kidnaping to get you people back. They control the Employment Board and you can be damned sure you're going to be undertrained or overtrained for any job opening that comes along. Except soldier."

"Are you sure?" Marygay asked. We both knew enough not to claim they couldn't do a thing like that.

"Sure as a Christian. I have a friend on the Luna division of the Employment Board. He showed me the directive; it's worded very politely. And it says 'absolutely no exceptions'. "

"Maybe by the time I get out of school——"

"You'll never get *into* school. Never get past the maze of standards and quotas. If you try to push, they'll just claim you're too old—hell, I couldn't get into a doctoral program at *my* age, and you're——"

"Yeah, I get the idea. I'm two years older."

"That's it. You've got the choice of either spending the rest of your life on relief or soldiering."

"No contest," Marygay said. "Relief."

I agreed. "If five or six billion people can carve out a decent life without a profession, I can too."

"They've grown up in it," Mike said. "And it may not be what you would call a 'decent life'. Most of them just sit around and smoke dope and watch the holo. Get just enough to eat to balance their caloric output. Meat once a week. Even on Class I relief."

"That won't be anything new," I said. "The food part, anyhow—it's exactly the way we were fed in the Army.

"As for the rest of it, as you just said, Marygay and I didn't grow up in it; we're not likely to sit around half-blown and stare at the cube all day."

"I paint," Marygay said. "I always wanted to settle down and get really good at it."

"And I can continue studying physics even if it's not for a degree. And take up music or writing or——" I turned to Marygay. "Or any of those things the sergeant talked about at Stargate."

"Join the New Renaissance," he said without inflection, lighting his pipe. It was tobacco and smelled delicious.

He must have noticed my hunger. "Oh, I'm being a hell of a host." He got some papers out of his purse and rolled an expert joint. "Here. Marygay?"

"No thanks—if it's as hard to get as they say, I don't want to get back into the habit."

He nodded, relighting his pipe. "Never did anybody any good. Better to train your mind, be able to relax without it." He turned to me "The Army *did* keep up your cancer boosters?"

"Sure." Wouldn't do for you to die in so unsoldierly a fashion. I lit up the slender cigarette. "Good stuff."

"Better than anything you'll get on Earth. Lunar marijuana is better, too. Doesn't mess you up so much."

Mother came in and sat down. "Dinner'll be ready in a few minutes. I hear Michael making unfair comparisons again."

"What's unfair? Earth marijuana, a couple of J's and you're a zombi."

"Correction: *you* are. You're just not used to it."

"Okay, okay. And a boy shouldn't argue with his mother."

"Not when she's right," she said, strangely without humor. "Well! Do you children like fish?"

We talked about how hungry we were, a safe enough subject, for a few minutes and then sat down to a huge broiled red snapper, served on a bed of rice. It was the first square meal Marygay and I had had in twenty-six years.

VIII

The next day, like everyone else, I went to get interviewed on the cube. It was a frustrating experience.

Commentator: "Sergeant Mandella, you are one of the most-decorated soldiers in the UNEF." True, all of us had gotten a fistful of ribbons at Stargate. "You participated in the famous Aleph-null campaign, the first actual contact with Taurans, and just returned from an assault on Yod-Four."

Me: "Well, you couldn't call it——"

Commentator: "Before we talk about Yod-Four, I'm sure the audience would be very interested in your *personal* impression of the enemy, as one of the very few people to have met them face-to-face. They're pretty horrible-looking, aren't they?"

Me: "Well, yes; I'm sure you've seen the pictures. About all they don't show you is the texture of the skin. It's pebbly and wrinkled like a lizard's, but pale orange."

Commentator: "What do they smell like?" Smell?

Me: "I haven't got the faintest idea. All you can smell in a spacesuit is yourself."

Commentator: "Ha-ha, I see. What I'm trying to get, Sergeant, is how *you* felt, the first time you saw the enemy . . . were you afraid of them, disgusted, enraged, or what?"

"Well, I *was* afraid, the first time, and disgusted. Mostly afraid—but that was before the battle, when a solitary Tauran flew overhead. During the actual battle, we were under the influence of hate-conditioning—they conditioned us on Earth and triggered it with a phrase—and I didn't feel much except the artificial rage."

"You despised them—and showed no mercy."

"Right. Murdered them all, even though they made no attempt to fight back. But when they released us from the conditioning . . . well, we couldn't believe we had been such butchers. Fourteen people went insane and all the rest of us were on tranquilizers for weeks."

"Ah," he said, absent-mindedly, and glanced over to the side for a moment. "How many of them did you kill, yourself?"

"Fifteen, twenty—I don't know; as I said, we weren't in control of ourselves. It was a massacre."

All through the interview, the commentator seemed a bit dense, repetitive. I found out why that night.

Marygay and I were watching the cube with Mike. Mom was off getting fitted with some artificial teeth (the dentists in Geneva supposedly being better than American ones). My interview was on a program called *Potpourri,* sandwiched between a documentary on Lunar hydroponics and a concert by a man who claimed to be able to play Telemann's *Double Fantasia in A Major* on the harmonica. I wondered whether anybody else in Geneva, in the world, was tuned in.

Well, the hydroponics thing was interesting and the harmonica player was a virtuoso, but the thing in between was pure drivel.

Commentator: "What do they smell like?"

Me (off-camera): "Just horrible, a combination of rotten vegetables and burning sulfur. The smell leaks in through the exhaust of your suit.''

He had kept me talking and talking in order to get a wide spectrum of sounds, from which he could synthesize any kind of nonsense in response to his question.

"How the hell can he do that?" I asked Mike when the show was over.

"Don't be too hard on him," Mike said, watching the quadruplicated musician play four different harmonicas against himself. "All the media are censored by the UNEF. It's been ten, twelve years since Earth had any objective reporting about the war. You're lucky they didn't just substitute an actor for you and feed him lines."

"Is it any better on Luna?"

"Not as far as public broadcast. But since everyone there is tied into UNEF, it's easy enough to find out when they're lying outright."

"He cut out *completely* the part about conditioning."

"Understandable." Mike shrugged. "They need heroes, not automatons."

Marygay's interview was on an hour later, and they had done the same thing to her. Every time she had originally said something against the war or the Army, the cube would switch to a closeup of the woman interviewing her, who would nod sagely while a remarkable imitation of Marygay's voice gave out arrant nonsense.

UNEF was paying for five days' room and board in Geneva, and it seemed as good a place as any to begin exploring this new Earth. The next morning we got a map—which was a book a centimeter thick—and took a lift to the ground floor, determined to work our way up to the roof without missing anything.

The ground floor was an odd mixture of history and heavy industry. The base of the building covered a large part of what used to be the city of Geneva, and a lot of old buildings were preserved.

Mostly, though, it was all noise and hustle: big g-e trucks

growling in from outside, shedding clouds of snow; barges booming against dock pilings (the Rhone River crawls through the middle of the huge expanse); even a few little helicopters beating this way and that, coordinating things, keeping away from the struts and buttresses that held up the gray sky of the next floor, forty meters up.

It was a marvel and more and we could have watched it for hours, but we would've frozen solid in a few minutes, with just light capes against the wind and cold. We decided we'd come back another day, more warmly dressed.

The floor above was called the first floor, in defiance of logic. Marygay explained that the Europeans had always numbered them that way (funny, I'd been a thousand light-years from New Mexico, and back, but this was the first time I'd crossed the Atlantic). It was the brains of the organism, where the bureaucrats and the systems analysts and the cryogenic handymen hung around.

We stood in a large quiet lobby that somehow smelled of glass. One wall was a huge holo cube displaying Geneva's table of organization, a spidery orange pyramid with tens of thousands of names connected by lines, from the mayor at top to the "corridor security" people at the base. Names flicked out and were replaced by new ones as people died or were fired or promoted or demoted. Shimmering, changing shape, it looked like the nervous system of some fantastic creature. In a sense, of course, it was.

The wall opposite the holo cube was a window overlooking a large room which a plaque identified as the *"Kontrollezimmer."* Behind the glass were hundreds of technicians in neat rows and columns, each with his own console with a semi-flat holo surrounded by dials and switches. There was an electric, busy air to the place: most of the people had on an earphone-microphone headset, talking with some other technician while they scribbled on a tablet or fiddled with switches; others rattled away on console keyboards with their headsets dangling from their necks. A very few seats were empty, their owners striding around looking important. An automated coffee tray slid slowly up one row and down the next.

Through the glass you could hear a faint susurrus of what must have been an unholy commotion inside.

There were only two other people in the lobby, and we overheard them say they were going to look at "the brain." We followed them down a long corridor to another viewing area, rather small in comparison to the one overlooking the control room, looking down on the computers that held Geneva together. The only illumination in the viewing area was the faint cold blue light from the room below.

The computer room was also small in comparison, about the size of a baseball diamond. The computer elements were featureless gray boxes of various sizes, connected by a maze of man-sized glass tunnels which had air locks at regular intervals. Evidently this system allowed access to one element at a time, for repair, while the rest of the room remained at a temperature near absolute zero, for superconductivity.

Though lacking the nervous activity of the control room, and far from the exciting hurly-burly on the floor below, the computer room was more impressive in its own static way: the feeling of vast, unknowable powers under constraint; a shrine to purpose, order, intelligence.

The other couple told us there was nothing else of interest on the floor, just meeting rooms and offices and busy officials. We got back on the lift and went to the second floor, which was the main shopping arcade.

Here, the map-book was very handy. The arcade was hundreds of shops and open-air markets arranged in a rectangular grid pattern, with interlacing slidewalks defining blocks where related shops were grouped together. We went to the central mall, which turned out to be a whimsical reconstruction of medieval village architecture. There was a Baroque church whose steeple, by holographic illusion, extended into the third and fourth floors. Smooth wall mosaics with primitive religious scenes, cobblestones laid out in intricate patterns, a fountain with water spraying from monsters' mouths . . . we bought a bunch of grapes from an open-air greengrocer (the illusion faltered when he took a calorie ticket and stamped my ration book) and walked along the narrow brick sidewalks, loving it. I was glad Earth still had time, and energy and resources, for this sort of thing.

There was a bewildering variety of objects and services for sale, and we had plenty of money, but we'd got out of the habit of buying things, I guess, and we didn't know how long our fortunes were going to have to last.

(We *did* have small fortunes, in spite of what General Botsford had said. Rogers' father was some kind of hot-shot tax lawyer, and she'd passed the word—we only had to pay tax at the rate set for our *average* annual income. I wound up with $280,000.)

We skipped the third floor, mostly communications, because we'd crawled all over it the day before, when we went for our interviews. I was tempted to go speak to the person who'd rearranged my words, but Marygay convinced me it would be futile.

The artificial mountain of Geneva is "stepped"—like a wedding cake—the first three floors and the ground level about a kilometer in diameter, rising about a hundred meters; floors four through thirty-two the same height but about half the diameter. Floors thirty-three through seventy-two make up the top cylinder, about three hundred meters in diameter by a hundred and twenty meters high.

The fourth floor, like the thirty-third, is a park; trees, brooks, little animals. The walls are transparent, open in good weather, and the "shelf" (the roof of the third floor) is planted in heavy forest. We rested for a while by a pond, watching people swim and feeding bits of grape to the minnows.

Something had been bothering me subliminally ever since we arrived in Geneva and suddenly, surrounded by all these gay people, I knew what it was.

"Marygay," I said, "nobody here is unhappy."

She smiled. "Who could be glum in a place like this? All the flowers and——"

"No, no . . . I mean in all of Geneva. Have you seen anybody who looked like he might be dissatisfied with the way things are? Who——"

"Your brother . . . ."

"Yeah, but he's a foreigner too. I mean, the merchants and workers and the people just hanging around."

She looked thoughtful. "I haven't really been looking. Maybe not."

"Doesn't that strike you as strange?"

"It is unusual . . . but. . . ." She threw a whole grape in the water and the minnows scattered. "Remember what that homosexual sergeant said? They diagnose and correct antisocial traits at a very early age. And what rational person wouldn't be happy here?"

I snorted. "Half of these people are out of work and most of the others are doing artificial jobs that are either redundant or could be done better by machine."

"But they all have enough to eat and plenty to occupy their minds. That wasn't so, twenty-six years ago."

"Maybe," I said, not wanting to argue. "I suppose you're right." Still, it bothered me.

IX

We spent the rest of that day and all of the next in the United Nations headquarters, essentially the capital of the world, that took up the whole top cylinder of Geneva. It would have taken weeks to see everything. Hell, it would take more than a week just to cover the Family of Man Museum. And every country had its own individual display, with a shop selling typical crafts, sometimes a restaurant with native food. I had been afraid that national identities might have been submerged; that this new world would be long on order and short on variety. Glad to have been mistaken.

Marygay and I planned a travel itinerary while we toured the UN. We decided we'd go back to the United States and find a place to stay, then spend a couple of months traveling around.

When I approached Mom for advice in getting an apartment, she seemed strangely embarrassed, the way Sergeant Siri had been.

But she said she'd see what was available in Washington (my father'd had a job there and Mom hadn't seen any reason to move after he died) when she got back, the next day.

I asked Mike about this reluctance to talk about housing and he said it was a hangover from the chaotic years between the food riots and the reconstruction. There just hadn't been enough roofs to go around; people had had to live two families to a room even in countries that had been prosperous. It had been an unstable situation and finally the UN stepped in, first with a propaganda campaign and finally with mass conditioning, reinforcing the idea that it was virtuous to live in as small a place as possible, that it was sinful to even *want* to live alone or in a place with lots of room. And one didn't talk about it.

Most people still had some remnant of this conditioning, even though they were detoxified over a decade before. In various strata of society it was impolite or unforgivable or rather daring, to talk about such things.

Mom went back to Washington and Mike to Luna while Marygay and I stayed on at Geneva for a couple of days.

We got off the plane at Dulles and found a monorail to Rifton, the satellite-city where Mom was living.

It was refreshingly small after vast Geneva, even though it spread over a larger area. It was a pleasingly diverse jumble of various kinds of buildings, only a couple more than a few stories high, arranged around a lake, surrounded by trees. All of the buildings were connected by slidewalk to the largest place, a Fullerdome with stores and schools and offices. There we found a directory that told us how to get to Mom's place, a duplex on the lake.

We could have taken the enclosed slidewalk but instead walked alongside it, in the good cold air and smell of fallen leaves. People slid by on the other side of the plastic, carefully not staring.

Mom didn't answer her door but it turned out not to be locked. It was a comfortable place, extremely spacious by starship standards, full of Twentieth-Century furniture. Mom was asleep in the bedroom, so Marygay and I settled in the living room and read for a while.

We were startled suddenly by a loud fit of coughing from the bedroom. I raced over and knocked on the door.

"William? I didn't"—coughing—"come in, I didn't know you were. . . ."

We went in and she was propped up in bed, the light on, surrounded by various nostrums. She looked ghastly, pale and lined.

She lit a joint and it seemed to quell the coughing. "When did you get in? I didn't know. . . ."

"Just a few minutes ago. But what about you? How long has this . . . have you been. . . ."

"Oh, it's just a bug I picked up in Geneva. I'll be fine in a couple of days." She started coughing again, drank some thick red liquid from a bottle. All of her medicines seemed to be the commercial, patent variety.

"Have you seen a doctor?"

"Doctor? Heavens, no, Willy. They don't have, it's not serious, don't——"

"Not serious?" At eighty-four. "For Chrissake, Mother." I went to the phone in the kitchen and with some difficulty managed to get the hospital.

A plain girl in her twenties formed in the cube. "Nurse Donaldson, General Services." She had a fixed smile, professional sincerity. But then everybody smiled.

"My mother needs to be looked at by a doctor. She has a——"

"Name and number, please."

"Bette Mandella." I spelled it. "What number?"

"Medical services number, of course," she smiled.

I called in to Mom and asked her what her number was. "She says she can't remember."

"That's all right, sir, I'm sure I can find her records." She turned her smile to a keyboard beside her and punched out some code.

"Bette Mandella?" she said, her smile turning quizzical. *"You're* her son? But she must be in her eighties."

"Please. It's a long story. She really has to see a doctor."

"Is this some kind of joke?"

"What do you mean?" Strangled coughing from the other room, the worst yet. "Really—this might be very serious, you've got to——"

"But, sir, Mrs. Mandella got a zero priority rating 'way back in 2010."

"What the hell is that supposed to mean?"

"S-i-r . . ." the smile was hardening in place.

"Look. Pretend that I came from another planet. What is a 'zero priority rating'?"

"Another—oh! I know you!" She looked off to the left. "Sonya—come over here a second, you'd never guess who. . . ." Another face crowded the cube, a vapid blond girl whose smile was twin to the other nurse's. "Remember? On the stat this morning?"

"Oh yeah," she said. "One of the soldiers—hey, that's really max, really max." The head withdrew.

"Oh, Mr. Mandella," she said, effusive. "No wonder you're confused. It's really very simple."

"Well?"

"It's part of the Universal Medical Security System. Everybody gets a rating on their seventieth birthday. It comes in automatically from Geneva."

"What does it rate? What does it mean?" But the ugly truth was obvious.

"Well, it tells how important a person is and what level of treatment he's allowed. Class three is the same as anybody else's; class two is the same except for certain life-extending——"

"And class zero is no treatment at all."

"That's correct, Mr. Mandella." And in her smile there was not a glimmer of pity or understanding.

"Thank you." I disconnected. Marygay was standing behind me, crying soundlessly with her mouth wide open.

I found mountaineer's oxygen at a sporting goods store and even managed to get some black-market antibiotics through a character in a bar in downtown Washington. But Mom was beyond being able to respond to amateur treatment. She lived four days. The people from the crematorium had the same fixed smile.

I tried to get through to Mike, but the phone company wouldn't let me place the call until I had signed a contract and posted a twenty-five-thousand-dollar bond. I had to get a credit transfer from Geneva. The paperwork took half a day.

I finally got through to him. Without preamble: "Mother's dead."

There was a lapse of about a second while the radio waves wandered up to the Moon and another lapse coming back. He started and then nodded his head slowly. "No surprise. Every time I've come down to Earth, the past ten years, I've wondered whether she'll still be there. Neither of us really had enough money to keep in very close touch." He had told us in Geneva that a letter from Luna to Earth cost a hundred dollars' postage—plus five thousand tax. It discouraged communication with what the UN considered to be a bunch of regrettably necessary anarchists.

We commiserated for a while and then Mike said, "Willy, Earth is no place for you and Marygay; you know that by now. Come to Luna. Where you can still be an individual. Where we don't throw people out the air lock on their seventieth birthday."

"We'd have to rejoin UNEF."

"True, but you wouldn't have to fight. They say they need you more for training. And you could study in your spare time, bring your physics up to date—maybe wind up eventually in research."

We talked some more, a total of three minutes. I got a thousand dollars back.

Marygay and I talked about it for hours. We went to bed and still talked, couldn't sleep, rattled on for hours saying the same things over and over.

Life on the Moon would be hard. Few luxuries, military discipline, long hours, constant danger from the environment.

Life on Earth was comfortable. We could sit back and have our needs taken care of, smoke the doctored dope until nothing looked wrong and we were as satisfied as all the other civilians seemed to be.

But right now our minds were clear and we could see that the price of this happy order was total surrender to the collective will. Who wants to be a happy zombi?

On the other hand, being realistic, we would have little enough "free will" back in UNEF. It would be better, of course, than before, being officers—but UNEF could honor its contract for a year or two and then suddenly have us back out in a Strike Force.

But maybe they were telling the truth and didn't want us for expensive cannon fodder; maybe they needed experienced soldiers to train new recruits, to crack the shell of Pollyannish conditioning that every civilian would have.

We talked about these things and for the first time we talked about love. Whether love would better flourish under one set of constraints or the other. Whether the game was worth the candle in either case.

Maybe our decision might have been different if we hadn't been staying in that particular place, surrounded by artifacts of Mother's life and death. But we stopped talking at dawn, when in the cold gray light the proud, ambitious, careful beauty of Rifton turned sinister and foreboding; we packed two small bags and had our money transferred to the Tycho Credit Union and took a monorail to the Cape.

X

"In case you're interested, you aren't the only combat veterans to have come back." The recruiting officer was a muscular lieutenant of indeterminate gender. I flipped a coin mentally and it came up tails.

"Last I heard, there had been nine others," she said in her husky tenor. "All of them opted for the Moon . . . maybe you'll find some of your friends there." She slid two simple forms across the desk. "Sign these and you're in again. Second lieutenants."

The form was a simple request to be assigned to active duty; we had never really gotten out of UNEF, since they had extended the draft law, but had just been on inactive status. I scrutinized the paper.

"There's nothing on here about the guarantees we were promised at Stargate."

"What guarantees?" She had that bland, mechanical Earth-smile.

"We were guaranteed assignment of choice and location of choice. There's nothing about that on this contract."

"That won't be necessary. The Force will. . . ."

"*I* think it's necessary, Lieutenant." I handed back the form. So did Marygay.

"Let me check." She left the desk and disappeared into an office. She was on a phone for a while and then we heard a printer rattle.

She brought back the same two sheets, with an addition typed under our names: "GUARANTEED LOCATION OF CHOICE [LUNA] AND ASSIGNMENT OF CHOICE [COMBAT TRAINING SPECIALIST]."

We got a thorough physical checkup and were fitted for new fighting suits. The next morning we caught the first shuttle to orbit, enjoyed zero-G for a few hours while they transferred cargo to a spidery tachyon-torch shuttle, then zipped to the Moon, setting down at Grimaldi base.

On the door to the Transient Officers' Billet, some wag had scratched, "Abandon hope all ye who enter." We found our two-man cubicle and began changing for chow.

Two raps on the door. "Mail call, sirs."

I opened the door and the sergeant standing there saluted. I just looked at him for a second and then remembered I was an officer and returned the salute. He handed me two identical 'faxes. I gave one to Marygay and our hearts must have stopped simultaneously.

"They didn't waste any time, did they?" Marygay said bitterly.

"Must be standing order. Strike Force Command's light-weeks away. They can't even know we've reupped yet."

"What about our. . . ." She let it trail off.

The guarantee. "Well, we *were* given our assignment of choice. Nobody guaranteed we'd have the assignment for more than an hour."

"It's so dirty."

I shrugged. "It's so Army." But I had two disturbing feelings: That all along we knew this was going to happen.

That we were going home.

The Birds

THOMAS M. DISCH

*There can be no theme to an annual anthology since it is assembled
after the act, after the stories have been written and published. The
stories that are collected here are selected for quality—not fash-
ionable content. If more than one story centers around a particular
idea this is because the idea is one that is disturbing authors.
Pollution bothers us all and no thinking writer can be indifferent to
mankind's continuous and casual destruction of the only world we
have. In the two stories that follow two different writers consider
the problem in two very different ways. Thomas Disch looks at it
wryly, darkly, humorously with his own particularly clear vision.*

"I fail to understand," Daffy said, in a kind of squawk, "how
they could have done this."

"People," Curtis commented. It was his explanation for everything.

"But *how?*" She plucked gluey pieces of down from the soft,
dead eggs.

"It's not *your* fault, darling. It's that spray they spray things
with. Science."

"Hate, I call it."

"Well, well." Curtis dug his beak into his oily brown feathers.
These outbursts of his wife's always rather embarrassed him.
"You've got to try and look at things from *their* point of view."

"All right, smartass, look at *this* from their point of view." And
she dug down savagely into the feeble shell and lifted out a
half-formed featherless duckling. "That's what all your damned

106

. . . ." But with the duckling in her beak she couldn't pronounce the word "objectivity."

Curtis, alarmed, spread his wings and rose a few feet into the air, but the oiled feathers did not permit sustained flight. He settled a few yards off on the slick surface of the pond.

Daffy dropped her lifeless burden back into the nest. She felt a hopelessness extremer than any sorrow. Everything she'd ever done, every instinct that had ever driven her, every scrap of down she'd ever plucked from her scrawny breast, had issued at last in this . . . futility.

Curtis, while his wife mooned about on the shore, kept diving down to the bottom and rooting about for something edible in the nonbiodegradable debris. He worked with a sullen, steady determination until he discovered a strand of weed quite two feet long. He waddled up to the shore with it, proud with accomplishment and coated with muck. He laid the weed at his wife's feet.

She gobbled down half its length greedily, then, gagging, spit out the whole black mulch. "It tastes like . . . !" she used an unprintable epithet.

Curtis nibbled at the weed. "I wish it did," he joked, cocking his head to one side. "I wish it tasted *half* that good."

Daffy laughed.

"Try and force yourself to eat it, darling," Curtis urged, resuming his manner of maddening reasonableness. "You must keep up your strength."

"*Why* must I? To what purpose?"

"Do you love me?"

Daffy turned her head away, almost tucking it under her left wing.

"Well? Do you?"

"Yes."

"That's why then. We've still got each other. As long as we've got each other, the world isn't coming to an end."

Her first impulse was to question even this. Love? Daffy's whole being was instinct with love—but not for Curtis, only for those poor lifeless creatures in the nest. But she couldn't expect her husband to understand this, and really, did she want him to? Stifling her protest, she bent down and forced herself to eat the putrid black weed.

It was autumn. Such leaves as had survived the summer had long since fallen from the trees. The ever-changing multitudes of insects that had sustained Daffy and Curtis through August and September had disappeared as suddenly and unaccountably as they had come. The bottom of the pond was scraped bare of all but its plastic and aluminum.

They knew what must be done. The necessity of flight tingled in the muscles of their wings and breasts like the thrill of sex, and yet a strange reluctance made them linger by the exhausted pond. Some counter-instinct, a kind of hysteria, as strong as the need that drove them upward ever and again, would force them each time to return, baffled, to the water still rippling from their departure.

Curtis proposed a number of theories to account for their aberrant behavior: panic syndrome, genetic alteration, their unaccustomed diet, a shift in the magnetic poles. But reason was no proof against what they *felt* each time they reached a certain altitude, the absolute, invincible terror.

"But we can't stay here," Daffy protested. Her only mode of argument was to repeat some incontestable fact. "I mean, we just can't."

"I know that."

"Something terrible will happen."

"I know that too."

"Well, I *feel* it—a kind of chill."

"Daffy, I'm *trying* to think."

"Think! You've been thinking for weeks, and where has it got us? Look at those trees! Feel this water—it's ice!"

"I know, I know."

"Tomorrow we've just got to. I mean we've *got* to."

"We say that every night, Daffy, and every morning it's the same old story—funk."

"I feel this incredible *urge*. To fly."

"That's it!"

Daffy nodded gloomily. "Of course that's it. So why don't we?"

"Flying: whenever we try to fly from here we always get up to a certain point and then the other thing sets in. Right?"

"But I thought you just said . . . ?" She was confused again.

"We'll walk."

"Walk? All that way?"

"As far as we can get. Maybe it's only right in this area that we can't lift off. Maybe it's the sight on the pond, I don't know."

"But I don't *like* to walk, not for any distance."

Curtis said no more. He tucked his feet up and buried his head and pretended to be asleep. Daffy, who liked to weigh all the pros and cons of any major decision, soliloquized restlessly, swimming around in abstracted circles, but at last she had to admit that Curtis was right.

In the morning they began to waddle south.

The highway stretched before them as far as the eye could see, parched and gray and unproviding, smooth as the calmest water. Gigantic machines hurtled past, so fast they seemed to fall toward the horizon. The two ducks trudged on, ignoring the machines and ignored by them. Daffy would have preferred keeping to the stubble, but Curtis insisted they'd make better time on the road. It wasn't so much that she felt threatened; it was just that the incessant zoom, zoom, zoom made any kind of conversation impossible.

They were both unutterably weary, and yet the urge to mount upward persisted as strongly as ever. Once, earlier, saying that she would just ruffle her wings a bit, Daffy had spread herself to the air and instinct had lifted her body like the updraught of a cyclone. Curtis had caught hold of the little metal band around her foot in the nick of time. For a while it had hung in the balance whether he would rise up with her or she fall back to earth with him. Then her wings had given out and she lay on the ground in an agony of shame and longing.

"I can't walk any more. I *can't*. You've broken my leg."

"Nonsense," Curtis said uncertainly.

"I think I'm dying. I've got to fly."

"If you fly now the same thing is going to happen."

"No, Curtis, I'm over that now. I really think I am."

"You'll get up there and you'll see the pond and just head right back to it. All this effort will have been wasted."

"I'll be careful. I promise."

"I won't argue about it any more, Daffy." And he had set off down the road. She had waited for him to look back, but he didn't, and finally she'd followed him, clenching her wings tightly to her side.

Toward evening the highway curved over to where the sun was sinking into smog. They'd been on the right side of the road, and so there was no way for them to continue south except by crossing it. The traffic, however, was worse than it had been at any point that day.

"If we flew," Daffy ventured.

"We'll wait," Curtis said in a tone that brooked no contradiction.

They waited and waited and waited, but there was never a letup in both directions at the same time. The cars had turned their headlights on, and Daffy grew dizzy watching her shadow swoop and disappear, swoop and disappear across the concrete. At last they gave up and climbed down into the ditch alongside the road, where by a stroke of luck they found a lovely puddle to sleep in.

The first thing Daffy saw when she awoke was the malevolent glint of a rat's eyes not one yard away. Without thinking she tried to spring up out of the water but her wings refused to move. She honked hysterically. Curtis woke and saw the rat, yet he too remained strangely immobile. So, for that matter, did the rat.

None of this is real, Daffy thought. I'm having a nightmare.

But Curtis, in his usual unruffled way, had come to a different conclusion. "The puddle froze during the night. That's why we can't move—we're trapped in ice."

"But the rat!"

"The rat is dead, Daffy."

"But look at it—those teeth!"

"*You* look at it. Better than that, smell it. I'd estimate that it's been lying there like that for a week."

Curtis methodically began pecking at the ice in which he was embedded, and in a little while he was able to come over and help Daffy extricate herself. She'd been sleeping in a shallower part of the puddle, and it was much harder work. In her haste she lost a good many feathers.

The whole length of the ditch was covered with rats in various stages of decomposition, as well as two dead weasels and a half-eaten owl. Daffy felt a disturbing mingling of pleasure and fear as she regarded the slain legions of her enemies. On the one hand the world was certainly better off without predators; she could not as easily define what it was on the other hand, but it was there.

"Daffy, look over here at this cave."

"For goodness' sake, Curtis, don't you know better than to—You're not going *in* there, are you? Curtis!" She rushed over to the opening too late to prevent him from entering.

"Look! At the other end. I can see light! This goes right under the highway to the other side."

"Curtis, come back!" She advanced a few steps into the darkness. Curtis was already yards ahead. She could see him silhouetted against the disc of light at the other end of the cave.

"We're going south, Daffy. *South!*" His voice echoed weirdly.

Daffy took another cautious step forward, right onto the furry body of a rat. She screamed and sprang up in terror, only to dash her head against the top of the culvert.

"Don't be afraid, darling. All these rats are dead, just like——"

At that moment the last living rat sprang for Curtis's throat. Curtis struggled to escape, rising again and again, battering his wings against the concrete and against his assailant, who clung with feeble tenacity. However often he was struck, however often

Curtis collapsed on top of him, he did not lose his purchase. Their struggle continued until they were both dead.

Daffy flew south. She had flown for days—past great gray lakes and greater, grayer cities, above the writhings of rivers and roads, through stinging clouds and blinding smoke: south. She had forgotten Curtis, it seemed, the moment she'd risen into the air. She became a rhythm of wings. Once or twice she knew an instant of panic, but it was not the old self-betraying urge to return to the nest moldering beside the pond. She simply felt lost, out of formation. In the first migrations of her youth she had been a single mote in a multitude of eight or nine, forming with the rest one entity, one action, one desire. But those panics subsided and were replaced by a growing certainty that the previous unity was somehow about to be restored to her.

She began to talk to herself. "Everything works out in the end," she would say. "You worry and you fret and you think the whole world is falling to pieces, and then lo and behold—the next day it's raining! I'm not saying that this is an *ideal* world. That would be silly. You only have to look around you to see, well, all sorts of things. But if you just keep going along and doing as best you can the thing you've *got* to do, it all works out."

She flew and she flew and in no time at all (though actually she was more tired than she cared to admit) she had come to the ocean. Her spirits soared. It would only be a little way now, another day at the most.

But as her flight took her out over the water something strange happened. At first she thought it was just a symptom of fatigue. Her wings would reach for the air—and miss. It was as though here above the ocean the nature of the atmosphere were changing. She became confused about her direction and had to veer far to the right and to the left to get back to a clear sense of the south. She seemed to hear thunder out of the cloudless sky, usually faint but sometimes so loud that if she'd closed her eyes she would have believed herself to be in the middle of a storm.

"This is absurd," she quacked irately. If there had been anything tangible to be afraid of, she would have been afraid. But there wasn't.

The air cracked and a few seconds were ripped out of the steady southern progression of time. The thunder became monstrous and then, just when she thought she couldn't bear any more, ceased.

"Well! Let's hope. . . ."

The sky collapsed. As the Concorde passed invisibly above her, Daffy plummeted, lifeless, into the ruined ocean.

The Wind and the Rain

ROBERT SILVERBERG

If we keep on attacking our environment as we have been doing, with no attempt to understand it or to live within its ecological bounds, we are going to destroy it. We have that ability. What will happen then? Robert Silverberg has received all of the writing awards in science fiction because he does it so well, as he does it here, looking with a very cool eye at just what we are doing to ourselves.

The planet cleanses itself. That is the important thing to remember, at moments when we become too pleased with ourselves. The healing process is a natural and inevitable one. The action of the wind and the rain, the ebbing and flowing of the tides, the vigorous rivers flushing out the choked and stinking lakes—these are all natural rhythms, all healthy manifestations of universal harmony. Of course, we are here too. We do our best to hurry the process along. But we are only auxiliaries, and we know it. We must not exaggerate the value of our work. False pride is worse than a sin: it is a foolishness. We do not deceive ourselves into thinking we are important. If we were not here at all, the planet would repair itself anyway within twenty to fifty million years. It is estimated that our presence cuts that time down by somewhat more than half.

The uncontrolled release of methane into the atmosphere was one of the most serious problems. Methane is a colorless, odorless gas, sometimes known as "swamp gas." Its components are carbon and hydrogen. Much of the atmosphere of Jupiter and

114

Saturn consists of methane. (Jupiter and Saturn have never been habitable by human beings.) A small amount of methane was always normally present in the atmosphere of Earth. However, the growth of human population produced a consequent increase in the supply of methane. Much of the methane released into the atmosphere came from swamps and coal mines. A great deal of it came from Asian rice fields fertilized with human or animal waste; methane is a by-product of the digestive process.

The surplus methane escaped into the lower stratosphere, from ten to thirty miles above the surface of the planet, where a layer of ozone molecules once existed. Ozone, formed of three oxygen atoms, absorbs the harmful ultraviolet radiation that the sun emits. By reacting with free oxygen atoms in the stratosphere, the intrusive methane reduced the quantity available for ozone formation. Moreover, methane reactions in the stratosphere yielded water vapor that further depleted the ozone. This methane-induced exhaustion of the ozone content of the stratosphere permitted the unchecked ultraviolet bombardment of the Earth, with a consequent rise in the incidence of skin cancer.

A major contributor to the methane increase was the flatulence of domesticated cattle. According to the U. S. Department of Agriculture, domesticated ruminants in the late twentieth century were generating more than eighty-five million tons of methane a year. Yet nothing was done to check the activities of these dangerous creatures. Are you amused by the idea of a world destroyed by herds of farting cows? It must not have been amusing to the people of the late twentieth century. However, the extinction of domesticated ruminants shortly helped to reduce the impact of this process.

Today we must inject colored fluids into a major river. Edith, Bruce, Paul, Elaine, Oliver, Ronald, and I have been assigned to this task. Most members of the team believe the river is the Mississippi, although there is some evidence that it may be the Nile. Oliver, Bruce and Edith believe it is more likely to be the Nile than the Mississippi, but they defer to the opinion of the majority. The river is wide and deep and its color is black in some places and dark green in others. The fluids are computer-mixed on the east bank of the river in a large factory erected by a previous reclamation team. We supervise their passage into the river. First we inject the red fluid, then the blue, then the yellow; they have different densities and form parallel stripes running for many hundreds of kilometers in the water. We are not certain whether these fluids are active healing agents—that is, substances which dissolve the solid pollutants lining the riverbed—or merely serve as markers permitting further chemical analysis of the river by the orbiting satellite system. It is not necessary for us to understand what we are doing, so long as we follow instructions explicitly. Elaine jokes about going swimming. Bruce says, "How absurd. This river is famous for deadly fish that will strip the flesh from your bones." We all laugh at that. *Fish?* Here? What fish could be as deadly as the river itself? This water would consume our flesh if we entered it, and probably dissolve our bones as well. I scribbled a poem yesterday and dropped it in, and the paper vanished instantly.

In the evenings we walk along the beach and have philosophical discussions. The sunsets on this coast are embellished by rich tones of purple, green, crimson, and yellow. Sometimes we cheer when a particularly beautiful combination of atmospheric gases transforms the sunlight. Our mood is always optimistic and gay. We are never depressed by the things we find on this planet. Even devastation can be an art form, can it not? Perhaps it is one of the greatest of all art forms, since an art of destruction *consumes* its medium, it *devours* its own epistemological foundations, and in this sublimely nullifying doubling-back upon its origins it far exceeds in moral complexity those forms which are merely productive. That is, I place a higher value on transformative art than on generative art. Is my meaning clear? In any event, since art ennobles and exalts the spirits of those who perceive it, we are exalted and ennobled by the conditions of Earth. We envy those who collaborated to create those extraordinary conditions. We

know ourselves to be small-souled folk of a minor latter-day
epoch; we lack the dynamic grandeur of energy that enabled our
ancestors to commit such depredations. This world is a symphony.
Naturally you might argue that to restore a planet takes more
energy than to destroy it, but you would be wrong. Nevertheless,
though our daily tasks leave us weary and drained, we also feel
stimulated and excited, because by restoring this world, the
mother-world of mankind, we are in a sense participating in the
original splendid process of its destruction. I mean in the sense that
the resolution of a dissonant chord participates in the dissonance of
that chord.

Now we have come to Tokyo, the capital of the island empire of
Japan. See how small the skeletons of the citizens are? That is one
way we have of identifying this place as Japan. The Japanese are
known to have been people of small stature. Edward's ancestors
were Japanese. He is of small stature. (Edith says his skin should
be yellow as well. His skin is just like ours. Why is his skin not
yellow?) "See?" Edward cries. "There is Mount Fuji!" It is an
extraordinarily beautiful mountain, mantled in white snow. On its
slopes one of our archaeological teams is at work, tunneling under
the snow to collect samples from the twentieth-century strata of
chemical residues, dust, and ashes. "Once there were over
seventy-five thousand industrial smokestacks around Tokyo,"
says Edward proudly, "from which were released hundreds of
tons of sulfur, nitrous oxides, ammonia and carbon gases every
day. We should not forget that this city had more than one and a
half million automobiles as well." Many of the automobiles are
still visible, but they are very fragile, worn to threads by the action
of the atmosphere. When we touch them they collapse in puffs of
gray smoke. Edward, who has studied his heritage well, tells us,
"It was not uncommon for the density of carbon monoxide in the
air here to exceed the permissible levels by factors of 250 percent
on mild summer days. Owing to atmospheric conditions, Mount
Fuji was visible only one day of every nine. Yet no one showed
dismay." He conjures up for us a picture of his small, industrious

yellow ancestors toiling cheerfully and unremittingly in their poisonous environment. The Japanese, he insists, were able to maintain and even increase their gross national product at a time when other nationalities had already begun to lose ground in the global economic struggle because of diminished population owing to unfavorable ecological factors. And so on and so on. After a time we grow bored with Edward's incessant boasting. "Stop boasting," Oliver tells him, "or we will expose you to the atmosphere." We have much dreary work to do here. Paul and I guide the huge trenching machines; Oliver and Ronald follow, planting seeds. Almost immediately, strange angular shrubs spring up. They have shiny bluish leaves and long crooked branches. One of them seized Elaine by the throat yesterday and might have hurt her seriously had Bruce not uprooted it. We were not upset. This is merely one phase in the long, slow process of repair. There will be many such incidents. Someday cherry trees will blossom in this place.

This is the poem that the river ate:

DESTRUCTION. I. *Nouns*. Destruction, desolation, wreck, wreckage, ruin, ruination, rack and ruin, smash, smashup, demolition, demolishment, ravagement, havoc, ravage, dilapidation, decimation, blight, breakdown, consumption, dissolution, obliteration, overthrow, spoilage; mutilation, disintegration, undoing, pulverization; sabotage, vandalism; annulment, damnation, extinguishment, extinction, invalidation, nullification, shatterment, shipwreck; annihilation, disannulment, discreation, extermination, extirpation, obliteration, perdition, subversion.
II. *Verbs*. Destroy, wreck, ruin, ruinate, smash, demolish, raze, ravage, gut, dilapidate, decimate, blast, blight, break down, consume, dissolve, overthrow; mutilate, disintegrate, unmake, pulverize; sabotage, vandalize; annul, blast, blight, damn, dash, extinguish, invalidate, nullify, quell, quench, scuttle, shatter, shipwreck, torpedo, smash, spoil,

undo, void; annihilate, devour, disannul, discreate, ex-
terminate, obliterate, extirpate, subvert; corrode, erode,
sap, undermine, waste, waste away, whittle away (*or*
down); eat away, canker, gnaw; wear away, abrade, batter, excoriate, rust.

III. *Adjectives*. Destructive, ruinous, vandalistic, baneful, cut-
throat, fell, lethiferous, pernicious, slaughterous, predat-
ory, sinistrous, nihilistic; corrosive, erosive, cankerous,
caustic, abrasive.

"I validate," says Ethel.
"I unravage," says Oliver.
"I integrate," says Paul.
"I devandalize," says Elaine.
"I unshatter," says Bruce.
"I unscuttle," says Edward.
"I discorrode," says Ronald.
"I undesolate," says Edith.
"I create," say I.

We reconstitute. We renew. We repair. We reclaim. We refur-
bish. We restore. We renovate. We rebuild. We reproduce. We
redeem. We reintegrate. We replace. We reconstruct. We retrieve.
We revivify. We resurrect. We fix, overhaul, mend, put in repair,
retouch, tinker, cobble, patch, darn, staunch, calk, splice. We
celebrate our successes by energetic and lusty singing. Some of us
copulate.

Here is an outstanding example of the dark humor of the ancients. At a place called Richland, Washington, there was an
installation that manufactured plutonium for use in nuclear
weapons. This was done in the name of "national security," that
is, to enhance and strengthen the safety of the United States of
America and render its inhabitants carefree and hopeful. In a
relatively short span of time these activities produced approximately fifty-five million gallons of concentrated radioactive

waste. This material was so intensely hot that it would boil spon-
taneously for decades, and would retain a virulently toxic character for many thousands of years. The presence of so much dangerous waste posed a severe environmental threat to a large area of the
United States. How, then, to dispose of this waste? An appro-
priately comic solution was devised. The plutonium installation
was situated in a seismically unstable area located along the
earthquake belt that rings the Pacific Ocean. A storage site was
chosen nearby, directly above a fault line that had produced a
violent earthquake half a century earlier. Here one hundred and
forty steel and concrete tanks were constructed just below the
surface of the ground and some two hundred and forty feet above
the water table of the Columbia River, from which a densely
populated region derived its water supply. Into these tanks the
boiling radioactive wastes were poured: a magnificent gift to
future generations. Within a few years the true subtlety of the jest
became apparent when the first small leaks were detected in the
tanks. Some observers predicted that no more than ten to twenty
years would pass before the great heat caused the seams of the
tanks to burst, releasing radioactive gases into the atmosphere or
permitting radioactive fluids to escape into the river. The designers
of the tanks maintained, though, that they were sturdy enough to
last at least a century. It will be noted that this was something less
than 1 percent of the known half-life of the materials placed in the
tanks. Because of discontinuities in the records, we are unable to
determine which estimate was more nearly correct. It should be
possible for our decontamination squads to enter the affected
regions in 800 to 1,300 years. This episode arouses tremendous
admiration in me. How much gusto, how much robust wit, those
old ones must have!

We are granted a holiday so we may go to the mountains of
Uruguay to visit the site of one of the last human settlements,
perhaps the very last. It was discovered by a reclamation team
several hundred years ago and has been set aside, in its original
state, as a museum for the tourists who one day will wish to view
the mother-world. One enters through a lengthy tunnel of glossy

pink brick. A series of airlocks prevents the outside air from penetrating. The village itself, nestling between two craggy spires, is shielded by a clear shining dome. Automatic controls maintain its temperature at a constant mild level. There were a thousand inhabitants. We can view them in the spacious plazas, in the taverns, and in places of recreation. Family groups remain together, often with their pets. A few carry umbrellas. Everyone is in an unusually fine state of preservation. Many of them are smiling. It is not yet known why these people perished. Some died in the act of speaking, and scholars have devoted much effort, so far without success, to the task of determining and translating the last words still frozen on their lips. We are not allowed to touch anyone, but we may enter their homes and inspect their possessions and toilet furnishings. I am moved almost to tears, as are several of the others. "Perhaps these are our very ancestors," Ronald exclaims. But Bruce declares scornfully, "You say ridiculous things. Our ancestors must have escaped from here long before the time these people lived." Just outside the settlement I find a tiny glistening bone, possibly the shinbone of a child, possibly part of a dog's tail. "May I keep it?" I ask our leader. But he compels me to donate it to the museum.

The archives yield much that is fascinating. For example, this fine example of ironic distance in ecological management. In the ocean off a place named California were tremendous forests of giant seaweed called kelp, housing a vast and intricate community of maritime creatures. Sea urchins lived on the ocean floor, one hundred feet down, amid the holdfasts that anchored the kelp. Furry aquatic mammals known as sea otters fed on the urchins. The Earth people removed the otters because they had some use for their fur. Later, the kelp began to die. Forests many square miles in diameter vanished. This had serious commercial consequences, for the kelp was valuable and so were many of the animal forms that lived in it. Investigation of the ocean floor showed a great increase in sea urchins. Not only had their natural enemies, the otters, been removed, but the urchins were taking nourishment from the immense quantities of organic matter in the sewage discharges dumped into the ocean by the Earth people. Millions of urchins were nibbling at the holdfasts of the kelp, uprooting the huge plants and killing them. When an oil tanker accidentally released its cargo into the sea, many urchins were killed and the kelp began to reestablish itself. But this proved to be an impractical means of controlling the urchins. Encouraging the otters to return was suggested, but there was not a sufficient supply of living otters. The kelp foresters of California solved their problem by dumping quicklime into the sea from barges. This was fatal to the urchins; once they were dead, healthy kelp plants were brought from other parts of the sea and embedded to become the nucleus of a new forest. After a while the urchins returned and began to eat the kelp again. More quicklime was dumped. The urchins died and new kelp was planted. Later, it was discovered that the quicklime was having harmful effects on the ocean floor itself, and other chemicals were dumped to counteract those effects. All of this required great ingenuity and a considerable outlay of energy and resources. Edward thinks there was something very Japanese about these maneuvers. Ethel points out that the kelp trouble would never have happened if the Earth people had not originally removed the otters. How naive Ethel is! She has no understanding of the principles of irony. Poetry bewilders her also. Edward refuses to sleep with Ethel now.

   In the final centuries of their era the people of Earth succeeded in paving the surface of their planet almost entirely with a skin of concrete and metal. We must pry much of this up so that the planet may start to breathe again. It would be easy and efficient to use explosives or acids, but we are not overly concerned with ease and efficiency; besides there is great concern that explosives or acids may do further ecological harm here. Therefore we employ large machines that insert prongs in the great cracks that have developed in the concrete. Once we have lifted the paved slabs they usually crumble quickly. Clouds of concrete dust blow freely through the streets of these cities, covering the stumps of the buildings with a fine, pure coating of grayish-white powder. The effect is delicate and refreshing. Paul suggested yesterday that we may be doing ecological harm by setting free this dust. I became frightened at the idea and reported him to the leader of our team. Paul will be transferred to another group.

Toward the end here they all wore breathing-suits, similar to ours but even more comprehensive. We find these suits lying around everywhere like the discarded shells of giant insects. The most advanced models were complete individual housing units. Apparently it was not necessary to leave one's suit except to perform such vital functions as sexual intercourse and childbirth. We understand that the reluctance of the Earth people to leave their suits even for those functions, near the close, immensely hastened the decrease in population.

Our philosophical discussions. God created this planet. We all agree on that, in a manner of speaking, ignoring for the moment definitions of such concepts as "God" and "created." Why did He go to so much trouble to bring Earth into being, if it was His intention merely to have it rendered uninhabitable? Did He create mankind especially for this purpose, or did they exercise free will in doing what they did here? Why would He want to take vengeance against his own creation? Perhaps it is a mistake to approach the destruction of Earth from the moral or ethical standpoint. I think we must see it in purely esthetic terms, i.e., a self-contained artistic achievement, like a *fouetté en tournant* or an *entrechat-dix,* performed for its own sake and requiring no explanations. Only in this way can we understand how the Earth people were able to collaborate so joyfully in their own asphyxiation.

My tour of duty is almost over. It has been an overwhelming experience; I will never be the same. I must express my gratitude for this opportunity to have seen Earth almost as its people knew it. Its rusted streams, its corroded meadows, its purpled skies, its bluish puddles. The debris, the barren hillsides, the blazing rivers. Soon, thanks to the dedicated work of reclamation teams such as ours, these superficial but beautiful emblems of death will have disappeared. This will be just another world for tourists, of sentimental curiosity but no unique value to the sensibility. How dull that will be: a green and pleasant Earth once more, why, why? The universe has enough habitable planets; at present it has only one Earth. Has all our labor here been an error, then? I sometimes do think it was misguided of us to have undertaken this project. But on the other hand I remind myself of our fundamental irrelevance. The healing process is a natural and inevitable one. With us or without us, the planet cleanses itself. The wind, the rain, the tides. We merely help things along.

A rumor reaches us that a colony of live Earthmen has been found on the Tibetan plateau. We travel there to see if this is true. Hovering above a vast red empty plain, we see large dark figures moving slowly about. Are these Earthmen, inside breathing-suits of a strange design? We descend. Members of other reclamation teams are already on hand. They have surrounded one of the large creatures. It travels in a wobbly circle, uttering indistinct cries and grunts. Then it comes to a halt, confronting us blankly as if defying us to embrace it. We tip it over; it moves its massive limbs dumbly but is unable to arise. After a brief conference we decide to dissect it. The outer plates lift easily. Inside we find nothing but gears and coils of gleaming wire. The limbs no longer move, although things click and hum within it for quite some time. We are favorably impressed by the durability and resilience of these machines. Perhaps in the distant future such entities will wholly replace the softer and more fragile life-forms on all worlds, as they seem to have done on Earth.

The wind. The rain. The tides. All sadnesses flow to the sea.

Ten Years Ago . . .

MAX BEERBOHM

It is a rare pleasure, on the anniversary of his hundredth birthday, to anthologize a new Max Beerbohm story copyrighted in this same year. This unusual circumstance came about through the picture reproduced here. It is by an unknown artist and hung for years in the Abinger cottage of Sydney and Violet Schiff where Max Beerbohm lived for most of World War II. He was so fascinated by the picture that he eventually had to write an explanation of it. He did this, telling no one, and pasted this story to the back of the frame where it was discovered many years later:

Ten years ago, on the edge of the world, a rather unsuccessful jerry-builder erected a small house. He built it with his own hands, and without consulting an architect, relying wholly on his own taste, which was bad, and on his own sense of measurement, which was even worse. But his commercial instinct was keen enough for him to realize that the house was unlettable. He cut his losses and went away.

Now it so happened that at that time a young man, named Edgar Smithson, who was a clerk in a provincial and rather unsuccessful bank, misappropriated a small sum of money, with which he purchased a suit from a branch of the firm of Mallaby Deely. He did not look well in the suit, for his legs were very badly formed. Also, his theft was quickly detected and he was discharged, but not prosecuted. He walked in deep dejection to the edge of the world, and saw there the vacant house. "At any rate," he muttered, "I can have a roof to my head." He was wrong. He could not enter the house, though he was rather below the middle height. The house was not tall enough for habitation. So he stood outside, staring down in deep dejection.

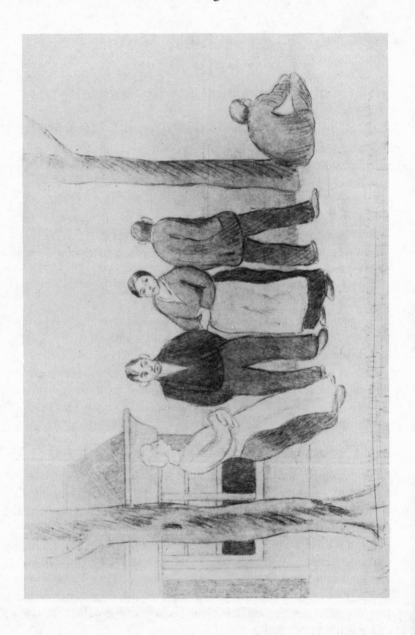

Now it so happened a few days later that to that edge of the world there came another discharged and malformed clerk. Neither of the two liked the look of the other. No words passed between them. The first-comer did not move. The newcomer passed by him and stood looking, for want of anything better to do, out across the edge of the world.

They were not long alone together. For it so happened that a malformed boy, who had recently escaped from Borstal, found his way to the spot where Smithson and the other man (who had no name at all) were standing. He liked the looks of neither of them and sat dully down beneath one of the two plane trees which were the only pleasant feature of the scene.

And on the following day it so happened that the scene became more populous, though perhaps not much more pleasant. Two females wandered into it. One was a discharged cook, of whom long ago, before she grew very stout, some short-sighted person had said that she looked rather like a Madonna. The other woman had not been discharged from any post, for she had never occupied one, had never been qualified for one. The fact that she had nothing to commend or discommend her but a Grecian profile, and a tin apron that was much too long for her, had prejudiced employers against her. She had never had anything to do. She felt it was time to do something now. She stationed herself on one side of Smithson. On his other side the discharged cook did likewise. They did not look at him, for they felt they had nothing in common with him. They did not look at each other, for the same reason. Yet these two had, though they refused to recognize it, one point in common. They were both of them instable. The ex-cook was always tumbling over sideways. The woman with the Grecian profile was forever falling down on her back.

They were not happy, these five persons outside the uninhabitable little new house. They often yearned to throw themselves over the edge of the world and explore infinity. But they lacked initiative. They had little will power. They are still standing where they stood. And from time to time Mr.—— comes to them and says to them brightly "You make a pattern."

Parthen

R. A. LAFFERTY

I can believe it, yes I can, I can believe it would happen in just this manner . . .

Never had the springtime been so wonderful. Never had business been so good. Never was the World Outlook so bright. And never had the girls been so pretty.

It is true that it was the chilliest spring in decades—sharp, bitter, and eternally foggy—and that the sinuses of Roy Ronsard were in open revolt. It is admitted that bankruptcies were setting records, those of individuals and firms as well as those of nations. It is a fact that the aliens had landed (though their group was not identified) and had published their Declaration that one half of mankind was hereby obsoleted and the other half would be retained as servants. The omens and portents were black, but the spirits of men were the brightest and happiest ever.

To repeat, never had the girls been so pretty! There was no one who could take exception to that.

Roy Ronsard himself faced it in a most happy frame of mind. A Higher Set of Values will do wonders toward erasing such mundane everyday irritations.

There is much to be said in favor of cold, vicious springtimes. They represent weather at its most vital. There is something to be said for exploding sinuses. They indicate, at least, that a man has something in his head. And, if a man is going to be a bankrupt, then let him be a happy bankrupt.

When the girls are as pretty as all that, the rest does not matter.

Let us make you understand just how pretty Eva was! She was a golden girl with hair like honey. Her eyes were blue—or they were green—or they were violet or gold and they held a twinkle that melted a man. The legs of the creature were like Greek poetry and the motion of her hips was something that went out of the world with the old sail ships. Her breastwork had a Gothic upsweep—her neck was passion incarnate and her shoulders were of a glory past describing. In her whole person she was a study of celestial curvatures.

Should you never have heard her voice, the meaning of music has been denied you. Have you not enjoyed her laughter? Then your life remains unrealized.

It is possible that exaggeration has crept into this account? No. That is not possible. All this fits in with the cold appraisal of men like Sam Pinta, Cyril Colbert, Willy Whitecastle, George Goshen, Roy Ronsard himself—and that of a hundred men who had gazed on her in amazement and delight since she came to town. All these men are of sound judgment in this field. And actually she was prettier than they admitted.

Too, Eva Ellery was but one of many. There was Jeannie who brought a sort of pleasant insanity to all who met her. Roberta who was a scarlet dream. Helen—high-voltage sunshine. Margaret —the divine clown. And it was high adventure just to meet Hildegarde. A man could go blind from looking at her.

"I can't understand how there can be so many beautiful young women in town this year," said Roy. "It makes the whole world worthwhile. Can you let me have fifty dollars, Willy? I'm going to see Eva Ellery. When I first met her I thought that she was an hallucination. She's real enough, though. Do you know her?"

"Yes. A most remarkable young woman. She has a small daughter named Angela who really stops the clock. Roy, I have just twenty dollars left in the world and I'll split it with you. As you know, I'm going under, too. I don't know what I'll do after they take my business away from me. It's great to be alive, Roy."

"Wonderful. I hate not having money to spend on Eva, but she's never demanding in that. In fact she's lent me money to smooth out things pertinent to the termination of my business.

She's one of the most astute business women I ever knew and has
been able to persuade my creditors to go a little easy on me. I won't
get out with my shirt. But, as she says, I may get out with my
skin.''

There was a beautiful, cold, mean fog and one remembered that
there was a glorious sun (not seen for many days now) somewhere
behind it. The world rang with cracked melody and everybody was
in love with life.

Everybody except Peggy Ronsard and wives like her who did
not understand the higher things. Peggy had now become like a fog
with no sun anywhere behind it. Roy realized, as he came home to
her for a moment, that she was very drab.

"Well?" Peggy asked with undertones in her voice. Her voice
did not have overtones like that of Eva. Only undertones.

"Well what? My—uh—love?" Roy asked.

"The business—what's the latest on it today? What have you
come up with?"

"Oh, the business. I didn't bother to go by today. I guess it's
lost.''

"You are going to lose it without a fight? You used not to be like
that. Two weeks ago your auditing firm said that you had all sorts
of unrealized assets and that you'd come out of this easily.''

"And two weeks later my auditing firm is also taking bank-
ruptcy. Everybody's doing it now.''

"There wasn't anything wrong with that auditing firm till that
Roberta woman joined it. And there wasn't anything wrong with
your company till you started to listen to that Eva creature.''

"Is she not beautiful, Peggy?''

Peggy made a noise Roy understood as assent, but he had not
been understanding his wife well lately.

"And there's another thing," said Peggy dangerously. "You
used to have a lot of the old goat in you and that's gone. A wife
misses things like that. And your wolfish friends have all changed.
Sam Pinta used to climb all over me like I was a trellis—and I
couldn't sit down without Willy Whitecastle being on my lap. And

Judy Pinta says that Sam has changed so much at home that life just isn't worth living any more. You all used to be such loving men! What's happened to you?''

"Ah—I believe that our minds are now on a higher plane."

"You didn't go for that higher plane jazz till that Eva woman came along. And that double-damned Roberta! But she does have two lovely little girls, I'll admit. And that Margaret, she's the one that's got Cyril Colbert and George Goshen where they're pushovers for anything now. She does have a beautiful daughter, though."

"Have you noticed how many really beautiful women there are in town lately, Peggy?"

"Roy, I hope those aliens get every damned cucumber out of that patch! The monsters are bound to grab all the pretty women first. I hope they're a bunch of sadist alligators and do everything that the law disallows to those doll babies."

"Peggy, I believe that the aliens (and we are told that they are already among us) will be a little more sophisticated than popular ideas anticipate."

"I hope they're a bunch of Jack the Rippers. I believe I could go for Jack today. He'd certainly be a healthy contrast to what presently obtains."

Peggy had put her tongue on the crux. For the beautiful young women, who seemed to be abundant in town that springtime, had an odd effect on the men who came under their influence. The goats among the men had become lambs and the wolves had turned into puppies.

Jeannie was of such a striking appearance as to make a man almost cry out. But the turmoil that she raised in her gentlemen friends was of a cold sort, for all that the white flames seemed to leap up. She was Artemis herself and the men worshiped her on the higher plane. She was wonderful to look at and to talk to. But who would be so boorish as to touch?

The effect of Eva was similar—and of Roberta and of Helen (who had three little daughters as like her as three golden apples)

and of Margaret and of Hildegarde. How could a man not ascend to
the higher plane when such wonderful and awesome creatures as
these abounded?

But the damage was done when the men carried this higher plane
business home to their comparatively colorless wives. The men
were no longer the ever-loving husbands that they should have
been. The most intimate relations ceased to take place. If continued long this could have an effect on the statistics.

But daily affairs sometimes crept into the conversations of even
those men who had ascended to the higher plane.

"I was wondering," Roy asked George Goshen, "when our
businesses are all gone—who do they go to?"

"Many of us have wondered that," George told him. "They all
seem to devolve upon anonymous recipients or upon corporations
without apparent personnel. But somebody is gathering in the
companies. One theory is that the aliens are doing it."

"The aliens are among us, the authorities say, but nobody has
seen them. They publish their program and their progress through
intermediaries who honestly do not know the original effectors.
The aliens still say that they will make obsolete one half of
mankind and make servants of the other half."

"Jeannie says—did you ever see her pretty little daughters?—that we see the aliens every day and do not recognize
them for what they are. She says that likely the invasion of the
aliens will have obtained its objective before we realize what that
is. What's the news from the rest of the country and the world?"

"The same. All business is going to pot and everybody is
happy. On paper, things were never more healthy. There's a lot of
new backing from somewhere and all the businesses thrive as soon
as they have shuffled off their old owners. The new owners—and
nobody can find out who or what they are—must be happy with the
way things are going. Still, I do not believe that anybody could be
happier or more contented than I am. Can you let me have fifty
cents, George? I just remembered that I haven't eaten today.
Peggy has gone to work for what used to be my company, but she's

a little slow to give me proper spending money. Come to think of it, Peggy has been acting peculiar lately.''

''I have only forty cents left in the world, Roy. Take the quarter. My wife has gone to work also, but I guess there will never be any work for us. Did you think we'd ever live to see the NO MALES WANTED signs on every hiring establishment in the country? Oh, well— if you're happy nothing else matters.''

''George, there's a humorous note that creeps into much of the world news lately. It seems that ours is not the only city with an unusual number of pretty young ladies this season. They've been reported in Teheran and Lvov, in Madras and Lima and Boston. Everywhere.''

''No! Pretty girls in Boston? You're kidding. This has certainly been an up-side down year when things like that can happen. But did you ever see a more beautiful summertime, Roy?''

''On my life I never did.''

The summer had been murky and the sun had not been seen for many months. But it was a beautiful murk. And when one is attuned to inner beauty the outer aspect of things does not matter. The main thing was that everyone was happy.

Oh, there were small misunderstandings. There was a wife —this was reported as happening in Cincinnati, but it may have happened in other places also—who one evening reached out and touched her husband's hand in a form of outmoded affection. Naturally the man withdrew his hand rudely, for it was clear that the wife had not yet ascended to his higher plane. In the morning he went away and did not return.

Many men were drifting away from their homes in those days. Most men, actually. However that old cohabitational arrangement had grown into being, it no longer had anything to recommend it. When one has consorted with the light itself, what can he find in a tallow candle?

Most of the men became destitute wanderers and loafers. They were happy with their inner illumination. Every morning the dead ones would be shoveled up by the women on the disposal trucks and carted away. And every one of those men died happy. That's

what made it so nice. To anyone who had entered higher understanding death was only an interlude.

It was a beautiful autumn day. Roy Ronsard and Sam Pinta had
just completed their fruitless rounds of what used to be called
garbage cans but now had more elegant names. They were still
hungry, but happily so for it was truly a beautiful autumn.

The snow had come early, it is true, and great numbers of men
had perished from it. But if one had a happy life, it was not a
requisite for it to be a long life. Men lived little in the world now,
dwelling mostly in thought. But sometimes they still talked to each
other.

"It says here—" Roy Ronsard began to read a piece of old
newspaper that had been used for wrapping bones—"that Professor Eimer, just before he died of malnutrition, gave as his opinion
that the aliens among us cannot stand sunlight. He believed it was
for this reason that they altered our atmosphere and made ours a
gloomy world. Do you believe that, Sam?"

"Hardly. How could anybody call ours a gloomy world? I
believe that we are well rid of that damned sun."

"And it says that he believed that one of the weapons of the
aliens was their intruding into men a general feeling of euphor—
The rest of the paper is torn off."

"Roy, I saw Margaret today. From a distance, of course.
Naturally I could not approach such an incandescent creature in my
present condition of poverty. But Roy, do you realize how much
we owe to those pretty girls? I really believe that we would have
known nothing of the higher plane or the inner light if it had not
been for them. How could they have been so pretty?"

"Sam, there is one thing about them that always puzzled me."

"Everything about them puzzled me. What do you mean?"

"All of them have daughters, Sam. And none of them have
husbands. Why did none of them have husbands? Or sons?"

"Never thought of it. It's been a glorious year, Roy. My only
regret is that I will not live to see the winter that will surely be the
climax to this radiant autumn. We have had so much—we cannot

expect to have everything. Do you not just love deep snow over you?''

"It's like the blanket of heaven, Sam. When the last of us is gone—and it won't be too long now—do you think the girls will remember how much light they brought into our lives?''

The Man Who Collected
the First of September 1973

TOR AGE BRINGSVAERD,
TRANSLATED BY ODDRUM GRONVIK

The author of this story is a well-known Swedish writer and playwright—in his most recent play, which opened in Oslo, it is discovered that Tarzan is a vampire. Although his works have been translated into seven languages this is his first appearance in English. A fitting international one, too, about a man who did just what the story's title indicates.

(1)

Ptk discovered that he was about to lose his grip on reality. In fact it had been building up for years (he suddenly realized)—without his caring, without his giving it a thought. Perhaps he hadn't even been aware of it. Now the gray film had thickened to a crust, a stocking cap stretched over and encasing his arms, a sagging tentlike umbrella dimming out the outside world. The hands of his wristwatch flamed, and he no longer knew on which side his hair was parted: the mirror said the right, his hand the left. In the paper he read about a Frenchman who for various reasons had had himself imprisoned, naked, inside a small chamber three hundred feet under the earth's surface. When he returned from isolation after three months, scientists were able to affirm that man has *"a natural rhythm—a built-in timekeeper"* and that this timekeeper *"is not adjusted to the sun, but counts thirty-one hours in the day-night cycle, instead of twenty-four."*

But no one dared to make the inference, the only logic possibility
. . . that man is a stranger, that Obstfelder was right, that our real
home is another (and slower) globe—which, lighted by an unknown sun, takes seven hours more than the Earth to rotate around
its own axis . . . that this is the genuine Eden—the garden we have
been turned out from. . . . PTK pointed in amazement at his own
mirror image, and neither Aspirins nor Valium was able to make
him think otherwise.

(2)

Ptk decided to face his every day, to try to orientate himself in
the reality he was stranded in. He went out, bought all of that day's
Oslo papers (Saturday, the 18th of August 1973), and went home.
He read them thoroughly—page by page, column by column.
When at last he felt that he had got some sort of grip on Saturday
the 18th of August, in the meantime Tuesday the 21st of August
had arrived—and reality had changed its face three times. Ptk
realized that the sum of information was too weighty for any single
man to balance on his head. News fell in heaps around his feet,
clung like ivy to his legs and tightened like a belt round his
stomach. He fought in despair against Wednedsay the 22nd and
Thursday the 23rd. He dared not blink for fear that Friday the 24th
might weigh down his eyelids. And even so . . . despite the best
will in the world . . . Saturday the 25th went over his head
completely.

(3)

Ptk realized that he'd acted in haste. He who consumes too
much news has no time for boiling, frying, or chewing it over, but
is obliged to swallow everything raw and whole. Having considered political digestion and protective fatty layers of tissue, he
decided to attack the problem from quite a different angle. Con-

fronted with reality as a many-headed beast he resigned, but chose instead to cut off one of the heads in order to get under the creature's skin by means of a detailed study of one single head. He selected the 1st of September 1973. In advance he had equipped a corner of his bedroom as a laboratory, and was all set with a typewriter, scissors, glue, paper, and a twenty-four-volume calf-bound encyclopedia at hand.

(4)

By the end of October Ptk had finished all the Norwegian papers from the 1st of September (including weekly papers). Without hesitation he delved into the study of papers from the rest of Scandinavia, primarily Denmark and Sweden. He had his fixed seat in the university library, and at night he stuck cuttings, notes, and Xerox copies on his bedroom walls. He developed an interest in curves and diagrams.

(5)

Soon his bedroom grew too small. In order to make his material for study as complete as possible, Ptk wrote to papers all over the world and asked for a copy from the 1st of September 1973 —whether he had command of the language or not. He went to evening classes in Spanish and Russian.

(6)

Four years later his flat had been exploited to the full. Apart from a cooker, a fridge, a bed, a coffee table, and a wooden chair there was no furniture; no ornaments. The rooms were divided with hundreds of partitions, and the passages were so narrow that Ptk had to walk sidelong (very carefully) when he wanted to remind himself of an important cutting or add a new note. Working hours apart (Ptk was an accountant), he spent all his time in his historical archives. He neglected friends and relatives, and when he met one of them in the street (going to or from his office) he found it hard to carry on a sensible conversation. He grew more and more appalled at how little people knew of the 1st of September 1973. In the end he cut himself off completely, ignored invitations, had the telephone removed, and made detours.

(7)

Twice he had to find a bigger flat. By 1982 he knew—more or less—twenty different languages and dialects. But all the time there were more things to learn. The subject turned out to be just about inexhaustible. Who would have guessed that so much had happened on exactly the 1st of September 1973? "What a coincidence!" Ptk said to himself (he hadn't talked to anyone else for six years). "What luck I had, choosing *that* particular day!" He still used the partition system, and busied himself organizing it all as systematically as possible. Not all subjects required the same amount of space. Some subjects, like temperature and wind, only needed half a wall, while others, as for instance business and finance, covered the whole dining room alone (all in all thirty walls, that is, about 4050 square feet).

(8)

On a gray and cloudy day in February 1983 a fire started in the games and sports department. Ptk was on his way home from a private lesson in Mongolian dialects. When he opened his front door the whole title fight in heavyweight was in flames, and champion George Foreman struck a powerful right hook when the Puerto Rican challenger as well as the picture curled up. It was an absolute storm of fire. Nothing was saved. Before the fire brigade got there, the whole archive was in ashes. (Apart from the two basement storerooms, of course. But here he had mainly deaths from the personal columns and unsorted obituaries. All of peripheral interest). Ptk was badly burnt, and spent the rest of his life (two years) in hospital.

(9)

During these two years both doctors and patients tried in vain to get through to him. But whenever anyone spoke of the war in South America, Ptk talked of Southeast Asia. If anyone mentioned the EEC, Ptk replied that he thought there still was a Norwegian majority against it—certainly *he* was. If the other patients talked about games, Ptk always shook his head and mumbled something about an illegal punch and the first world championships in synchronized swimming starting in Belgrade. He now and then talked about two Englishmen rescued after being trapped in a minisubmarine on the floor of the Atlantic, he referred to the king as the crown prince, and always spoke of the president as "Nixon." If he was willing to reply at all. Most of the time he was not. "A hopeless case," the doctors said. "There's nothing we can do."

(10)

And when no one tried any more, Ptk was allowed the peace he so ardently yearned for. He spent his last three months lying happily on his back. One by one he brought forth the fragments, one by one he painstakingly put them together, starting at the back right-hand corner of his brain and working leftward. The picture of the 1st of September 1973 slowly grew in his mind, getting bigger and clearer day by day. Names and numbers melted into maps and diagrams. Border disputes and cinema advertisements merged. Ptk smiled. The picture filled his head. Some bits were still missing. He found them. His head became too small. The picture shattered his head and filled the whole hospital. Still some bits were missing. A few. He found them. The picture shattered the hospital and filled all of the park outside, unfolded like a transparent film and became one with the trees, the birds, and the sky. But then he'd already been dead . . . a quarter of an hour, one doctor said. Ten minutes, said the other. And neither noticed that it was autumn.

Captain Nemo's Last Adventure

JOSEF NESVADBA,
TRANSLATED BY IRIS URWIN

Josef Nesvadba is that one-of-a-kind writer whose stories are all different yet all unqualifiedly his. He will be remembered for his "The Lost Face" in Best SF: 1970. *It is a pleasure to welcome him to these pages again with this perceptive glimpse at the future of space travel.*

His real name was Feather. Lieutenant Feather. He was in charge of transport between the second lunar base and the airfields on Earth, both direct trips and transfers via Cosmic Station 36 or 38. It was a dull job, and the suggestion had been made that the pilots of these rockets be replaced altogether by automatic control, as the latter was capable of reporting dangerous meteorites or mechanical breakdowns sooner and with greater accuracy, and was not subject to fatigue.

But then there was the famous accident with Tanker Rocket 272 BF. Unable to land on Cosmic Station 6, it was in danger of exploding and destroying the whole station, which would have held up traffic between the Moon and the Earth for several weeks and brought the greatest factories on Earth to a standstill, dependent as they are on the supply of cheap top-quality Moon ore. How would the Moon crews carry on without supplies from Earth? Were their rations adequate? How long would they be cut off? Everyone asked the same questions; there wasn't a family on Earth who didn't have at least one close relative on one lunar station or another. The Supreme Office of Astronautics was criticized from all quarters, and it looked as though the chairman would have to resign.

Just then the news came through that an unknown officer, one Lieutenant Feather, had risked his life to land on the tanker rocker in a small Number Four Cosmic Bathtub (the nickname for the small squat rockets used for short journeys). After repairing the rocket controls, Feather had landed safely on one of the Moon bases. Afterward he spent a few weeks in the hospital; apparently he had tackled the job in an astronautical training suit. On the day he was released, the chairman of the Supreme Office of Astronautics himself was waiting for him, to thank him personally for his heroic deed and to offer him a new job.

And so Lieutenant Feather became Captain Feather; and Captain Feather became Captain Nemo. The world press services couldn't get his Czech name right, and when news got out that Captain Feather was going to command the new *Nautilus* rocket to explore the secrets of Neptune, he was promptly rechristened Nemo (Jules Verne was en vogue just then). Reuter even put forth another suggestion: Captain Feather de Neptune (it was meant to look like a title of nobility). But no one picked up on the idea.

Readers all over the world soon got used to Captain Nemo, who discovered the secrets of Neptune, brought back live bacteria from Uranus, and saved the supplies of radon on Jupiter during the great earthquake there—or rather, the planetquake. Captain Nemo was always on the spot whenever there was an accident or catastrophe in our solar system—whenever the stakes were life or death. He gathered together a crew of kindred spirits, most of them from his native Skalice, and became the idol of all the little boys on our third planet (as the scientists sometimes called Earth).

But progress in automation and the gradual perfection of technical devices made human intervention less and less necessary. Feather/Nemo was the commander of the rescue squads on Earth, but for some years he had had no opportunity to display his heroism. He and his crew were the subjects of literary works, the models for sculptors and painters, and the most popular lecturers among the younger generation. The captain often changed his place of residence—and his paramours as well. Women fell for him. He was well-built and handsome, with a determined chin and hair that had begun to gray at the temples: the answer to a maiden's prayer. And unhappy at home; everybody knew that.

That was really why he had become a hero. At any rate, a psychologist somewhere had written a scholarly article about it: "Suicide and Heroism. Notes on Cause and Effect." That was the title of the study. The author cited the case of Captain Nemo: if only this great cosmic explorer had been more happily married, he said, if instead of a wife from Zatec, where the hops grow, he had married a wife from Skalice, where they are brought up with the vine, if only his wife were not such a narrow specialist in her own field (she was a geologist), but had the gift of fantasy, and if only the son had taken after his father—Mr. Feather would be sitting quietly by the family hearth, and no one would ever have heard of Captain Nemo. As it was, his wife was of no particular use to him, and he was always trying to slip away from home. His son was nearsighted, had always had to wear thick spectacles, and was devoted to music. He was also composing symphonies that nobody ever played; his desk was full of them by now, and the only thing he was good for was to occasionally play the harp and to teach youngsters to play this neglected old instrument at music society meetings. The son of a hero, a harpist—that was another good reason for Captain Nemo to be fed up with life. And so he looked for distraction elsewhere. His most recent affair was said to have been with a black girl mathematician from the University of Timbuctoo, but everyone knew that even this twenty-year-old raven beauty could not hold him for long. He was famous for his infidelity—a relatively rare quality at this stage in history, since people usually married only after careful consideration and on the recommendation of the appropriate specialists, so that the chances of a successful marriage were optimal. Naturally the experts always tried to adjust the interests of those in love. Heroism was no longer considered much of a profession; it was a bit too specialized, and in fact no longer fulfilling. Today's heroes were those who designed new machines or found the solution to some current problem. There was no longer any need to risk one's life. Thus Captain Nemo had become somewhat obsolete in the civilization he had so often saved from destruction; he was a museum piece women admired because they longed for excitement, because they still remembered that lovemaking and the begetting of children were the only things that had not changed much since men emerged from the jungle. Feather and his men were the constant recipients of love letters from all over the Earth—in fact, from all over the solar system. Needless to say, this did nothing to make their own marriages any more stable, quite the reverse: because they were so popular, they longed to be able to return over and over again as conquering heroes. Finally even the raven-skinned girl in Timbuctoo began to think of setting up house as the necessity for heroic journeys began to dwindle: even this adventurous young lady wanted to bind Nemo with love, just as the geologist from Zatec had managed to do once upon a time. But that was not what the captain wanted at all. That would mean the end of adventure, and the beginning of old age and illness. He could not imagine what he would do with a happy marriage; he would have to upset it so as to have a reason for flying off again and risking his life, just as a drunkard invents a reason for getting drunk. Nemo knew the stories of all the great adventures of the past, he knew how to build up a convincing argument, and he used to say that in the end humanity would realize that this vast technical progress that kept them living in ease required, demanded, an equally vast contrast; that man must give rein to his aggressive instincts; that men need adventure in order to remain fertile—in other words, that risking one's life in the universe (or anywhere else) was directly bound up with the fate of future generations. It was an odd sort of philosophy; very few people took it up, and as time went on there were fewer and fewer arguments in its favor. In fact, for the last five years Nemo and his men had simply been idle. The men were discontented. And so they were all delighted when one night quite suddenly their captain was called to the chief ministry, just like in the old days of alarms.

*　*　*

PIRATES

"This time, Captain Nemo," the minister addressed him ceremoniously, "we are faced with an unusual and dangerous mystery. For this time it is apparently not only Earth that is threatened, but the sun itself, the source of all life in our solar system, the source of all we see around us." The minister solemnly signaled to the assistant secretary of science to continue. Nemo and his adjutant were sitting facing them on the other side of the conference table. The four men were alone in the room. The assistant secretary walked over to a map of the Universe.

"Of course we didn't believe it at first, but we were wrong, gentlemen. The facts you are about to be given are well founded. About a year ago, one of the universities sent us a paper written by a young scientist about the incidence of novas. The papers quoted old Egyptian astronomical maps as well as recent observations in the constellation of Omega Centauri and the galaxy of Andromeda. The writer concluded that novas do not simply explode of their own accord, but that they are touched off according to a plan. Like someone going along the hilltops who lights a beacon to signal back to the valleys below. Some sort of rocket seems to have been entrusted with the task—or a satellite with an irregular course, something moving independently through space and destroying the stars one by one. It is interesting to note that a similar idea occurred to the writers of antiquity. Since according to this paper the next victim of these cosmic pirates would be the immediate neighborhood of our own solar system, we quickly set up a secret telescope near Jupiter, without the knowledge of the public, in order to observe the regions in which this body appears to be moving. Today we reviewed the information provided by that telescope." The assistant secretary picked up a long pointer and turned back to the astronomical map. The minister could control his excitement no longer. He leapt to his feet.

"They're coming!" he shouted. "They're coming closer! We've got to catch them!" He was so excited that his chest was

heaving, and he had to wipe his brow with his handkerchief.
"Damn them," he said and sat down again.

"If the reports from ancient Egypt are reliable, this body has
been wandering around the universe for about nine hundred
thousand years," the assistant secretary of science went on.
"We've managed to calculate the precise course it has followed to
date. It cannot possibly be the satellite of some distant sun—it's a
body that moves under its own power."

"Its own power? Then it *is* a rocket," Nemo's young adjutant
breathed.

"But seven thousand times the size of any rocket we are presently capable of constructing," said the assistant secretary. "And
it detonates the stars from an immense distance. In one year our
sun will come within its orbit. In one year, it can cause an
explosion of our solar system."

"What are our orders, sir?" said Nemo briefly, taking out his
notebook as though it were all in the day's work to tackle cosmic
pirates seven thousand times his own size.

"Orders? Don't talk nonsense," the minister burst out. "How
could we send anyone to attack it? You might just as well send an
ant to deal with an elephant."

"Why not, if the ant is clever enough and you give it enough
oxygen?" Nemo laughed.

"There's no question of building a miracle missile for you," the
minister went on.

"We can give you the latest war rockets equipped with radio-
activite missiles, but of course they're over a hundred years old,"
the assistant secretary said. The young officer at Nemo's side
frowned.

"Haven't you got any bows and arrows?" Nemo savored his
joke. He was notorious for telling funny stories when things were
really dangerous.

"This is a serious matter, Captain Nemo," said the minister.

"I can see that. Your automatic pilots are no good to you now,
are they? You can't send them out that far because they'd never be

able to keep in touch with you, I suppose. Only a human crew can fly that kind of distance.''

''Naturally.'' The assistant secretary looked grim. ''That's why it's a volunteer's job. Nobody must be allowed to know anything about it. We don't want to frighten the public now, when people have only been living without fear of war for a few generations. We'll issue a communiqué only if your mission fails.''

''You mean if we don't manage to render them harmless?''

They explained that is was not a matter of rendering the aliens harmless. It would be far better if they could come to terms and avoid making enemies in the universe unnecessarily. But they did not want to tell Nemo what to do: they appreciated to the utmost not only his heroism, but his common sense as well. The moment the pirates turned away from our solar system, they assured him, everything would be all right.

''We shall send in a report, I suppose?'' the adjutant asked.

''I hardly think so,'' said Nemo.

''Why not?'' The adjutant was just over twenty. The other three looked at him—the minister, his assistant secretary, and Captain Nemo.

''My dear boy, there's such a thing as relativity, you know. By the time you get anywhere near that thing you'll have been moving practically at the speed of light, and more than a thousand years will have passed on Earth.''

''A thousand years?'' the adjutant gasped, remembering that a thousand years earlier Premysl Otakar had been on the throne of Bohemia.

''It's a job for volunteers only, Captain Nemo.''

''It's a magnificent adventure——''

''And I'm afraid it will be our last,'' Captain Nemo replied, getting to his feet and standing at attention. He wanted to get down to the details of the expedition.

''What do we tell the folks at home?'' His adjutant was still puzzled.

''Surely you don't want to upset them by suggesting that in a year or two somebody's going to blow our Sun to bits? You'll set out on a normal expedition, and in a month we'll publish the news of your death. Or do you think it would be better for your loved ones to go on hoping for your return, until they themselves die? Your grandchildren won't know you, and in a thousand years everyone will have forgotten you anyway."

"If we get the better of the pirates." Nemo laughed. "If not, we'll all be meeting again soon."

"Do you still believe in life after death?" The minister smiled.

"An adventurer is permitted his little indulgences," Captain Nemo answered. "But if you really want to know—no, I don't believe in it. That's precisely why I love adventure: you risk everything."

"But this isn't an adventure," his adjutant interrupted in an agitated voice. "This is certain death. We can't destroy an entity that has detonated several suns in the course of the ages from an enormous distance—and even if we managed to do it, we'd be coming back to a strange land, to people who won't know us from Adam. . . ."

"You will be the only human beings to experience the future so far ahead," said the minister.

"And it is a volunteer expedition," added the assistant secretary pointedly.

"If you can suggest any other way out, let us hear it. The World Council has been racking its brains for hours."

"And then they remembered us. That's nice." Captain Nemo felt flattered. "But now I'd like to know the details. . . ." He turned to the assistant secretary like the commander of a sector ready to take orders from the commander in chief of an offensive.

FAREWELL

"Can't they leave you alone?" Mrs. Feather grumbled crossly as she packed her husband's bag. "Couldn't they find anybody younger to send? You'd think they could find somebody better for the job when you're getting on to fifty . . . I thought we were going to enjoy a little peace and quiet now, in our old age, at least. We could have moved to the mountains, the people next door are going to rent a cottage, and we could have had a rest at last. . . ."

"There'll be plenty of time to rest when we're in our graves," Captain Nemo yawned. Ever since he'd come home he'd been stretched out on the couch. He always slept for twenty-four hours before an expedition. He used to say it was his hibernation period, and that the only place he ever got a decent rest was in his own house. And his wife knew that whenever he came home he would drop off somewhere. In the last few years, though, he'd been stopping by on Sundays and at Christmas as well.

"For heaven's sake, Willy, are you going to carry on like an adolescent forever? When are you going to settle down?"

He got to his feet in anger. "I wish I knew why you never let me get a bit of rest. If you had any idea how important this expedition is——"

"That's just what you said before you went to Jupiter and Neptune, and then there was the moonstorm business and the time those meteors were raining. . . . It's always the most important expedition anyone's ever thought of, and it's always a good reason for you to run away from home again. . . ."

"Do you call this home?" He looked around. "I haven't set eyes on the boy since morning."

It appeared his son had finally found a music group that was willing to perform one of his symphonies, and they'd been rehearsing ever since the previous day.

"You mean he isn't even coming to say good-bye to me? Didn't you tell him?"

"But he's getting ready for his first night at last, don't you understand?" His mother tried to excuse him.

"So am I," answered Nemo, who did not quite know how to describe his gala last performance. But in the end he tried to find his son. To listen to the rehearsal, if nothing else.

The concert hall was practically empty; one or two elderly figures were dozing in the aisle seats. The orchestra emitted peculiar sounds while young Feather conducted from memory, absorbed in the music and with his eyes closed, so that he did not see his father gesticulating at him from one of the boxes. He heard nothing but his own music; he looked as though he were quite alone in the hall. Nemo went out and banged the door in disgust. An elderly attendant came up.

"How do you like the symphony?" he asked the old man.

"It's modern, all right; you've got to admit that."

"Yes, but I wanted to know whether you liked it." At that moment, a wave of particularly vile noise came screeching out through the door, and Nemo took to his heels.

In front of the hall, the girl from Timbuctoo was waiting for him. She had flown over that morning by special rocket. He recalled how she had wept the last time he'd refused to marry her.

"We're off to repair some equipment between Mercury and Venus." Nemo laughed. "We'll get pretty hot this time. When I get back, Timbuctoo won't even look warm by comparison."

"I know you're not coming back, Captain." She had always called him Captain. "I was the one who passed the report on to the authorities."

"What report?"

"About the cosmic pirates seven thousand times our size." She smiled. "I thought it would be an adventure after your own heart at last. I could have sent the whole thing back, you know—a very young student submitted it. I could have won a little more time for us to spend together. But we have our responsibilities, as you've always told me."

"You're perfectly right."

"But we must say good-bye properly. I'm not coming to see you off; I want to be alone with you when we part. . . ."

So once again Nemo did not go home to Mrs. Feather, nor did he see his son again before he left. His adjutant brought his bags to the rocket, since he hadn't found the captain at home. Nemo turned up looking rather pale and thin, and the crew commented on it, but he had always been like that whenever they were about to take off, and he was used to their good-natured jokes.

This time the ministry prepared an elaborate farewell. No expense was spared. The World Government Council turned up in a body, together with all the relatives of the men, and crowds of admirers: women, girls, and young boys. Enthusiastic faces could be seen between the indifferent countenances of relatives, who were used to such goings-on, and the serious, almost anxious faces of those who knew the secret behind this expedition. The minister's voice almost shook with emotion as he proposed the toast. He did not know how to thank the crew enough, and promised that their heroism would never be forgotten. His hand trembling by the time he gripped Nemo's in farewell, and he actually began to weep.

Once the relatives and curious onlookers had vanished, the crew had a final meeting with the leaders of the world government.

"All our lives are in your hands—the lives of your families, your children and your children's children, for generations to come. Men have often died for the sake of future generations, and often the sacrifice has been in vain. You can rest assured that this is not the case today. That's the only comfort we can offer you. I wish I were going with you myself, but it would cause too much talk, and we can't risk a panic. Still, it's better to fight than to wait passively in the role of victim."

Then they played famous military marches in honor of the crew—it an international team—but the gesture fell a bit flat; not a tear was shed at the sound of "Colonel Bogey" or the "Radetzky March." With sudden inspiration, the bandmaster struck up the choral movement from Beethoven's *Ninth Symphony,* and the band improvised from memory as best it could. In those few moments, everyone present realized that for more than a generation man had been living in the age of true brotherhood, and that fear had suddenly reared its head again.

THE FLIGHT

In half an hour they had gained the required speed—the rocket had been adapted for its job after all. When sixty minutes had passed, the adjutant brought a telegraph message to the commander. On Earth, where several years had already passed since their departure, an official communiqué reporting the loss of the *Nautilus III* had been issued.

"So now we're dead and gone."

"Am I to inform the crew?" the adjutant asked in embarrassment.

"Of course. We need have no secrets from each other here."

The first reaction of the crew to the news of their own deaths was a roar of laughter. If you survive your own death, you live long, as the saying goes. And it was a fact that if they survived their meeting with the space pirates, they would return to Earth as thousand-year-old ancients, ancients at the height of their powers. But the topic soon palled, and the usual effects of space flight appeared. The men began to be tired and to feel sorry for themselves, to be touchy and depressed. There was only one way to deal with this state of affairs when humor failed. The captain always pointed out that if it didn't matter to anyone that the flight from Prague to Moscow made you age two hours in the old days, why should you mind aging a couple of years? The main thing was not to feel any older. But when his jokes failed, he had to make the day's routine tougher. Hunger and fear left no room for useless brooding. For this reason, the captain had made it a practice to invent all kinds of problems in the spaceship (which was in perfect order, of course). One day the deck equipment threatened to break down, and had to be adjusted while it was running. All the parts were changed, one by one; general rejoicing followed. The next time he thought up an imminent collision with a meteorite: all supplies had to be moved from the threatened side to the other side, and after the supposed danger had passed, everything had to be put back in its place again. A third time he invented an infectious disease the men must have brought on board with them and which required reinoculation for everyone; or the food would be infested, which meant going on a diet of bread and water for two days. The captain had to continually think up minor forms of torment to liven their days and keep the men occupied so there was no time for brooding.

But there was no one there to think up a way to lift Feather's days. He had to bear everything alone: the feeling that their expedition and his own life were utterly senseless, that he was to remain alone forever; despair at the hopelessness of the task he had undertaken and at the hopelessness of the life he had left behind him on Earth. He and the ship's doctor had made a pact: whenever the doctor thought the captain's depression was reaching alarming proportions, he would discover an attack of gallstones that called for special radiation treatment in the sick bay. And then while the captain got very drunk in the sick bay—he refused all medication but whiskey—his adjutant took over command of the ship. In two days the captain had usually gotten rid of his hangover and came up on deck again to think up some new danger to throw the men into a sweat, to be overcome, and to provide cause for celebration.

After his most recent hangover, however, Nemo did not have to bother to think up a new trick. The meeting with the pirate ship seemed imminent at last. They could see it now—a rocket that looked more like a blimp, shaped like a cigar and about the size of a small planetoid: half the size of our moon. It was moving very slowly in the direction of our solar system. There could be no doubt about it: it was aiming at the sun.

Nemo gave orders for a message to be sent down to Earth at once by means of their special equipment. It was an experiment, for the chance of communication at that distance was extremely dubious. Then he called all hands on deck. The crew had to take turns at the machines and sleep in their spacesuits with weapons ready. He turned the heaviest long-range catapults on the giant, and slackened speed.

THE ENCOUNTER

There were several courses open to them. They were all discussed by the staff officers, and the computers offered an endless list of possible combinations. They all really boiled down to two: either to attack the ship outright, or to come to terms.

In view of the damage the pirate ship had already done in space, most of the officers were in favor of direct attack. The test explosions were still very much alive in their minds, and they could not imagine anything in the whole of the universe that could stand up to their nuclear weapons. There was, of course, the question whether the attacking ship could survive the explosion. Would the *Nautilus* hold out? No one could offer an answer, because no one had any idea what material the pirate ship was made of. It was also quite possible that the crew of the super-rocket would be reasonable, intelligent, and willing to reach an agreement. But suppose the pirates seized and killed the emissaries? That was the risk involved in the second alternative. The first, however, involved an even greater risk: they would all be blown to pieces.

Nemo finally decided to fly to the strange vessel in the company of a few of his most stalwart men, armed to the teeth and ready to open negotiations. They set off in an old-fashioned Cosmic Bathtub—the one in which he had first made his name.

They were all amazed to see that the rocket was very similar to certain types that were used for transport on Earth, only many times larger. They flew around it like a satellite and found no sign of life. Either there had been no lookouts, or the pirates were willing to come to terms. Or they were all dead, thought Nemo.

"We'll land there by the main entrance." He pointed to an enormous gap yawning in the bow. The entrance was unguarded, and the five men easily found their way inside. Roped together and maintaining radio contact with the Bathtub, they went down into the bowels of the rocket one by one. The first to disappear was the adjutant. He came back in a few minutes. His eyes were staring wildly and he was spitting blood, as far as they could make out through the thick lenses of his spacesuit goggles. They had to send him back to the Bathtub at once. No one felt like going down after that. They stood there hesitating, their feet weighted down and little batteries in their hands to allow them to move about; their automatic rifles were slung over their shoulders. No one stirred. Then Nemo himself stepped forward and slowly sank into the abyss.

He was barely ten feet down when a persistent thought began to circle in his mind, as though somebody were whispering to him:

"We are friends . . . we are friends . . . we are friends . . ." he seemed to hear. But of course he didn't really hear anything. It was like having a tune stuck in the mind. The words went on and on in his head like a broken phonograph record.

He began to feel frightened by the words as they swirled around. At last he landed on a sort of platform. The moment he felt his feet touch ground, the opposite wall began to open; it was several yards thick. He shut his eyes and went quickly through the opening. At first he threw a thin stream of light ahead with his flashlight, but in about three minutes he was blinded by light.

He was at the side of an enormous hall—impossible to see how far it stretched. And up front was a group of monsters.

At least they looked like monsters to him. But he was equally sure that he looked like a monster to them. What surprised him most, though, was that the creatures were not all alike. One was almost the size of a whale and looked something like a swollen ciliaphore; another was covered with flagella, while another featured eight feet. They were all transparent, and he could see a strange liquid pulsating through their bodies. They did not move. If it had not been for the liquid, he would have thought they were dead.

"They're only asleep—frozen. You can wake them up if you warm them, they'll wake up right away. . . ." He heard the words in his mind. He had already realized that they came from microtransmitters on the brain surface. He switched his battery off. He did not want to wake them up; he did not even want to warm the place they were in with his torchlight. He gave a couple of sharp tugs at the cable he had fastened to his body. The minute the men pulled him up, he heard the insulating wall close behind him.

"They really are monsters," he said to the others, taking a swig of whiskey. "Enormous protozoa. When I was a boy, someone showed me a drop of water under the microscope. It's like a drop of water seven thousand times enlarged," he added, and almost believed his own words. They hurried off to the Bathtub, and returned to the rocket to call a staff officer's meeting.

"My suggestion," said the adjutant, who had come to himself

in the meantime, "is to fix all the explosives we've got to the surface of their rocket, fix the time fuses for a week from now, and get back to Earth as quickly as we can."

"But suppose they're friendly," Nemo objected. "We have no right to destroy them just like that. Suppose they're bringing us a message—or a warning?" Finally, he decided to fix the explosives to the giant ciliaphore spaceship, but to attempt to negotiate at the same time. "Who wants to come along with me and talk to them?" he asked at last. He looked at his hardened band of adventurers, but not one of them could meet his eye. It was the first time in all those years that they had felt fear. The adjutant had been in a terrible state when they got him to sick bay. He had raved about monsters and terrible creatures, and they could see what horrors he had gone through.

"I'll go with you." It was the adjutant himself who spoke. They were all astonished. "I've got to make good. . . ."

THE SPHINX

The two men stood at the edge of the great hall, near the whale-ciliaphore and the elephant-flagellula, with the giant podia of the third creature lying in the background. They didn't even try to distinguish the rest of the monsters. Once again they heard the two messages echo in their minds. Slowly, they began to warm the air. They had brought an active accumulator with them, and in less than an hour the liquid in the ciliaphore's body had begun to course more rapidly, while the unknown creature's podia began to tremble and the flagellula stretched itself with lazy delight.

Up to this point the crew of the *Nautilus III* had been able to follow the encounter, because the adjutant had taken a television transmitter with him, but when the flagellula moved a second time the picture seemed to mist over, as though water were pouring over it, and communication was interrupted.

The second officer immediately called a meeting. Since the two emissaries had ceased to respond to signals on the cable, the men on the *Nautilus* wondered whether they should attack. Finally they decided to send another party. The men who went discovered that the wall was closed. It would not open, and even withstood the oxyacetyle lamps they had brought along with them from the spaceship, and which were capable of dissolving any material known to man. They decided to wait by the entrance to the giant rocket for an hour longer, and then to attack.

Precisely fifty-nine minutes later the two men inside were heard again. They came out and boarded the Bathtub. When they reached the *Nautilus*, Nemo called the whole crew on deck and gave the order to return home.

"What about the explosives?"

"We can leave them behind. They know all about it, anyway," and shut himself up in his cabin with the doctor and the adjutant. They spent nearly ten hours in consultation.

Meanwhile, the men observed that the crew of the giant rocket was not idle. The enormous cigar-shaped vessel seemed to bend suddenly, straightened itself out, and moved off at top speed in the direction from which it had come, away from our Sun. The *Nautilus* had apparently succeeded in its task. But the mystery of the giant pirate ship had not yet been solved. They were all impatient to hear what the captain would have to say, and hurried on deck for evening roll call.

"I'm afraid you're going to be disappointed," Nemo addressed them. "We only spoke a few words to the foreign ambassadors. They answered us by telepathy, and I must say they seem to have made much greater progress there than we have. We asked them whether they were flying toward our solar system, and why. They explained that a long time ago they had been sent into space from their planet to visit our system, which according to their reports seemed to be the only one in the universe inhabited by intelligent animals—that is to say, by living creatures who are aware of themselves, their surroundings, and their own actions.

"We asked them what they wanted, and why they had undertaken such a long journey to see us—whether there was anything we could do to help them, whether they wanted to move to our planet—and of course we pointed out immediately that it would never work out. It seemed to us, you see, that nothing short of mortal danger could have sent these creatures on so long and difficult a journey.

"They replied that they wanted to know our answer to the fundamental question of life." The captain blushed as he said that, like a schoolboy who has suddenly forgotten the answer when the teacher calls on him. "I'm sorry. I know it sounds silly, but that's really what they said. . . ." He glanced at his adjutant, who nodded and repeated:

"They said they wanted to know our answer to the fundamental question of life."

"Naturally we didn't know what they meant," the captain went on. "We thought they were asking us about the purpose of life. Everyone knows that the purpose of life is to transform nature. But that didn't seem to be what they wanted. Maybe they wanted to find out how much we know about life. So we offered them the doctor's notes: we have mastered the problem of tissue regeneration; we can prolong human life and heal even the most seriously damaged animal. But that wasn't what they wanted either. *The fundamental question of life!* They seemed to be shouting the words at us, like a crowd at a football game, or a pack of mad dogs. They wanted to know the answer. And we didn't even know what they meant."

"The fundamental question of life." The adjutant interrupted him. "Of course it occurred to us that it might all be strategy, a way of distracting us by philosophical arguments. They couldn't expect us to believe they'd been en route from some damn spiral nebula for at least two hundred thousand years, or that they were tagging the stars as they went so folks back home would know they were going on with their task; they couldn't expect us to believe they'd volunteered to be put into suspended animation just to ask the kind of question that no one on Earth bothers with except idlers, drunkards, and philosophers. I thought it might be a trick—that they were really out to take us prisoner and destroy the rocket. I tried to give you orders—"

"And that's just what you shouldn't have done!" Nemo shouted at him angrily. "The ciliaphore next to us immediately opened the insulating door and pushed us out."

" 'Tell them we have detached their explosives,' he said. 'It is clear to us that life in your solar system is not yet completely reasonable. . . .' "

"We would have attacked if they'd kept you one minute longer."

"You're all fools," answered the captain. "Fools and idiots. Nothing would have happened. Can't you understand that these creatures are much more technologically advanced than we are? We were at their mercy, and they spared us, simply because they gave up killing and destruction long ago. They're interested in other things." He was silent for a moment and then apologized quickly to the crew. "It was an unnerving experience, and I'm getting old. You know I've never shouted at you before. But I've got the feeling those creatures could have told us much more. Perhaps life asks more questions, the more perfect it gets."

"The main thing is, we saved our homes," said the second officer.

"Saved them? From what? Questions aren't dangerous to anyone."

"They're starting up again!" The doctor ran in from the watch room without knocking or saluting. "They're not going back to Andromeda—they're heading out into space again. And they're slowing down."

"That means they still think they'll find the answer to their questions somewhere in the universe."

"Fundamental questions, sir," his adjutant reminded him.

"Fundamental questions." Captain Nemo was still angry with his adjutant. He turned to the crew and read the orders for the next day. Never before had they heard him speak so quietly.

"He's getting old," they said to each other. But they were wrong. The captain had just begun to think.

* * *

NAUTILUS 300

On the journey home no one bothered to think up any problems for the crew, and no one bothered to keep the men from worrying. The captain sat in his cabin all day long, watching through the window the dark void that surrounded them, the mysterious depths of eternity—perhaps not so eternal after all—: the utter infinite. The cooks began to hand out better food, the officers relaxed, roll call was held when the men turned up for it, and nobody bothered much about the flight itself. At first the men were contented; then they began to feel afraid, lost their appetites—the mess hall was next to empty at mealtimes—suffered from insomnia and were prey to disquieting thoughts. And in this state they landed. Needless to say, the rocket returned to the point where it had taken off. It was late evening; so far as they could see, there had been no changes at the base since the day they left. The moment they landed, old-fashioned luggage trailers drove up from the hangars and men in overalls helped them down and into the trailers. They smiled and shook hands with the newcomers warmly, looking very friendly. But that was all. There was no crowd of welcoming officials, no reporters, no curious onlookers, and not even a government delegation complete with military band. Nothing. Just a run-of-the-mill arrival, as though they had come back from a stroll around Mars. The captain felt injured.

"Didn't you know we were going to land?"

"Of course we knew. You interrupted traffic on the main line to Mercury. We had to take five rockets off, since we had no guarantee you'd be on time."

"We're always on time!" the captain shouted angrily. "Is there no higher officer coming to thank us?" he added in a haughty voice.

"Tomorrow, tomorrow morning. In your quarters," replied the man he had been talking to. He was tall, with an ashen face, and did not look well. He asked the crew to take their places in the trailers and take only essential luggage with them. They drove off with mixed feelings. This was not the way they had imagined their return to the Earth they had saved.

"We might just as well have sent the monsters instead. They'd probably have made a bigger impression." They had just turned into the main road when they heard an explosion behind them. The captain swung around to look. At the base, someone had set fire to the *Nautilus*: the tanks had just gone up. Nemo and the men with him beat on the door of the truck in a rage, but the trailer only picked up speed.

"And we didn't even bring a gun with us," the second officer growled. The captain's adjutant leaned over and tried to jab a penknife into the rear tire as they drove along at top speed. A voice came from the loudspeaker:

"Please behave reasonably, men. We must ask you to remember that you come from an era that sent several rockets a day into space. If we tried to save all of those that return to Earth, there would soon be no landing room left. You are the three-hundredth crew to have returned after hundreds of years in space. We cannot understand why you people were so anxious to fly around—in fact, we find it incomprehensible. But we do try to make allowances, and you must also try to understand our position."

The adjutant gave up: the trailer had solid rubber tires, and now they were drawing up in front of the camp. It was a huddle of low buildings similar to those of the era they had known. Porters came running toward them and picked up their bags. They all looked pale. The captain liked their quarters.

"I should like to thank your commanding officer," he said to the drivers.

"You must wait until tomorrow." They smiled shyly. "Tomorrow morning, please." And they saluted and drove off.

As Nemo approached the dormitory he heard loud laughter. He opened the door: his men were standing silently, hesitantly by their bunks, and in one corner lay an elderly bearded fellow in the tattered remains of an astronaut's suit, rocking with laughter.

"He says——"

"Do you know what he's been telling us?"

"—that they aren't men," the captain heard someone say.

"Robots or something like that . . . 'Black and white servants' . . . 'Gray doubles' . . .''

Nemo strode over to the old man, who was holding his sides in uncontrollable laughter, and dealt him several resounding slaps. The man jumped to his feet and clenched his fists. But a glance at the captain's broad shoulders calmed him down, and he could see that the rest were all against him.

"They don't even know what *this* means—brawling," he snapped. "And they don't like it if we fight."

"Who's 'we'?" asked the captain.

"Who are we? The small crew of a private rocket from California that set out to see whether there was anything to be exploited on Mercury. Only our joystick went out of action and we bounced back and forth between Mercury and Earth for years before someone happened to notice us and bring us down. I can tell you we felt pretty foolish when we found out that the people who had saved us, who played cards with us and drank grapefruit juice with us all the way here were really machines from a factory. Yes, gentlemen, you'll hear all about it from Dr. Erasmus tomorrow. Just wait until morning."

THE FUNDAMENTAL QUESTION OF LIFE

"You've come back to Earth at a time when technical progress has been completed," Dr. Erasmus told them the next morning. He was almost paler than his black-and-white servants. "Man began to invent machines to save him drudgery. But work was really ideal for man. Man is best suited to do his own work; the only thing he cannot stand is the humiliation. As soon as machines had been invented that could in fact do all jobs, there was only one problem left: what the machines should look like. It didn't seem appropriate to create models of attractiveness; some people might fall in love with their own servant-machines, might hate them, punish them, take revenge on them—in short, transfer human emotions to their relationships with the machines. It was also suggested—this simply to give you the whole picture—that the form of a monkey or a dog be used. But the monkey was not considered efficient enough, and the dog, though he has been man's companion for ages, cannot clean up after man, or do his work for him, or look after him so well that man can devote himself to the two things only man can do: create and think. Finally, the servants were built, in black and white, and each man was given one so like himself as to be indistinguishable from himself, a gray double, as it were, who did all his work and looked after the man in whose image it was made. You can order doubles like that for yourselves, if you like our society and decide to try to adapt to it. You won't need to take care of anything; all the servants are directed from a common computer center which follows a single chief command: *look after humanity*. Thus the technical problems have been solved for good, and man is free of work for all time.

"Of course, if you prefer to go on living in your old way—many elderly people do find it difficult to adapt themselves to something new—you can remain here. This camp has been set aside for you and anyone else who may return to Earth from space."

It sounded so strange. What did people do with their time, then? Nemo asked.

"I can show you," answered Dr. Erasmus, and switched on the telewall. They saw a garden, where Dr. Erasmus's double was strolling along deep in discussion with several friends. Only then did they realize that the man they were watching on the telewall was the real Dr. Erasmus and the one talking to them his gray double. Dr. Erasmus on the telewall suddenly turned around and smiled at the crew, waving a friendly hand before going on with his talk as though there was nothing more important on Earth. . . .

The crew of the *Nautilus* decided to have a look at the new society. Dr. Erasmus's double smiled: everyone started out this way; but, alas, not all retained their initial enthusiasm.

The captain's first errand was to the Historical Institute. There he asked to see the records of his last flight—the date of their takeoff and the date on which their death was announced. He could find nothing to fall back on. There was no mention of cosmic pirates anywhere; the minister had been so afraid of creating a panic that he had forgotten to leave any evidence which could help the men now.

"Look up Feather for me," he ordered. The double looked at him in perplexity. "Leonard Feather, the famous hero, also known as Nemo," the captain went on, looking around to see if anyone he knew happened to be listening. But the double still looked blank.

"Don't you mean Igor Feather?" Igor was the name of the captain's half-blind son. "Dvořák, Janáček, Feather? The three greatest Czech musicians?" the robot asked politely.

"Musicians?"

"Composers, that is . . . Feather is certainly the greatest of the three, as every child knows today. The house where he was born has been preserved for a thousand years in its original state; concerts and evening discussions on music are arranged there. You will find the place full of people," the robot stressed the word *people*. And so the captain came home after a thousand years.

Fortunately, there was no concert scheduled for that day. He was afraid that even after so many years he would not have been able to stand the caterwauling. Their old home now stood in a park, and all the adjacent houses had been torn down. While he was still a long way off, he could see two gold plates gleaming on the front of the house. One commemorated his son and the music he had written, celebrating the young man's service to the cause of music. The other—Nemo approached it with quickening pulse—commemorated his wife. No one had put up a plaque to the memory of Captain Nemo. He looked around thoroughly, but he could find no mention of himself.

"She died a year before the first performance of Igor's concerto in Rudolfinum Hall . . ." somebody said behind him. He started and looked around to see his adjutant walking out of the shadow of the bushes. "She had to take care of your son, who had gone completely blind. She looked after him for twenty years, and he died in her arms. She didn't even live to see his name established: he became famous a year after her death. That woman was a saint, sir."

"Why are you telling me this?"

"Because I loved her."

"You never said anything about it."

"Of course you never saw anything strange in my coming to see you at home, but I was happy just to be near her. And you deceived her with that black girl who got married a week after you started out on your last flight."

"That's a lie."

"It's the truth. She had twelve children. You can trace her descendants if you like. There'll be hundreds of them by now. I was one of your officers on the *Nautilus* only because of your wife, sir. I wanted to show her it wasn't so hard to be a hero, and that I could stand as much as you could, even if my shoulders weren't so broad. But she only loved you. And you loved that other girl."

"Another one of life's puzzles, isn't it? Another fundamental question."

"There's no question about it. It's a fact. You helped to kill her . . . . It's a filthy business, and that's the truth. You behaved shamefully to her." His adjutant had never spoken in that tone before. Nemo turned on his heel and walked away. He saw that once more he would have to do something for his crew, find them another difficult task, for this new age was too much like those empty days out there in space.

In the Astronautics Institute they would not even hear of taking him on. "We have our own robot crews. Why risk your life? Why bother with things that can be done better by machines, while you neglect those things that only the human mind can do?"

"Here are my papers." He showed them his records like a desperate man who had aged prematurely. "I can pilot a rocket as well as any of your robots. And I've got a crew of men who'll follow me to hell if need be."

"No human organism could hold out in our current program of space flight. We have no job you could do. We're investigating the curvature of space, the qualities of light, whether even higher speeds can be reached—all tasks beyond your powers. Devote yourself to philosophy, art, aesthetics. That's the coming field, after all. . . ."

"I'm too old," replied the captain, rising from his chair. The gray robot said he was sorry. The wall of his office yawned and his human image leaned into the room. He was about fifty, a Bohemian with a palette and brush in his hand, and an enormous canvas behind him. He had a ringing voice.

"If anyone says that the time for philosophy has not yet arrived, or that it has passed, it's as good as saying that the time for happiness has not yet come, or that there is no longer any such thing. . . . That's Epicurus, my friend, wisdom that's thirty-five hundred years old. Find yourself something creative to do. Everyone has some sort of talent—something that makes him aware he is alive, that proves his own existence to him, something he can express himself best in. Leave those technical toys to machines and children; there's nothing in them to interest a grown man. We have more serious problems. The most urgent are the fundamental questions of life. . . ." Nemo had heard that before.

"Has anybody found any answers yet?" he asked.

"My dear sir, humanity is still too young for that. It's not like smashing the atom or orbiting around Jupiter. These questions need time and patience, they require a man's whole being. The answer is not only given in words, but in the way you live. . . ."

"I'm too old to change. I'm prepared to turn up at the old takeoff ramp tomorrow, with my whole crew," Captain Nemo decided with finality.

The painter shrugged his shoulders, as if to say he was sorry that he had wasted his time. He turned back to his canvas, and the wall closed behind him. His gray servant bowed the captain out.

"As you wish. But I've warned you: it is suicide."

THE FINAL ANSWER

The captain could not sleep in the morning. He recalled how little enthusiasm his men had shown the evening before, how unconvinced some of them were that it would be better for them to move off. Still, in the end he managed to persuade them, and they had promised to come. He dashed out before it was light and stumbled up to the ramp on foot. Robots were already hard at work there. The rocket they were preparing for flight did not look anything like a rocket: it was more like a globe, or a huge drop of liquid. It made him feel a twinge of fear. The firing mechanism was altogether different as well; he could not understand how it worked. The gray robots let him go wherever he wished and look at anything he cared to look at. Their smiles were strangely apologetic, as though it were not quite right for such a serious-looking man to be wasting his time with such foolishness as rockets. Nemo went back to the rendezvous point. His men were coming up in the morning mist, one by one. They were wearing their old suits again. This time they would be leaving without the fanfare, without the flags, but it would be better for them all. They couldn't possibly stay on Earth, they would never be able to adjust to this strange life. . . .

That was more or less what he said to them on the little rocket base. The mist almost choked him and he had to clear his throat. Then he read off the roll: the men were to answer to their names and step forward to shake hands with him. They answered and stepped forward to shake his hand.

But they were robots. They were the gray doubles of his men, who had sent the robots rather than come themselves. Not one of those ungrateful sons of bitches had reported for duty. The captain rubbed his eyes. It must be the mist, he thought. And he sat down on the nearest stone because he found himself somehow unable to breathe properly.

"Captain Feather?" A broad-shouldered fellow bent over him. He was wearing a beautifully brushed uniform, covered with gold braid, such as Nemo had never seen before.

"Yes." He looked at him closely.

"They sent me over from the central office. With your permission, I'll take over the command. . . ." Yes, of course, it was himself. Just a bit grayer, that was all.

"If you wish. If they wish," answered the captain, who felt defeated. His double saluted respectfully and stood smartly to attention just as Feather always did. In a short time he heard his own voice coming from the rocket, giving brief, staccato commands, reports and orders, just as he had done in previous years. In a few minutes the rocket silently moved away from the ground—*what kind of fuel do they have in there?*—and slowly rose toward the clouds. He waved after it. And looked around, just in case anyone was watching. It was silly, after all, to wave at a machine that worked so precisely all by itself.

He turned away and went slowly back to his old home. This time there were crowds of people in the house. His son's last symphony was being performed. He recognized those strange sounds that had upset him so much before he had left on his last flight. But now they no longer seemed so odd: he found himself beginning to listen attentively. He remained where he was, standing by a tree, at a considerable distance from the audience; the breeze carried snatches of music to him. Far up in the sky he saw the rocket pass out of sight.

And it occurred to him suddenly that if his son had stood before those pilgrims from distant galaxies, he might have been able to answer their questions.

I must tell them not to send rockets out to look for the answer to the fundamental question of life, he thought. We must find the answer down here, on Earth.

The orchestra fell silent and the harp sang out alone. It reminded him of something very beautiful.

La Befana

GENE WOLFE

There are certain tired science fiction plots—everyone dies except two people are left and his name is Adama and hers Eva—that every editor sees over and over again and rejects instantly. If any editor is asked he will quickly supply a list of stories he has seen a thousand times, which he will never buy. Yet—if a writer of some genius takes a plot that has been done before. . . .

When Zozz, home from the pit, had licked his fur clean, he howled before John Bannano's door. John's wife Teresa opened it and let him in. She was a thin, stooped woman of thirty or thirty-five, her black hair shot with gray; she did not smile, but he felt somehow that she was glad to see him. She said, "He's not home yet. If you want to come in we've got a fire."

Zozz said, "I'll wait for him," and six-legging politely across the threshold sat down over the stone Bananas had rolled in for him when they were new friends. Maria and Mark, playing some sort of game with beer-bottle caps on squares scratched on the floor-dirt, said, "Hi, Uncle Zozz," and Zozz said, "Hi," in return. Bananas's old mother, whom Zozz had brought here from the pads in his rusty powerwagon the day before, looked at him with piercing eyes then fled into the other room. He could hear Teresa relax, the wheezing out-puffed breath.

He said, half-humorously, "I think she thinks I bumped her on purpose yesterday."

"She's not used to you yet."

"I know," Zozz said.

170

"I told her, Mother Bannano, it's their world, and they're not used to *you*."

"Sure," Zozz said. A gust of wind outside brought the cold in to replace the odor of the gog-hutch on the other side of the left wall.

"I tell you it's hell to have your husband's mother with you in a place as small as this."

"Sure," Zozz said again.

Maria announced, "Daddy's home!" The door rattled open and Bananas came in looking tired and cheerful. Bananas worked in the slaughtering market, and though his cheeks were blue with cold, the cuffs of his trousers were red with blood. He kissed Teresa and tousled the hair of both children and said, "Hi, Zozzy."

Zozz said, "Hi. How does it roll?" And moved over so Bananas could warm his back. Someone groaned, and Bananas asked a little anxiously, "What's that?"

Teresa said, "Next door."

"Huh?"

"Next door. Some woman."

"Oh. I thought it might be Mom."

"She's fine."

"Where is she?"

"In back."

Bananas frowned. "There's no fire in there; she'll freeze to death."

"I didn't tell her to go back there. She can wrap a blanket around her."

Zozz said, "It's me—I bother her." He got up. Bananas said, "Sit down."

"I can go, I just come to say hi."

"Sit down." Bananas turned to his wife. "Honey, you shouldn't leave her in there alone. See if you can't get her to come out."

"Johnny——"

"Teresa, dammit!"

"Okay, Johnny."

Bananas took off his coat and sat down in front of the fire. Maria and Mark had gone back to their game. In a voice too low to attract their attention, Bananas said, "Nice thing, huh?"

Zozz said, "I think your mother makes her nervous."

Bananas said, "Sure."

Zozz said, "This isn't an easy world."

"You mean for us. No, it ain't, but you don't see me moving."

Zozz said, "That's good. I mean, here you've got a job anyway. There's work."

"That's right."

Unexpectedly Maria said: "We get enough to eat here, and me and Mark can find wood for the fire. Where we used to be there wasn't anything to eat."

Bananas said, "You remember, honey?"

"A little."

Zozz said, "People are poor here."

Bananas was taking off his shoes, scraping the street mud from them and tossing it into the fire. He said, "If you mean us, us people are poor everyplace." He jerked his head in the direction of the back room. "You ought to hear her tell about our world."

"Your mother?"

Bananas nodded. Maria said, "Daddy, how did grandmother come here?"

"Same way we did."

Mark said, "You mean she signed a thing?"

"A labor contract? No, she's too old. She bought a ticket—you know, like you would buy something in a store."

Maria said, "That's what I mean."

"Shut up and play. Don't bother us."

Zozz said, "How'd things go at work?"

"So so." Bananas looked toward the back room again. "She came into some money, but that's her business—I didn't want to talk to the kids about it."

"Sure."

"She says she spent every dollar to get here—you know, they haven't used dollars even on Earth for fifty, sixty years, but she still says it, how do you like that?'' He laughed, and Zozz laughed too. ''I asked how she was going to get back, and she said she's not going back, she's going to die right here with us. What could I say?''

''I don't know.'' Zozz waited for Bananas to say something, and when he did not he added, ''I mean, she's your mother.''

''Yeah.''

Through the thin wall they heard the sick woman groan again, and someone moving about. Zozz said, ''I guess it's been a long time since you saw her last.''

''Yeah—twenty-two years Newtonian. Listen, Zozzy. . . .''

''Uh-huh.''

''You know something? I wish I had never set eyes on her again.''

Zozz said nothing, rubbing his hands, hands, hands.

''That sounds lousy, I guess.''

''I know what you mean.''

''She could have lived good for the rest of her life on what that ticket cost her.'' Bananas was silent for a moment. ''She used to be a big, fat woman when I was a kid, you know? A great big woman with a loud voice. Look at her now—dried up and bent over; it's like she wasn't my mother at all. You know the only thing that's the same about her? That black dress. That's the only thing I recognize, the only thing that hasn't changed. She could be a stranger—she tells stories about me I don't remember at all.''

Maria said, ''She told us a story today.''

Mark added: ''Before you came home. About this witch.''

Maria said: ''That brings the presents to children. Her name is La Befana the Christmas Witch.''

Zozz drew his lips back from his double canines and jiggled his head. ''I like stories.''

''She says it's almost Christmas, and on Christmas three wise men went looking for the Baby, and they stopped at the old witch's door, and they asked which way it was and she told them and they said come with us.''

The door to the other room opened, and Teresa and Bananas's

mother came out. Bananas's mother was holding a teakettle; she edged around Zozz to put it on the hook and swing it out over the fire.

"And she was sweeping and she wouldn't come."

Mark said: "She said she'd come when she was finished. She was a real old, real ugly woman. Watch, I'll show you how she walked." He jumped up and began to hobble around the room.

Bananas looked at his wife and indicated the wall. "What's this?"

"Some woman. I told you."

"In there?"

"The charity place—they said she could stay there. She couldn't stay in the house because all the rooms are full of men."

Maria was saying, "So when she was all done she went looking for Him only she couldn't find Him and she never did."

"She's sick?"

"She's knocked up, Johnny, that's all. Don't worry about her. She's got some guy in there with her."

Mark asked, "Do you know about the baby Jesus, Uncle Zozz?"

Zozz groped for words.

"Giovanni, my son. . . ."

"Yes, Mama."

"Your friend. . . . Do they have the faith, Giovanni?"

Apropos of nothing, Teresa said, "They're Jews, next door."

Zozz told Mark, "You see, the baby Jesus has never come to my world."

Maria said: "And so she goes all over everyplace looking for him with her presents, and she leaves some with every kid she finds, but she says it's not because she thinks they might be him like some people think but just a substitute. She can't never die. She has to do it forever, doesn't she, Grandma?"

The bent old woman said, "Not forever, dearest, only until tomorrow night."

Five Poems

This department of SF poetry is now well established and flourishing. The selections this year contain two poems—the Auden and the Haden-Guest—that were commissioned by a London newspaper to commemorate the annual Motor Show. The others are from that excellent little magazine, Cornudo.

A CURSE

W. H. Auden

Dark was that day when Diesel
conceived his dread engine that
begot you, grim invention,
more vicious, more criminal
than the camera even,
metallic monstrosity,
bale and bane of our Culture,
chief woe of our Commonweal.
How dare the Law prohibit
hashish and heroin yet
licence your use who inflate
all weak inferior egos?
Their addicts only do harm
to their own lives, you poison
the lungs of the innocent,
your din dithers the peaceful,
and on choked roads hundreds must
daily die by chance-medley.

Nimble technicians, surely
you should hang your heads in shame.
Your wit works mighty marvels,
has landed men on the moon,
replaced brains by computers,
and can smithy a "smart" bomb.
It is a crying scandal
that you cannot take the time
or be bothered to build us,
what sanity knows we need,
an odourless and noiseless
staid little electric brougham.

AUTO-APOTHEOSIS

Anthony Haden-Guest

Today my soul has transmigrated
Into a milk-white Chevrolet
My instruments are platinum-plated
My ornaments come from Fabergé
My benzine is Napoleon brandy
My exhaust smells like cotton candy

My binary metamorphosis
Is a flesh-coloured Cadillac
Fat kid upholstery, stuffed with roses,
And Auto-drive by BRAINIAC
My soul is scented like a lotus
My body comes from General Motors

Drear hordes of Dodge and Studebaker,
Hispano-Suiza, Edsel Ford,
Make way! I drive to meet my Maker
In the garages of the Lord . . .

I'll drive thru an Eternal Day
That infinite-laned Motorway!

TWO POEMS

William Jon Watkins

I.

We have a colony
on the face of the sun,
comfortable as an old dog
under the stove.
It floats in a bubble
of energy
like an ad
for Consolidated Edison.
People like it so much there,
no one ever comes back.
Some people think it's unfair
that only troublemakers
got to go there
and the Government never built a second ship.

II.

First, they danced around him like St. Elmo's fire.
Then they buzzed his head.
Finally, they hailed him on all civilized frequencies,
then shrugged
and left.

"Some days," St. Francis said,
"the world fairly buzzes
with the radiant glory of God."

SPORT

Steven Utley

Poor man

brought low by laughing wolverines
wielding hatchets

carved, opened and eaten on the spot,
not far from the cooling carcasses
of his she and his manling—
both brained for sport,
and to the great satisfaction
of passenger pigeons, auks,
and other interested parties

The Window in Dante's Hell

MICHAEL BISHOP

Too much science fiction is about the future from the point of view of the present; too few are stories of the future as though written in that future. Michael Bishop does this—and does it very well indeed.

1/*the combcrawlers*

We received notification of the woman's death on the Bio-monitor Console in the subsidiary control room on West Peach-tree. A small cherry-red light went on; it glowed in the blue halflight that hangs about the console like the vague memory of fog. "Someone's dead," Yates's son said. "That light just came on." Yates's son is fourteen years old. His broad face was purplish in the fog of the control room, the sheen of flesh over forehead reflecting back a small crescent of the red that had just come on. Only a moment before, the boy had entered the building, stopped at my elbow, and waited for an opportunity to talk. Yates is my boss, the head of the city's Biomonitor Agency. Because our interests were similar, his son frequently came around to talk to me: I girderclimbed on the weekends, and the boy was just learning. But he had never come into the console area before, and when the red light began faintly pulsing on the monstrous board, his lank body had stooped toward it.

"Yes," I said. "Someone's dead. The board don't lie. 'Deed it don't." To sentimentalize the death of a cubicle-dweller is a soul-destroying business. I try to keep it light.

"I've never seen a dead person. Papa says that people get sick,

179

that the board reports that all the time—but people don't die very often.''

"People die all the time.''

"I've never seen a dead person,'' Yates's son said. "Never at all.''

"You're lucky you haven't seen a girderclimbing accident, Newlyn. You'd see death and terror and plummeting human beings all in one fell swoop.'' I am nine years older than Newlyn, and those nine years have taught me one or two things that I'm not always capable of communicating to those younger than myself. But I try—for their benefit, not mine. "When I was your age, I saw a party of six combcrawlers, hooked together with a glinting golden cord, lose either the magnetic induction in their girderboots or else all sense of the teamwork involved in dome-traversing.''

Newlyn looked away from the board. His heavy forehead turned toward me; his African lips framed a faint exhalation: "What happened?''

"The climbers,'' I told him, "had reached a section of honeycombing about three hundred yards from the very apex of the Dome. Their backs were down, and inside the spun-iron gloves their hands were probably clinging like crazy to the track of the navigational girder they had chosen. They had worked out a complicated, a truly beautiful assault on the apex. They were high above the city, bright specks on the artificial sky, and suddenly the fourth man in the contingent fell away from the group and bobbed on the elastic gold cord that held them together—bobbed just like a spider weighting the center of its web.

"From the top of the new Russell Complex, my father and I watched them—even though we hadn't gone up there for that purpose.

"The combcrawlers couldn't recover, Newlyn. The fifth and sixth men broke away, flailing their arms around. It was amazing how slowly—how really distinctly—their fates overtook them. The first three men in the chain were sucked down toward us, and the whole broad sky under the Dome seemed to hold them up for a while. Then they fell, twirling around and around each other like

the strands of one of those Argentine *bolas*, hypnotizing everybody in the streets. At last they fell through the canyon of buildings
to our north and disappeared toward the concrete that I could *feel*
impacting against them. It was terrifying, but it was beautiful. I
resolved to become a combcrawler myself. All unbeknownst to my
father, of course—he'd've suffered a multiple aneurysm if he'd
known about that resolution. You see, Newlyn, you're lucky.
Your father approves.''

"But did you see them after they fell?" Newlyn asked, unawed.
"Did you see them lying in the street, dead?"

Annoyed, I said: "Hell no, I didn't see them! If my father was
the sort to frown on combcrawling, do you think he'd bundle me
off to ogle six crumpled, blood-spattered husks of humanity in
some crappy alley?"

Newlyn smiled. "Then you haven't seen a dead person,
either."

"Certainly I have."

"Where?"

"On the board," I said, smiling too. "There's one right there,
that pulsing red light."

"And who is it, then?" the boy said, continuing his interroga-
tion. "And where does he live?"

"Just a minute, lad." I leaned forward, recorded the coordinates of the light, and at last gave it permission to go dead, its dull
cherry sheen fading out of the naked crystal and leaving us, the boy
and me, swimming in the blue dimness. (Wherever possible, you
see, the city conserves its resources.) I ran the coordinates through
the appropriate computer and found that the dead person lay in a
cubicle somewhere on Level 8. To be exact: Concourse E-16,
Door 502, Level 8. Another computer gave me the corpse's name,
age, and vital statistics—though there weren't many of the latter.

"Well, who is it?" Newlyn asked.

"Almira Longhope. One hundred and seven years old. Unmar-
ried. No relatives. Caucasian. Came into the city at the age of
thirty-one with the refugees of the first Evacuation Lottery. . . .''

"Let's go see her!"

"What?"

"Let's go see her. Somebody's got to go get her, don't they?"

"Somebody. Not us."

"Look, Mr. Ardrey, that old woman died down on Level 8 because she was old and alone, probably. I've never seen a dead person, you've never seen a dead person. Let's go and retrieve her and keep them servo-units from eating her up like a wad of dust. Okay?"

"Newlyn, we're not going anywhere to gawk at an old woman who couldn't get any higher than Level 8 in seventy years."

"It wouldn't be any gawking," Newlyn said. "It wouldn't."

And with that as a prologue and only a little more argument, I finally consented. The Biomonitor Agency does not ordinarily send human beings to dispose of the human beings who have died in their cubicles—nor does the Agency refrain from want of sufficient manpower or out of callousness. The problem is that human beings are invariably *too* compassionate; they represent feeling, and when that feeling confronts a corpse and all its attendant suggestions of loneliness, the living human beings suffer—and suffer profoundly. Therefore, the Agency usually dispatches servo-units to the cubicles of the kinless and the forgotten. It is best.

I appointed Arn Bartholomew to take my place at the console. I gathered from our files and resource rooms some of the things we would need. Then Newlyn and I went into the street.

Because it was winter and because our meteorologists maintain internal conditions that correspond with the external passing of the seasons, we wore coats. Newlyn, in his navy pea jacket, strode ahead of me like an adolescent tour guide, spindly, purposeful, curt. We walked across one marble square, circumnavigated a huge fountain whose waters were frozen in fantastic loops and falls, and jogged toward the monolithic lift-terminal that dispatches its passengers up and down the layered levels of the city in crystal lift-tubes. We jogged because it was cold. We jogged because it is difficult to talk while jogging, and we did not believe

that we had, in actuality, committed ourselves to the viewing and
the disposal of a . . . *dead person*. Jogging, we tried not to look at
each other.

The Dome glowered above us; it seemed that it hung down with
the weight of its own honeycombing, threatening to crush us. No
one was up there. No one was crawling over the girders.

Then we reached the lift-terminal, found an open tube, and
descended into the great hive of the city—descended in utter
silence, descended through a nightmare halflight, a halflight
freaky as the cold simulation of dawn. On Level 8, one stratum
above the nethermost floor of the hive, we disembarked.

2/*the glissadors*

We found the concourse; we found the corridor. The people we
passed in the corridor refused to look at us, passing us like wisps of
smoke against the smudge-red illumination that contained us all.

Many of those who passed us were ghostly glissadors, hive
inhabitants who spend so much of their time going up and down
and about and through the various hallways that they have donned
nearly soundless skates to conserve their energy and speed their
labors. The skates are pieces of simulated cordovan footwear with
a multitude of miniature ball bearings mounted in the soles. The
city issues these glierboots to its sublevel employees. And Newlyn
and I watched the graceful glissadors sweep past us through the
gloom, their heads down.

Each time that one went past, Newlyn turned in a slow circle to
watch. He said, "That looks like fun."

"It gets to be work," I said. "Everything gets to be work."

Still, I caught the next effortlessly volplaning figure by the
elbow and spun him about before he could disappear into the dim
distance. A small sound of protest escaped his lips, but he controlled his turn and wheeled about like a mute ballet performer. He

was tall. Like Newlyn, he was the intense color of ripe wet grapes.

"Almira Longhope," I said. "Do you know her cubicle?"

The glissador stared at me: "What's her number, *sur-facesider*?"

I told him.

"Then you keep following these here doors till you reach it." He threw up his arm and spun away. He looked at us briefly. Turning with sinuous skill, he strode out forcefully and skated off, off forth on swing.

"Why'd you stop him?" Newlyn asked. "We knew where we were."

I said nothing for a moment, trying to pick out the departing glissador's figure in the crimson light.

Newlyn said: "Well? Why'd you do that?"

"I wanted one of them to . . . to acknowledge us. I wanted to watch how one of them resumed his skating. Maybe it is fun," I said. And stopped. Newlyn was watching me. "Never mind. Let's follow the goddamn doors."

We did. We walked. Our feet *tap-tap-tapped* on the tiles, mundanely coming down one foot after another. In this fashion we eventually reached Door 502, a door which looked uncannily like the two doors on either side.

I extracted from my pocket the obscenely rubberoid sheath upon which were embossed the whorls of Miss Almira Longhope's right thumbprint, and slipped this sheath over my forefinger so as not to distort the print with my own outsized thumb. Then I held my forefinger to the electric eye for scanning, and the panel slid back, admitting us to the cubicle in which the dead woman must necessarily lie: unwept, unhonored, very nearly unborn. Newlyn preceded me into the odd closet just inside the cubicle's door.

At first we saw nothing. After our trip through the murky, glissador-haunted catacombs, the room's bright midday glare struck at us cruelly. We squinted. We blinked. And then there was the inevitable resolution of detail (in itself a haunting experience) as our eyes came back to us.

We found ourselves in an environment immensely strange. We

were in a cramped artificial foyer. The walls on the inside of the cubicle had been altered so that they formed an octagonal area of space rather than a square one. Moreover, just inside the cubicle's doorway Newlyn and I stumbled upon a crude wooden step which we had to mount in order to see more than the tops of the wall sections opposite us. We climbed the step.

We stood then on a narrow dais, approximately one foot from the cubicle's real floor, that made an octagonal circuit about the entire room and provided an odd catwalk for the unexpecting, and certainly unexpected, intruder into Miss Longhope's spendidly insane sanctuary. It was a sanctuary unlike any that one would expect to find on the lower levels of the hive—or anywhere else, for that matter.

Banks of computerlike gadgetry, from which there emanated the faint and fitful winking of orange and red lights, stood against two facets of the octagonal wall. Against two more sections—the two flanking us—we saw tall glass cylinders that were polarized so that we could not see into them; these cylinders could have been anything, from models of the city's lift-tubes, to gigantic chemical beakers, to containers for space travelers in suspended animation. The mystery intrigued us, but something else drew our attention away. In the remaining four facets of the octagonal wall, directly across the room, we looked upon four distinct and different windows: view screens that permitted us to see panoramas that no living inhabitant of the Dome had ever gazed upon, unless he were possessed of a vivid clairvoyance.

Newlyn and I drank in these panoramas quickly.

From left to right these "windows" demonstrated a progression based on an expanding consciousness of the universe. The screen on the far left depicted a view of our own domed city, but from the *outside*, as if from a distant hilltop in the wilderness that we had so long ago fled; and darkness swirled over the Dome's imposing hump like a disturbed gas, uneasily hovering.

The second window showed us the dead face of the Moon from about ten thousand miles away. No man had set foot there for more than eighty, ninety, perhaps one hundred years.

The third window gave us the ethereal aloofness of Saturn and its incandescent rings.

And the fourth window, the one on the far right, made us look into the cruel depths of outer space—where the glassy indifference of a thousand sharp stars somehow stung us back into the here-and-now, sucking away our breaths. And since the biomonitor units in the cubicle had begun to refrigerate the air to compensate for the onset of the old woman's physical decay, our breaths were chill.

Newlyn reacted noisily: "What kind of place does this old woman live in, Mr. Ardrey? What's it supposed to be?" As in the hallway, his body revolved out of the impulse of sheer wonder. "What the heck is all this stuff for?"

"I don't think it's exactly *for* anything."

"Everything's for something, Mr. Ardrey. What's this stuff supposed to be? What's it do?"

I tried to make sense of my suspicions. We had stumbled into what was evidently an elaborate mockup, and the octagonal room could have been a wide variety of things: the hall of planets in a second-rate surfaceside museum, some sort of wildly improbable computer chamber, or——

"—The command pit of a spaceship," I said. "It's supposed to be the command pit of——"

Newlyn cut me off with a cry that might have come out of the mouth of someone a great deal younger: "Look, there she is!" He pointed down into the pit which I had been trying to identify; he pointed at the back of the huge swivel chair that dominated this intriguing area. Visible above the back of this chair, the back of a woman's head, matted over with frowzy iron-gray pleats, caught my eye and sent a cold wrinkle unwinding up my spine. Newlyn jumped from the dais, jumped into the command pit before I could say anything. As I had spun the glissador about in the hallway, he spun the arm of the chair and turned the ruined face of Almira Longhope, glassy eyes open, lower lip twisted, toward me—toward *me!*

I stared at the dead woman, feeling her accusation.

"She's really dead," Newlyn told me excitedly, running a finger over the silver lamé sleeve of her gown. "She's really dead."

"I know. I can see that."

Newlyn turned impulsively around, forgetting the old woman. He did not spin the chair in the direction of his turn. Instead, he simply walked around the chair and paused momentarily at the semicircular panel of "instruments" over which the dead woman had been gazing before he had disturbed her. He looked toward the four viewing screens. Dome, Moon, planet, stars. The last three could have meant almost nothing to Newlyn, even though he had undoubtedly seen the night sky in visicom presentations and read about the "promise of space" in preEvacuation literature. Besides, the four windows had no reality. The stars on the far right were sharp and cold, yes, but they existed only as glossy points on a piece of lusterless mounted silk. Each window, in fact, was just such a piece of lusterless mounted silk. Despite this, Newlyn stared at the viewing screen on the far right for a long while. "Look at that," he said before turning away. "Look at all that distance, all that space." At last he did turn away. He brought his attention back to the semicircular console in front of the old woman's command chair.

Reaching over it, he pushed buttons. One or two of them seemed to operate lights in the walls. He fiddled with levers. One of the levers controlled two mobiles that hung from the ceiling, seemingly as navigational devices, since each one represented a miniature spaceship moving gyroscopically inside a glass sphere divided into sections by thin blue lines. "Look at all this stuff," Newlyn said over and over again. He made low whistling noises, articulations of pleased astonishment.

Meanwhile, the corpse of Almira Longhope continued to stare at me. I was certain now that the bitch's stare was single-mindedly accusatory, even though her sunken features contained less malice than disappointment.

But for Newlyn's oblivious cluckings, the room was deathly still. And cold. The orange and red lights on the phony computers made no noise; none of the instruments on the semicircular panel hummed, or clicked, or whirred. I grew uneasy.

"Newlyn!"

He did not even look up. "What?"

"Get away from there. We've got things to do."

"Just a second, Mr. Ardrey. This thing's got a purpose, I can tell." He was manipulating a dial on the command console. Soundlessly the scenes depicted in the four windows opposite us slipped into another continuum; to take their places there came the images of (1) an alien planetscape, (2) the craggy moon of a world not belonging to Sol, (3) an eerie double binary, and (4) a minute spiral galaxy as seen from the loneliness of open space. How far outward the old woman had permitted herself to venture! These new images—or perhaps simply the changes he had worked —exhilarated Newlyn. "Climbersguts!" he said, a bit of irritating slang.

"Goddammit, Newlyn, will you get away from there!"

He looked up hurriedly and faced me, his chin tilted a little. I had never spoken to him like that before. His eyes betrayed his hurt and bewilderment.

"You were the one," I reminded him, "who said we weren't going to come down here to gawk. Do you remember that? You were the one who wanted to make sure the servo-units didn't vacuum her up like a piece of dirt."

The boy dropped his head, chastened.

I was still angry. My fists were clenching and unclenching of their own accord. It was difficult not to look into the corpse's vein-woven eyes, lose all resolution, and return surfaceside to the control room on West Peachtree. Especially since we had stumbled on the mausoleum of an aged lunatic with an adolescent pituitary where her brains should have been. No wonder that Almira Longhope, at the age of one hundred and seven, still resided in a three-room cubicle on Level 8: she had exhausted her monetary and spiritual resources constructing a tomb with faster-than-light-speed capabilities, patching together an epitaph out of old screenplays and pulp magazine stories, paying homage to the

very worst of the products of the pre-Evacuation mass media. No
wonder that she stared at me with accusation and disappointment;
the dream, too, had finally died, and we had walked in on its naked
remains.

Still chastened, Newlyn said: "All right, Mr. Ardrey, what do
we have to do now?" Finally he looked up. "I'm sorry. I'm sorry
I——"

This time I cut *him* off. "Don't be sorry. It was a natural
response, Newlyn, a very natural response." Then I told him that
the first thing I wanted him to do was face the old woman toward
her windows once again, and he did this for me. "The computer
said that she had no relatives," I went on, "so we don't have to try
to contact anyone. All we have to do is go through her belongings
and determine if she's left a will or any papers. Then we must see
that her body goes into the waste converter on Level 9 and file a
report so that her cubicle can be sprayed. All this junk will have to
be destroyed."

"It doesn't look like junk, Mr. Ardrey."

"It's junk."

He didn't protest a second time, but his eyes, though superfi-
cially still penitent, cut away from me at an angle of vague
reprimand. I ignored this silent cavil. He was young.

It took us a little while to find the entrance into her sleeping
quarters because the artificial hull of her "spaceship" had been
erected in front of the cubicle's internal doorways. (The entrance
from the outer corridor, through which Newlyn and I had originally come, was disguised as the facing of an airlock, for the
artifices of Miss Longhope were nothing if not thoroughgoing.)
We walked around the catwalk that circled the vessel's command
pit. We tested the firmness of the walls with our hands and knees.
We scrutinized the phony computer banks and puzzled over the
two glass cylinders. And, at last, we did find the doorway to the
old woman's bedchamber.

Newlyn made the discovery. Running his hands over the surface
of one of the cylinders, he was surprised to find a vertical seam. He
pressed this seam, and the cylinder split apart and opened out.

"Mr. Ardrey!" he called. I went to him. Together we found that the other half of the cylinder also opened out, but in the direction of the concealed sleeping chamber.

We went through this unorthodox portal, down a single step, and into the old woman's private alcove. Newlyn dialed up the lights.

The alcove contained a low bed, a study area, and the standard visicom console on which one can display reading material or run his choice of entertainment visuals. However, the visicom's screen was silver-gray. And dead. The fanaticism manifested so tangibly in the main living area did not appear so virulent here. I looked at Newlyn. The disappointment on his face mirrored the look on the old woman's corpse. In truth, however, he had nothing to be disappointed *about*. Almira Longhope's ruling passion had merely secreted itself away into drawers, boxes, diaries, packets of photographs, and a heavy blue ledger. One of two testimonies of this passion remained shamelessly in the open, although Newlyn had not noticed them.

"Cheer up," I said. "Look there."

Beside the old woman's bed, resting on her night table, there was a spherical lamp mounted on a tripod base. The lamp had hundreds of tiny holes in its surface, for in reality it was not a lamp at all but a simple version of the star-projectors that one of the old networks had marketed in such profiteering quantities before the Last Days of our great-grandfathers. Newlyn asked what the thing was: I told him. Then he wanted to see how the thing worked. Therefore, after he had dimmed the lights, I turned the projector on. At once stars appeared on the walls and ceiling—the constellations all misshapen and askew, however, because Miss Longhope had apparently not been able to devise a curved surface on which to project them. To Yates's son, the resulting distortion made no difference. Even after I had made him dial the lights up again, he stood over the star-projector with all the solicitude of a nursing mother for her newborn whelps. His face was silly with concern.

"How did she think up all these things?" he asked.

"She didn't. She just copied them."

"From what?"

"From a style of entertainment that existed before the Domes went up—similar to our visual entertainment tapes. Most of this stuff has its origin in one of their *shows* . . . back when they believed in interstellar travel and galactic civilizations. Or at least when some of them did. She's just copied everything from that one particular series of tapes—and from magazines and movies."

"When was it? When was all this stuff thought up?"

"Eighty years ago. Ninety years ago. I don't know, Newlyn."

He stared at the star-projector. He looked back toward the half-open cylinder beyond which lay the spaceship's command pit. His lips scarcely moved. "It's neat," he said pontifically. "It's some of the neatest stuff I've ever seen."

"That old woman wasted her life," I said. "She wasted it."

Turning my back on Yates's son, I sat down at the study center and began pulling drawers open. What I found confirmed my judgment. Newlyn, sullen and belligerent now, looked over my shoulder as I arranged the contents of the drawers and of several crumpled manila envelopes on the surface of the desk. The stench of another time flew out of these envelopes like the moths that still flutter from the surfaceside grasses in April. I coughed. Like moths, the photographs and slips of precious paper seemed to beat about my head with their dusty hard-edged wings. In Miss Longhope's blue ledger I flipped randomly to one of the pages of broad childish handwriting.

I read one of the paragraphs on the page.

Log entry: Tonight I saw the episode entitled "Between the Star Mirrors" for the third time. Is there an alternate Almira somewhere in the universe? I wish that I could break through for a moment and visit my other self. The Rigelian first officer is an honorable man in both universes. What would I be? Sometimes I am afraid that I am empty of stars in both places, but this is not true. Even my other self, just as I do here, would have all her alternate universe to reach into and to wonder at. But she would probably need to have help to reach out—just as I do. I hate the image that the mirror I hold up to the world returns to me. The image in the mirror clouds over every day, like the dirty sky and the people's ugly wrinkled unhappy faces.

I read this passage aloud to Newlyn. "Neat, huh?"

He said nothing. He picked up one of the laminated photographs, bent and yellowed in spite of the lamination, and ran his finger over the heavy intense face of one of the actors who had been in the series. In the photograph, the actor had a smooth triple-lobed cranium and no discernible eyebrows; he had signed his name across the bottom of the picture. Newlyn touched the signature, too—or tried to touch it; the dull plastic prevented him. Stymied, he studied the face.

"Look at this man's head, Mr. Ardrey." He had forgotten his resentment of my skeptical attitude toward Miss Longhope's memorabilia. "Look at his head, Mr. Ardrey. Where did this man come from?"

"A makeup room, Newlyn. It's just an actor pretending to be a member of a humanoid species that never existed. A nonexistent friendly alien."

He continued to look at the actor's picture. "Can I have this?"

"No," I said. "It isn't mine to give you. What do you want with it, anyway?" I took it out of his hands, gently.

He shrugged and looked at the other items on the desk. He feigned an interest in the ledger containing the old woman's "log entries," but I could tell that the writing there bored him.

I sorted the papers and photographs and put them back into the dingy manila envelopes. There was nothing in the old woman's possessions of any conceivable value to the city. We had innumerable collections of such maudlin remnants of the pre-Evacuation days, should anyone actually wish to see such things. Museums. Chronos galleries. Pedestrian corridors lined with glass cases and curio-boards. No one was denied information about the past. And if Almira Longhope had anything at all worth saving, I supposed it to be the blue ledger. However miserable and cramped, at least it was a document of human suffering and therefore of some value to the urban archives.

But as I had mentally predicted he would, Newlyn had grown weary of this document. He had left the sleeping cubicle and gone back to the command pit of the *Sojourner II*. I finished putting away the old woman's possessions, the inconsequential leftovers of a lifetime misspent and horrifyingly sad.

Everything but the ledger.

That I carried with me, out to where Newlyn prowled among the winking lights and the ghostly crewmen who rode their drifting derelict through the ruinous voids of that lifetime.

Newlyn said: "What do we have to do now?"

"Find a telecom unit. The old bitch must have tried to make it an integral part of the equipment on this 'vessel.' Why don't you see if you can find it?"

This request pleased Yates's son; it gave him an excuse to finger the dials and levers, to examine the intricacy of the total construct. Meanwhile, the old woman surveyed us regally from the command chair. I realized that she was attired after the fashion of some anonymous producer's concept of a Rigelian priestess; a sort of scepter, or abbreviated staff, lay across her thin thighs. How magnificently, how pettily, she had met her death. In the cubicle's cold air her face seemed to be carved of ice. I had just looked away from her twisted lower lip when Newlyn called, "Here it is, Mr. Ardrey. In this box over here. Where it says 'Communications.' "

"Where it says 'Communications,' " I echoed. "Very apt."

I mounted the catwalk, sat down, and made three brief calls. One to the main control room. One to the office of the administrative head of the glissadors on Level 8. One to the city agency of Flame-Decontamination and Refurbishing.

Newlyn said: "You're going to have them burn out the old woman's cubicle? You're going to let them set fire to all this stuff she's made?"

"She's done with these things, Newlyn. Somebody else should have access to what she can't use any more. Even though this is

Level 8, there are people waiting to live here. People from the level beneath us.''

"Maybe they'd like it the way she has it now."

"Grow up," I said.

He wouldn't talk to me through the waiting that followed. He wouldn't talk to me when the glissadors came with their silent cart to carry Miss Almira Longhope's corpse through the murky corridors to the pneumatic scaffolding that would drop her to the waste converters on Level 9. He remained silent through the waiting that followed the glissadors' departure.

And when the men from F-D&R came into the cubicle with their canisters of the bactericidal combustgens, and their flame-suits, and their unbelieving goggled-over eyes, Newlyn cut his own eyes in reprimand and stalked out. He went into the corridor—went with blatant contempt for my colloquy with these men—and waited outside in the smoky half light that drifted there. I explained the situation to the men from F-D&R. I gave directions. They nodded their insectlike heads. My explanation done, I went into the silent corridor and, with considerable difficulty, found Newlyn leaning in a crimson shadow against the opposite wall. I said something, but he wouldn't talk to me.

"All right," I said. "I'm going up. You can do what you like."

The *tap-tap-tap* of my footfalls was overwhelmed, just then, by the carnivorous *whooshing* of the F-D&R handtorches. The corridor filled with this noise, and the tightly closed panel of cubicle 502 gave me the momentary illusion that the panel itself was glowing with unnatural heat, unnatural light. I hesitated briefly. Then I resumed walking. Seconds later, it became apparent that another series of footfalls was echoing my own, albeit in a reluctant and irregular way: *taptap tap taptaptap*.

3/*the hoisterjacks*

In the domed cities (not simply in Atlanta, but in all the Urban

Nuclei) there exist among the affluent surfacesiders, particularly among the adolescent boys of the wealthy and/or enfranchised, a significant few who have more leisure and more adrenalin than they can intelligently deal with. These few release their energy and defile their time in inutile pursuits that frequently terrorize the innocent, the unprepared, the preoccupied. They do not pick pockets. They do not engage in vandalism. They do not kill.

Instead, they practice the grotesque art of instilling a wholly meaningless terror in all those whom they assault with mad gestures and mad nylon-distorted faces. These boys—and, sadly, these few perverse adult males—go by the name of *hoisterjacks*, primarily because of their inclination to leap out of the darkness of the catacombs, to cling reasonlessly to the crystalline face of a lift-tube, arms full out, fingers gripping the maintenance handles on either side of the lift-tube door, and to scream like ravening hyenas as they press their already misaligned features against the glass.

One can in no way make adequate psychological preparation for the coming of a hoisterjack—even if one sees him beforehand.

I had entered the central concourse on Level 8, the concourse leading to the lift-station from which we had earlier disembarked, when I became aware of an echo on the tiles. An echo in addition to Newlyn's tentative *taptap-taptapping*. The echo was coming to me from the direction in which I moved, not from behind me. I looked down the ill-lit corridor, through the haze of red light. I saw the deeper glimmering of the lift-station and the translucent outline of the waiting lift-tube itself. I thought the cylinder's presence a fine piece of luck; we would not have to wait for transportation —and I would not have to make inane conversation to cover the depressing childishness of Newlyn's funk.

Then I saw, or believed I saw, two wraithlike figures cross the glimmering backdrop of the lift-station and disappear into an auxiliary hallway. I could not be sure. I paid little heed.

When I reached the lift-tube, I entered and held my thumb on the thin silver operating panel so that the door would not close. From out of the fog of halflight Newlyn came. He entered the cylinder and stood to one side, away from me. I did not remove my thumb from the operating panel.

"Let go of it," Newlyn said. "Send us up."

"What do you mean, 'Let go of it'? Who are you talking to?" Newlyn didn't answer. I repeated my self-defeating straightline: *"Who are you talking to, Newlyn?"*

"A bigshot *fire*man. A burnheaded topsider."

He spoke with such incredible malice, enunciating each consonant and each vowel as if they would carve flaming signs in the air, that I could say nothing. My thumb was on the panel; the door remained open. At last, gathering a little strength against my embarrassment, I said: "You knew what we had to do. And what we found in Almira Longhope's cubicle didn't make any difference. In fact, it deserved the combustgens and the spray even more than the ordinary furnishings of one of these places. What a waste, Newlyn! That sort of thing, that sort of crap, has to be burned out, cut away, buried. Everyone goes through that, Newlyn."

Yates's son sprang toward me and knocked my hand away from the control panel. The glass door slid into place. I dropped the old woman's blue ledger.

Then a number of things happened simultaneously.

A huge shadow leaped at us from the corridor and affixed itself to the surface of the lift-tube. Another shadow, less quick, fell away behind the first and disappeared as the lift-tube began, seemingly of its own accord, to ascend. An hysterical, mocking scream pierced the thin wall of glass that contained the boy and me.

And then (beneath the terrifying scream) another sound: Newlyn was trying to quench the sobs that rose in his throat. Unsuccessfully.

"It doesn't have to be——" he said. "It doesn't have to be . . . to be . . . unless you make it——"

I'm afraid that I pushed him. He was leaning into my chest, and all my attention had shifted from him to the droop-lipped, acromegalic hoisterjack who clung to our lift-tube, leering, insupportably leering.

I shoved Newlyn aside and began pounding on the glass between me and the hoisterjack's hooded face. I wanted him to lose his grip. I wanted him to fall down the terminal shaft to the concrete of Level 9, there to split and pulp open like an overripe radish. I wanted to murder his iconoclasm and turn his impudence to bile.

Then I felt a fist against the side of my head and heard Newlyn shouting and sobbing at once: "Leave him alone, you bastard! Leave him alone!"

We grappled. The boy struck me again. I pushed him down. He came back and pummeled my chest. Now I realized exactly what I was doing, and the pain that it gave me could not have been more real, more cruel, more excruciating. I knew that we would not go combcrawling with each other this weekend, nor any weekend to come. I struck Newlyn solidly under the chin, and it was like striking myself.

He crumpled and sat on the crystalline floor, making low noises.

The lift-tube continued to ascend. I picked up Almira Longhope's ledger. I raised my eyes. The hoisterjack clinging to our little prison was grinning at me, grinning at me in cryptic triumph.

Sister Francetta
and the Pig Baby

KENNETH BERNARD

*A brief story demands a brief introduction. Kenneth Bernard is a
teacher and a playwright—and a very witty short-story writer.*

Let me get right into it. When Sister Francetta was a little girl
she looked into a baby carriage one day and saw a baby with a pig
head. It wore dainty white clothes, had little baby hands and feet, a
baby's body. Of course the sounds it made were strange, but the
main thing was the pig head. It lay there on its back, kicking its
feet, waving its arms, and staring at the world through a pig head.
Now Sister Francetta taught us her morality through stories. For
example, little boys and girls who put their fingers in forbidden
places sometimes found that their fingers rotted away. That was
the moral of a story about a boy who picked his nose. However,
rotting fingers were a comparatively mild consequence. Sister
Francetta's childhood world was filled with sudden and horrible
attacks of blindness, deafness, and dumbness. Ugly purple
growths developed overnight anywhere inside or outside of
people's bodies. Strange mutilations from strange accidents were
common. It absolutely did not pay to be bad. Sinful thoughts were
the hardest to protect against. Prayer and confession were the
surest remedies. As I grew older, Sister Francetta's tales gradually
subsided into remote pockets of my mind, occasionally to crop up
in dream or quaint reminiscence. Except for the pig baby. The pig
baby is still with me. It was different from her other stories. For
example, it had no moral, it was just there: there had once been a

198

baby with a pig head. Also, whereas Sister Francetta told her other stories often, and with variations, she told the story of the pig baby only once. And she told it differently, as if she herself did not understand it but nevertheless felt a tremendous urgency to reveal it. The other stories she told because they were *useful*. The story of the pig baby she told because she had *faith* in it. It captured my imagination totally. I tried to find out more, but she usually put me off. And I thought a great deal about it. Since Sister Francetta is dead now, I suppose I am the only expert in the world on the pig baby, and what I know can be listed very quickly:

1. The pig baby was apparently Caucasian.
2. Its parents were proud of it and in public seemed totally unaware of its pig head.
3. I do not know how long it lived. It apparently never went to school.
4. It always snortled noticeably but never let out any really piglike sounds like *oink*.
5. It ate and drank everything a regular baby ate and drank.
6. Its parents were not Catholic.
7. Everyone pretended not to notice that the baby had a pig head. For some reason it was not talked about either.
8. At some early point the family either moved away or disappeared.
9. No one said anything about that either.

Sister Francetta died a few years after I had her as a teacher. She was still young. It was whispered among us that she had horrible sores all over her body. I became an excellent student and went on to college. There I developed more sophisticated ideas about the pig baby, the two most prominent of which were (1) that Sister Francetta herself was the pig baby, and (2) that the pig baby was Jesus Christ. There is no logic to either conclusion. Since college I have more or less given up the pig baby. Nevertheless it is a fact that I never look into a carriage without a flush of anxiety. And I cannot get rid of the feeling that Sister Francetta is angry with me.

Escape

ILYA VARSHAVSKY,
TRANSLATED BY LELAND FETZER

All too little Russian science fiction has been published in translations in this country, while too much of what has been published is second rate to begin with. All this despite the fact that the popularity of SF is very high in the Soviet Union. The situation seems to be that the people who know Russian science fiction are not translators—while the translators know nothing about Russian SF. Happily, this situation is changing. Leland Fetzer, who holds a doctorate in Russian from the University of California and who is a translator of note, will be offering a course this year on Eastern European SF at San Diego State University. His translation of Gennady Gor's best novel, The Statue, *will be published soon. When asked if there was any current Russian story of quality suitable for this year's best he suggested this effective tale by Ilya Varshavsky, one of the Soviet Union's most popular SF writers —and he was right.*

"One, two, pull! One, two, pull!"

It was a simple device—a beam, two ropes—but with its help the heavy block of ore was quickly hoisted into the wagon.

"Get moving!"

The load was not exceptionally heavy, but the little man in a striped uniform who leaned his chest into the wagon's crossbar was unable to move it at all.

"Get moving!"

Lending his aid, one of the other prisoners put his shoulder to the crossbar. It was too late! A guard had turned their way.

"What happened?"

"Nothing."

"Well, then, get going!"

The little man once more attempted to move the load, lunging at the crossbar. It was impossible and exhausted by an effort beyond his capabilities, he began to cough. He covered his mouth with his hand.

Silently the guard waited until his coughing spell had passed.

"Show me that hand."

Blood was on the hand that the prisoner extended.

"So . . . turn around."

On the back of the prisoner's jacket was a number which the guard wrote in his notebook.

"Report to the doctor!"

Another prisoner took the sick man's place.

"Get going!" This was to both of them, to the one who now would pull the wagon and to the one who was no longer capable of it.

The wagon began to roll.

"Excuse me, sir, would it be possible——"

"I told you to report to the doctor!"

He followed the bent back as it disappeared, verifying the entry in his notebook: A 0 15/13264. This was obvious enough: A—desertion, 0—life imprisonment, barracks No. 15, prisoner No. 13264. Life imprisonment. Yes, he had it correct, but for this prisoner his sentence was nearing its end. This meant the cotton fields.

"One, two, pull!"

Gleaming, polished metal, glass, the diffused light of fluorescent lamps, a kind of peculiar, palpable, sterile cleanliness.

The gray, somewhat fatigued eyes of the man in the white coat peered attentively out of his thick glasses. Here, in Medena's underground camps, human life was highly valued. Of course! Every prisoner, until his soul presented itself before the highest tribunal, had to expiate his guilt before those who in the distant

reaches of the universe were engaged in an unprecedented struggle
for the hegemony of the planet. And the planet needed uranium.
Every prisoner was given work to do, and therefore his life was as
valuable as the precious ore. But unfortunately there were cases
like this. . . .

"Put your clothes on!"

His long thin arms hastily drew the jacket over his emaciated
body.

"Stand here."

A slight depression of a pedal and the sacred number was
obliterated by a red cross. Henceforth prisoner A 0 15/13264
would once more be addressed as Arp Zumbi. This was only a
natural expression of humane feeling for a man who was to labor in
the cotton fields.

The cotton fields. Really no one knew anything reliable about
them except those who never returned after they had been sent
there. It was said that in their hot desiccating climate a man's body
in twenty days was transformed into a dry stick, fit fuel for the
crematoria.

"Here is your work release. Get out."

Arp Zumbi presented the work release to the guard at the
barracks door and plunged into the familiar odor of disinfectant.
The barracks resembled a public lavatory with its oppressive odor
of disinfectant and hot stoves. The monotony of its white walls was
relieved only by a large sign: "Torture and Death is the Punishment for Attempted Escape." This was yet additional evidence for
the high regard in which human life was held here: it could be taken
only when accompanied by the greatest possible effect.

Along one of the walls was something resembling a huge
honeycomb—these were sleeping places divided into individual
cells. Both convenient and hygienic. The slightest speck of dirt
was apparent on the white plastic. But the cells were not meant for
comfort. This was a prison and not a rest home, as the voice loved
to repeat which conducted the daily psychological exercises.
Separating the sleeping places into cells made it impossible for the

prisoners to communicate with one another at night when the guards' alertness was somewhat dulled.

It was forbidden to remain in the sleeping places during the day and Arp Zumbi passed his time sitting on a bench. He thought about the cotton fields. Usually prisoners were collected and sent there once every two weeks when prisoners were brought together from all the camps. Then two days later replacements would arrive. It seemed to him that this had occurred most recently five days earlier, when that strange individual had appeared near Arp in the sleeping places. He was a little touched. Yesterday he had given Arp half of his own bread at the dinner hour. "Take it," he said, "you're so thin your pants are going to fall off." That was something! Giving away your own bread! Arp had never heard of that before. He was probably insane. Last night he was singing before he fell asleep. Imagine, singing in a place like this.

Arp's thoughts once more returned to the cotton fields. He knew that this meant the end, but for some reason he was not saddened. You get accustomed to death after ten years in the mines. But still he was curious about life there in the cotton fields.

During his entire imprisonment this was the first day without work. That was probably why it was passing so slowly. Arp would have liked to lie down and sleep, but that was impossible, even with a work release. This was a prison and not a rest home.

Arp's comrades returned from their work and to the odor of the disinfectant was added the sweetish odor of liquid decontaminant. Every prisoner who worked with uranium ore had to take a precautionary shower in the decontaminant every day. This was one of the measures which increased the prisoner's average life span.

Arp took his place in the line and set off for dinner.

Breakfast and dinner—at these times the guards largely ignored the restriction on conversation. Besides, it was hard to say much with your mouth full.

Arp silently ate his portion and waited for the command to rise.

"Take it!" And once more the crazy man gave him half his bread ration.

"I don't want it."

The command to fall into formation was given. It was only now that Arp noticed that everyone was staring at him. Doubtless because of the red cross on his back. We are always intrigued by a corpse.

"Lively there!"

This was meant for Arp's friend. His line had already formed, but he still sat at the table. He and Arp rose simultaneously and as Arp was taking his place he heard the almost inaudible whisper: "You could escape."

Arp pretended that he hadn't heard. The camp was full of informers and he didn't want to die under torture. The cotton fields would be better than that.

The voice either rose to a scream which made your head ache or it dropped to a barely audible whisper, which you involuntarily had to strain to hear. It issued from a loudspeaker which was fastened at the head of the sleeping places. This was the evening psychological exercise.

A nauseatingly familiar baritone elucidated for the prisoners the utter gravity of their fall. You could neither flee nor hide from the voice, nor could you simply exclude it from your consciousness like the shouting of the guards. You would begin to think about something else besides life in the camp and suddenly your attention would be seized by the voice with its unexpected fluctuations in volume. And that is the way it was three times a day: in the evening before sleep, at night when you slept, and in the morning five minutes before awaking. Three times, because this was a prison and not a rest home.

Arp lay, his eyes closed, and tried to think about the cotton fields. The exercise was nearing its end, but through it he could hear someone tapping rhythmically on the partition between the cells. It was the psycho again.

"Well, what do you want?" he said through his hands, held in the shape of an ear trumpet against the partition.

"Go to the latrine."

Arp himself did not know what compelled him to go downstairs to the doorway where he could hear the sound of running water.

In the latrine it was so hot that it was impossible to bear it for more than two minutes. In a moment they were bathed in sweat.

"Do you want to escape?"

"Get out of here. . . ."

Arp Zumbi was a veteran of the camps and he knew all the informers' tricks.

"Don't be afraid," the man whispered quickly. "I'm a member of the League of Liberation. Tomorrow we're going to try to smuggle out our first group of prisoners and transport them to a safe place. You don't have anything to lose: you will be given poison. If the attempted escape fails. . . ."

"What then?"

"Take the poison. It will be better than death in the cotton fields. Agreed?"

Unexpectedly, even for himself, Arp nodded.

"You'll get your instructions tomorrow in your bread ration. Be careful."

Once more Arp nodded and then he left.

For the first time in ten years he was so lost in his dreams that he did not even hear the second and third psychological exercises.

Arp Zumbi stood last in the breakfast line; now his place was at the end of his lines. Anyone who was released from work was the last to receive food.

The convict dispensing the soup looked attentively at Arp and then, with a quick grin, threw him a piece of bread which had lain separate from the rest.

As he ate his soup, Arp carefully crumbled the bread. It was there. He placed the rolled-up paper inside his mouth against his cheek.

Then he had to wait until the file of prisoners had left for their work.

He heard the command to rise. Arp left the cafeteria at the end of the column and, reaching a cross corridor, turned to the left, while the others continued ahead.

Here, around the corner, Arp was relatively safe. The trustees were cleaning the barracks and the new shift of guards had not yet appeared.

The instructions were very terse. Arp read them three times, and confident he could remember them, he rolled the paper into a ball and swallowed it.

Now, when it was necessary to act, he was overcome by fear.

He wavered. Death in the cotton fields seemed more desirable than the threat of torture.

"The poison!"

The recollection of the poison calmed him immediately. When all was said and done, what did he have to lose?

Fear—disgusting, clinging, strangling fear—welled over him again as he presented his work release to the guard at the edge of his zone.

"Where are you going?"

"To the doctor."

"On your way."

Arp felt as though his legs were made of cotton. He wandered through the halls feeling danger behind his back. Any moment he expected a shout and a round of automatic fire. In such cases they aimed at the legs. For attempted escape the penalty was torture and death. It was impossible to deprive the prisoners of an instructive spectacle; this was a prison and not a rest home.

Turn here!

Arp rounded the corner and leaned against the wall. He could hear his heart pounding and he felt that any minute he might vomit up that crucial ball of paper together with the bile that rose from his stomach. Cold sweat covered his body and his teeth would not cease their chattering. It was to the sound of a drum that prisoners apprehended in an attempted escape were led to the place of execution.

An eternity passed before he could bring himself to move on.

Somewhere here in an alcove there were supposed to be garbage containers. Arp repeated the instructions once more to himself. But again he was touched by doubt. What if this was all arranged? He could climb into a container and then they would have him! And as yet he had no poison. Fool! He should not have agreed to this until he had the poison in his hand. What an idiot he was! He was ready to pound his head against the wall—to fall like this into an informer's trap.

Here were the containers. Near the one on the left someone had placed a painters's trestle, just as in the instructions. Arp stood irresolute. Probably the best thing to do would be to turn back.

Suddenly he heard loud voices and the barking of a dog. A patrol! He had no time to think, but with unexpected agility he climbed onto the trestle and from it leaped into the container.

The voices came closer. He could hear the wheeze of the dog straining against its leash and the ringing of iron heels.

"Back, Gar!"

"There's somebody in one of those containers."

"Just rats, there are plenty of them here."

"No, he would bark differently if it were rats."

"Stupid! Let's get going! And shut up the dog!"

"Quiet, Gar!"

The sound of their steps died away.

Now Arp could inspect this refuge. The container was only one-fourth full and he could not hope to climb out of it, since it was the height of two men. Arp passed his hand along its wall and found two small holes which were described in the note. They were located in the battered sign which read "Labor Camps" girdling the container. Arp was to breathe through these openings when the cover was closed.

When the cover was closed Arp felt himself more than ever in a trap. Who knew how this folly would end? What was the League of Liberation? He had never heard of it in the camp before. Was it perhaps the same people who had helped him desert? He had been wrong not to listen to them and to tell his mother what he had done. That's when someone had informed on him. If he hadn't been such a fool everything could have been different.

Once more he heard voices and the sound of wheels. Arp put his eye to one of the openings and stood still. Two prisoners were pulling a tub with garbage; obviously they were trustees in this zone. They were in no hurry. Making themselves comfortable on the cart they passed back and forth a cigarette butt discarded by one of the guards. Arp watched the pale streams of smoke and his mouth filled with saliva. Some people have all the luck!

They got all they could from the butt. Then they hoisted the tub with the aid of a cable which passed through a pulley over Arp's head. He covered his head with his arms as the contents of the tub fell onto him.

It was only after the prisoners had left that he noticed the foul odor in his hiding place.

The breathing holes were located a little higher than Arp's mouth and he had to scrape some of the rubbish together under his feet to reach them comfortably.

Now he had to be alert. The garbage collection ended at ten o'clock and then the full containers would be sent up.

He did not know where the broad, rough plank, smeared with plaster, came from. One end of it was wedged into a corner of the container while the other was above Arp's head. The plank, like the trestle, was evidence that someone was concerned about the fate of the fugitive. Arp felt this especially keenly when through the garbage a sharp metal rod was driven which caught on the plank and then probed it from top to bottom. If the plank had not been there. . . . It seemed to him that the search would never end.

"What's inside there?" asked an old man's hoarse voice.

"Nothing, just a plank."

"Let's go!"

A light blow, the creaking of a gate, and the container, rocking back and forth, began to move upward. At times it hit against the walls of the shaft and Arp, his face pressed against the side of the container, felt every shock. Between his head and the plank there was a small area free of garbage, and this made it possible for him to pull his head away from the openings when the container swung particularly sharply.

Then it stopped! A final, very incisive blow, and the lid drew open with a rumble. Once more the iron bar probed the container's interior. Once more the friendly plank concealed the man who huddled under it shaking with fear.

Now the openings were turned to a concrete wall and all of Arp's world was limited to a gray, rough surface.

But that world was full of forgotten sounds. Among them Arp could make out the hum of automobile tires, the voices of people walking by, and even the chirping of sparrows.

A steady, persistent beating on the container's lid drove him to roll himself into a ball. The knocking came faster, more insistent, more impatient, and he realized it was rain. It was only then that he perceived how desirable and how close lay freedom.

Everything that night seemed to him like a dream. From the moment that he found himself thrown out of the container, he was either unconscious or awakened by the touch of rats' feet. The dump was full of rats. Somewhere not far away a highway passed and at times the automobiles' headlights outlined the heap of trash behind which Arp was hidden. Squeaking, the rats would throw themselves into the darkness, raking his face with their sharp claws, biting if he attempted to frighten them away, and then returning as soon as the heap was plunged into darkness.

Arp realized that by now his flight would have been discovered. He imagined what was happening in the camp. It occurred to him that dogs might pick up his trail leading to the containers, and then. . . .

Two bright bursts of light stunned him. Arp leaped to his feet as the headlights were extinguished. In their place gleamed a flashlight inside the truck. It was an army van, the kind that was ordinarily employed to haul supplies. The man behind the wheel beckoned to Arp to come closer.

Arp sighed with relief; this was the truck described in his instructions.

He came up behind the van as its rear door opened. Arp seized the hands extended to him and once more found himself in darkness.

The van was very crowded. Sitting on the floor, Arp could hear heavy breathing, and feel other bodies behind him and to the sides. Swaying softly on its springs, the van quietly advanced through the darkness. . . .

Arp was awakened by a flashlight turned onto his face. Something had happened! The sense of movement, which he had already grown accustomed to, had ceased.

"Time to stretch!" said the man with the flashlight. "You have five minutes."

Arp felt no eagerness to leave the vehicle, but many bodies were pressing against him and he was compelled to leap onto the ground.

Everyone milled around the cab; no one dared to go far from the van.

"Listen, friends!" said their rescuer, illuminating the figures in convicts' clothing with his flashlight. "Everything has gone well so far, but before we get you to a safe place anything might happen. Do you know the punishment for attempted escape?"

No one answered.

"You know. Therefore the Committee has poison for you. One pill for each of our friends. It will work instantly. Take it only in case of extreme need. Do you understand?"

Arp took his allotment wrapped in silver foil and climbed back into the van.

The pill which he held in his clenched fist gave him a feeling of personal power. Now the guards had no sway over him. He fell asleep with that idea on his mind. . . .

Danger! It was apparent in everything: the stopping of the van, the pale faces of the prisoners illuminated by the light coming in through the cracks in the van's panels, in the loud voices, there, on the road.

Arp tried to move, to get up, but a score of hands waved to tell him not to stir.

"You know military supplies are not subject to inspection." That was the driver's voice.

"But I'm telling you that we have our orders. Tonight. . . ."

The van roared ahead and automatic rifle fire crackled in pursuit. Chips flew off the ceiling of the van.

When Arp finally lifted his head he noticed that his hand held someone's small palm. From under a shaved skull dark eyes framed in long lashes looked at him and the prison clothing could not hide the girl's rounded body. On her left sleeve was the green star of the inferior race.

Arp involuntarily released his hand and wiped it on his trousers. Any communication with the inferior race was forbidden by Medena's laws, and that was why everyone who wore the star was born and died in the camps.

"Then they won't catch us? Is it true?"

The trembling little voice was so pitiful, that Arp, forgetting the law, shook his head.

"What's your name?"

"Arp."

"Mine is Ghetta."

Arp lowered his head onto his chest and pretended that he was drowsing. Who knows how they would look upon such contacts when the prisoners reached their destination?

Without reducing speed, the van left the highway and began to bounce over a bumpy road. Arp was hungry. Thanks to lack of food and the rough road, he began to feel ill. He tried to suppress his coughing, which offended those around him, but his efforts only made it worse. His body was bent double and the coughs tore from his throat along with a spray of blood.

This coughing spell so exhausted Arp that he did not have the strength to push away the hand which was wiping the sweat from his face, the hand of the girl who wore a green star.

The warm night air was saturated with the odors of exotic flowers, filled with the sounds of cicadas singing.

The prisoners' clothing had been discarded and the long linen gowns reaching to their heels were cool on bodies which had come hot from the baths. With his spoon Arp carefully scraped the last of the groats from his dish.

At one end of the cafeteria near a stage constructed from old barrels and planks stood three figures. A tall gray-haired man with a farmer's sun-burned face was obviously in charge. The second was a mild-visaged lad in a Medena army uniform, the driver of their van. The third was a little woman with thick red hair worn in a braid wound around her head. Her white medical gown suited her very well.

They waited until the dinner was completed.

Finally the clatter of spoons subsided, and the man in charge leaped gracefully onto the stage.

"Greetings, my friends!"

A pleasant murmur of voices served to answer that unusual greeting.

"I want to tell you, first of all, that you are completely safe. The government does not know the location of our evacuation camp."

There was such an expression of happiness on the gray, emaciated faces that they almost seemed beautiful.

"You will remain here at our evacuation camp for a period of five to ten days. The exact length of your stay will be determined by our physician because you have a lengthy and difficult transition ahead of you. The place we are taking you to, of course, is not paradise. You will have to work. We have carved every foot of our settlements out of the jungle. But there you will be free, you may rear families and labor to your own advantage. Your residences have been prepared for you by those who have gone before you. This is our tradition. And now I will answer your questions."

As others were asking questions Arp was torn with indecision. He wanted to know if it would be possible at the settlements to marry a girl of the inferior race. But when he finally got his courage to the sticking point and hesitantly raised his hand, the tall man with the farmer's face was already leaving the stage.

Now the woman addressed the fugitives. She had a low sing-song voice and Arp had to strain to understand what she said.

The woman asked everyone to lie down and await physical examinations.

Arp found a cot with his name tag on it, lay down on the crisp cool sheets, and immediately fell asleep.

In his sleep he sensed that he was being turned onto his side, he felt the cold touch of a stethoscope, and opening his eyes, he saw the little woman with the red braid who was writing something in a notebook.

"Are you awake?" She smiled, revealing brilliant even teeth.

Arp nodded.

"You are very worn down. And your lungs are not in good condition. You will sleep for seven days. We'll put you to sleep now."

It was only then that Arp noticed some kind of a machine which had been advanced to his bed.

The woman pressed several buttons on a white panel and a strange hum entered Arp's brain.

"Go to sleep!" said a remote and melodious voice and Arp fell asleep.

He had an amazing dream, full of sunshine and happiness.

Only in a dream could there be such ravishingly measured moments, such as absence of earth-bound gravity, such an ability to float through the air.

A huge meadow was sown with blinding white flowers. In the distance Arp could see a lofty tower flashing with all the lights of the rainbow. Arp pushed himself away from the earth and then slowly descended. He was irresistibly drawn to the radiant tower from which streamed ineffable bliss.

Arp was not alone. From all ends of the meadow toward the tower streamed people dressed like he in long white robes. Among them was Ghetta, the skirts of her robe overflowing with white flowers.

"What is it?" Arp asked her, pointing to the tower.

"The Tower of Freedom. Come!"

They took each other's hands and floated together through the air bursting with the rays of the sun.

"Wait!"

Arp also gathered flowers, filled the skirts of his robe with them, and they continued their way.

They lay the flowers at the foot of the tower.

"Who else!" cried Ghetta, fluttering through the gray-stemmed plants. "Come with me!"

The others were infected by their example. Only a short time passed and the tower's foundation was piled with flowers.

Then they built fires and roasted great pieces of meat skewered on long thin wands. The captivating odor of the meat blended with the smell of burning branches and aroused memories, very old, very pleasant.

Sated, they lay on the ground near the fire, watched the stars, great unknown stars in a black, black sky.

When Arp fell asleep near the smouldering fire, a little warm hand rested in his.

The fires went out. Variegated lights near the tower were illuminated. Near the ground, doors opened and two gigantic mechanical arms extended to rake in the cotton.

In the glassed-in tower the man with the sun-burned face watched the indicator on the automatic scales.

"Five times greater than any other group," he said, turning on the conveyor. "I'm afraid at that insane rate they won't last a week."

"I'll bet two bottles of wine on that," said the mild-visaged young man in uniform, grinning brightly. "They'll make it the usual twenty days. Hypnosis is a marvelous thing! Isn't it amusing the way they ate those roasted turnips! Anything can be done with hypnosis, isn't that so, Doctor?"

The little woman with the heavy braid of red hair coiled around her head did not hasten to answer. She came to the window, turned on a searchlight, and attentively observed the faces below, their skin drawn tight, like skulls.

"You're exaggerating the possibilities of electro-hypnosis," she said, revealing as she smiled a vampire's sharp teeth. "The powerful radiation of the psi-field can only provide rhythm for the work and determine a certain commonality of effort. What is most important is the preliminary psychological conditioning. The feigned escape, the staged dangers—it all creates a sense of freedom obtained at a dear price. It is impossible to know in advance what enormous reserves in the organism may be aroused by the higher emotions."

Early Bird

THEODORE R. COGSWELL AND THEODORE L. THOMAS

This year saw the publication of Astounding: John W. Campbell Memorial Anthology *in which a number of the Golden Age contributors to that magazine wrote stories, more in the spirit of* Astounding *than of* Analog, *in memory of the editor. Cogswell, infamous for his "The Specter General," and Thomas—as well known for his "The Weather Man"—teamed up to write an utterly fascinating sequel to the Cogswell story.*

When the leader of a scout patrol fell ill two hours before takeoff and Kurt Dixon was given command, he was delighted. More than a year had passed since the Imperial Space Marines had mopped up the remnants of the old Galactic Protectorate, and in spite of his pleasure at his newly awarded oak leaves, he was tired of being a glorified office boy in the Inspector General's office while the Kierians were raiding the Empire's trade routes with impunity. After a few hours in space, however, his relief began to dwindle when he found there was no way to turn off Zelda's voice box.

Zelda was the prototype of a new kind of command computer, the result of a base psychologist's bright idea that giving the ship's cybernetic control center a human personality tailored to the pilot's idea of an ideal companion would relieve the lonely tedium of being cooped up for weeks on end in a tiny one-man scout. Unfortunately for Kurt, however, his predecessor, Flight Leader Osaki, had a taste for domineering women, and the computer had been programmed accordingly. There hadn't been time for replacement with a conventional model before the flight had to scramble.

216

Kierian raids on Empire shipping had only begun six months before, but already the Empire was in serious trouble. Kierians bred like fruit flies, looked like mutated maggots, and ate people. Nobody knew where they came from when they came raiding in. Nobody knew where they went when they left with their loot. All that *was* known was that they had a weapon that was invincible and that any attempt to track down a raiding party to the Kierian base was as futile as it was suicidal. Ships that tried it never came back.

But this time it looked as if the Empire's luck might have changed. Kurt whistled happily as he slowly closed in on what seemed to be a damaged Kierian destroyer, waiting for the other scouts of his flight to catch up with him.

Zzzzzt!

The alien's fogger beam hit him square on for the third time. This close it should have slammed him into immediate unconsciousness, but all it did was produce an annoying buzz-saw keening in his neural network.

Flick! Six red dots appeared on his battle screen as the rest of his flight warped out of hyperspace a hundred miles to his rear.

An anxious voice came over his intercom. "Kurt! You fogged?"

"Nope. Come up and join the picnic, children. Looks like us early birds are just about to have us some worms for breakfast."

"He hits you with his fogger, you're going to be the breakfast. Get the hell out of there while you still have a chance!"

Kurt laughed. "This one ain't got much in the way of teeth. Looks like he's had some sort of an engine-room breakdown because his fogger strength is down a good 90 percent. He's beamed me several times, and all he's been able to do so far is give me a slight hangover."

"Then throw a couple of torps into him before he can rev up enough to star hop."

"Uh, uh! We're after bigger game. I've got a solid tracer lock on him and I've a hunch, crippled as he seems to be, that he's going to run for home. If he does, and we can hang on to him, we may be able to find the home base of those bastards. If just one of us can get back with the coordinates, the heavies can come in and chuck a few planet-busters. Hook on to me and follow along. I think he's just about to jump.''

Flick! As the tight-arrow formation jumped back into normal space, alarm gongs began clanging in each of the tiny ships. Kurt stared at the image on his battle screen and let out a low whistle. They'd come out within fifty miles of the Kierian base! And it wasn't a planet. It was a mother ship, a ship so big that the largest Imperial space cruiser would have looked like a gnat alongside it. And from it, like hornets from a disturbed nest, poured squadron after squadron of Kierian destroyers.

"Bird leader to fledglings! Red alert! Red alert! Scramble random 360. One of us has to stay clear long enough to get enough warper revs to jump. Zelda will take over if I get fogged! I. . . .'' The flight leader's voice trailed off as a narrow cone of jarring vibration flicked across his ship, triggering off a neural spasm that hammered him down into unconsciousness. The other scouts broke formation like a flight of frightened quail and zigzagged away from the Kierian attackers, twisting in a desperate attempt to escape the slashing fogger beams. One by one the other pilots were slammed into unconsciousness. Putting the other ships on slave circuit, Zelda threw the flight on emergency drive. Needles emerged from control seats and pumped anti-G drugs into the comatose pilots.

A quick calculation indicated that they couldn't make a sub-space jump from their present position. They were so close to the giant sun that its gravitational field would damp the warper nodes. The only thing to do was to run and find a place to hide until the pilots recovered consciousness. Then, while the others supplied a diversion, there was a chance that one might be able to break clear. The computer doubted that the Imperial battle fleet would have much of a chance against something as formidable as the Kierian mother ship, but that was something for fleet command to decide. Her job was to save the flight. There were five planets in the system, but only the nearest to the sun, a cloud-smothered giant, was close enough to offer possible sanctuary.

Setting a corkscrew evasion course and ignoring the fogger beams that lanced at her from the pursuing ships, she streaked for the protective cloud cover of the planet, programming the computers of the six ships that followed her on slave circuit to set them down at widely separated, randomly selected points. Kierian tracer beams would be useless once the flight was within the violent and wildly fluctuating magnetic field of the giant planet.

Once beneath the protective cloud cover, the other scouts took off on their separate courses, leaving Zelda, her commander still slumped in a mind-fog coma, to find her own sanctuary. Then at thirty thousand feet the ship's radiation detector suddenly triggered off a score of red danger lights on the instrument panel. From somewhere below, a sun-hot cone of lethal force was probing for the ship. After an almost instantaneous analysis of the nature of the threat, Zelda threw on a protective heterodyning canceler to shield the scout. Then she taped an evasive course that would take the little ship out of danger as soon as the retrorockets had slowed it enough to make a drastic course change possible without harm to its unconscious commander.

II

Gog's time had almost come. Reluctantly she withdrew her tubelike extractor from the cobalt-rich layer fifty yards below the surface. The propagation pressures inside her were too great to allow her to finish the lode, much less find another. The nerve stem inside the extractor shrank into her body, followed by the acid conduit and ultrasonic tap. Then, ponderously, she began to drag her gravid body toward a nearby ravine. She paused for a moment while a rear short-range projector centered in on a furtive scavenger who had designs on her unfinished meal. One burst and its two-hundred-foot length exploded into a broken heap of metallic and organic rubble. She was tempted to turn back—the remnants would have made a tasty morsel—but birthing pressures drove her on. Reaching the ravine at last, she squatted over it.

Slowly her ovipositor emerged from between sagging, armored buttocks. Gog strained and then moved on, leaving behind her a shining, five-hundred-foot-long egg.

Lighter now, her body quickly adapted for post egg-laying activities as sensors and projectors extruded from depressions in her tung-steel hide. Her semi-organic brain passed into a quiescent state while organo-metallic arrays of calculators and energy producers activated and joined into a network on her outer surfaces. The principal computor, located halfway down the fifteen-hundred-meter length of her grotesque body, activated and took over control of her formidable defenses. Then, everything in readiness, it triggered the egg.

The egg responded with a microwave pulse of such intensity that the sensitive antennae of several nearby lesser creatures grew hot, conducting a surge of power into their circuits that charred their internal organs and fused their metallic synapses.

Two hundred kilometers away, Magog woke from a gorged sleep as a strident mating call came pulsing in. He lunged erect, the whole kilometer of him. As he sucked the reducing atmosphere deep into the chain of ovens that served him as lungs, meter-wide nerve centers along his spinal columns pulsed with a voltage and current sufficient to fuse bus bars of several centimeters' cross section. A cannonlike sperm launcher emerged from his forehead and stiffened as infernos churned inside him. Then his towering bulk jerked as the first spermatozoon shot out, followed by a swarm that dwindled to a few stragglers. Emptied, Magog sagged to the ground and, suddenly hungry, began to rip up great slabs of igneous rock to get at the rich vein of ferrous ore his sensors detected deep beneath. Far to the east, Gog withdrew a prudent distance from her egg and squatted down to await the results of its mating call.

The spermatoza reached an altitude of half a kilometer before achieving homing ability. They circled, losing altitude until their newly activated homing mechanisms picked up the high-frequency emissions of the distant egg. Then tiny jets began pouring carbon dioxide, and flattened leading edges bit into the atmosphere as they arced toward their objective.

Each was a flattened cylinder, twenty meters long, with a scythe-shaped sensing element protruding from a flattened head, each with a pair of long tails connected at the trailing edge by a broad ribbon. It was an awesome armada, plowing through the turbulent atmosphere, homing on the distant signal.

As the leaders of the sperm swarm appeared over the horizon, Gog's sensors locked in. The selection time was near. Energy banks cut in and fuel converters began to seethe, preparing for the demands of the activated weapons system. At twenty kilometers a long-range beam locked in on the leading spermatozoon. It lacked evasive ability and a single frontal shot fused it. Its remnants spiraled to the surface, a mass of carbonized debris interspersed with droplets of glowing metal.

The shock of its destruction spread through the armada and stimulated wild, evasive gyrations on the part of the rest. But Gog's calculators predicted the course of one after another, and flickering bolts of energy burned them out of the sky. None was proving itself fit to survive. Then, suddenly, there was a moment of confusion in her intricate neural network. An intruder was approaching from the wrong direction. All her reserve projectors swiveled and spat a concentrated cone of lethal force at the rogue gamete that was screaming down through the atmosphere. Before the beam could take effect, a milky nimbus surrounded the approaching stranger and it continued on course unharmed. She shifted frequencies. The new bolt was as ineffective as the last. A ripple of excited anticipation ran through her great bulk. This was the one she'd been waiting for!

Gog was not a thinking entity in the usual sense, but she was equipped with a pattern of instinctive responses that told her that the gamete that was flashing down through the upper skies contained something precious in defensive armament that her species needed to survive. Mutations induced by the intense hard radiation from the nearby giant sun made each new generation of enemies even more terrible. Only if her egg were fertilized by a sperm bearing improved defensive and offensive characteristics would her offspring have a good chance of survival.

She relaxed her defenses and waited for the stranger to home in on her egg; but for some inexplicable reason, as it slowed down, it began to veer away. Instantly her energy converters and projectors combined to form a new beam, a cone that locked onto the escaping gamete and then narrowed and concentrated all its energy into a single, tight, titanic tractor. The stranger tried one evasive tactic after another, but inextricably it was drawn toward the waiting egg. Then, in response to her radiated command, the egg's shell weakened at the calculated point of impact. A moment later the stranger punched through the ovid wall and came to rest at the egg's exact center. Gog's scanners quickly encoded its components and made appropriate adjustments to the genes of the egg's nucleus.

Swiftly—the planet abounded in egg eaters—the fertilized ovum began to develop. It drew on the rich supply of heavy metals contained in the yoke sac to follow the altered genetic blueprint, incorporating in the growing embryo both the heritage of the strange gamete and that developed by Gog's race in its long fight to stay alive in a hostile environment. When the yolk sac nourishment was finally exhausted, Gog sent out a vibratory beam that cracked the shell of her egg into tiny fragments and freed the fledgling that had developed within. Leaving the strange new hybrid to fend for itself, she crawled back to her abandoned lode to feed and prepare for another laying. In four hours she would be ready to bear again.

III

As Kurt began to regain consciousness, mind still reeling from the aftereffects of the Kierian fogger beam, he opened his eyes with an effort.

"Don't say it," said the computer's voice box.

"Say what?" he mumbled.

" 'Where am I?' You wouldn't believe it if I told you."

Kurt shook his head to try to clear it of its fuzz. His front vision screen was on and strange things were happening. Zelda had obviously brought the scout down safely, but how long it was going to remain that way was open to question.

The screen showed a nightmare landscape, a narrow valley floor crisscrossed with ragged, smoking fissures. Low-hanging, boiling clouds were tinged an ugly red by the spouting firepits of the squat volcanoes that ringed the depression. It was a hobgoblin scene populated by hobgoblin forms. Strange shapes, seemingly of living metal, crawled, slithered and flapped. Titanic battles raged, victors ravenously consuming losers with maws like giant ore crushers, only to be vanquished and gulped down in turn by even more gigantic life forms, no two of which were quite alike.

A weird battle at one corner of the vision screen caught Kurt's attention, and he cranked up magnification. Half tank, half dinosaur, a lumbering creature the size of an imperial space cruiser was backed into a box canyon in the left escarpment, trying to defend itself against a pack of smaller but swifter horrors. A short thick projection stuck out from between its shoulders, pointing up at forty-five degrees like an ancient howitzer. As Kurt watched, flame suddenly flashed from it. A black spheroid arced out, fell among the attackers, and then exploded with a concussion that shook the scout, distant as it was. When the smoke cleared, a crater twenty feet deep marked where it had landed. Two of the smaller beasts were out of action, but the rest kept boring in, incredibly agile toadlike creatures twice the size of terrestrial elephants, spouting jets of some flaming substance and then skipping back.

This spectacular was suddenly interrupted when the computer said calmly, "If you think that's something, take a look at the rear scanner."

Kurt did and shuddered in spite of himself.

Crawling up behind the scout on stumpy, centipede legs was something the size of a lunar ore boat. Its front end was dotted with multifaceted eyes that revolved like radar bowls.

"What the hell is *that?*"

"Beats me," said Zelda, "but I think it wants us for lunch."

Kurt flipped on his combat controls and centered the beast on his cross hairs. "Couple right down the throat ought to discourage it."

"Might at that," said Zelda. "But you've got one small problem. Our armament isn't operational yet. The neural connections for the new stuff haven't finished knitting in yet."

"Listen, smart ass," said Kurt in exasperation, "this is no time for funnies. If we can't fight the ship, let's lift the hell out of here. That thing's big enough to swallow us whole."

"Can't lift either. The converters need more mass before they can crank out enough juice to activate the antigravs. We've only five kilomegs in the accumulators."

"Five!" howled Kurt. "I could lift the whole damn squadron with three. I'm getting out of here!"

His fingers danced over the control board, setting up the sequence for emergency takeoff. The ship shuddered but nothing happened. The rear screen showed that the creature was only two hundred yards away, its mouth a gaping cavern lined with chisel-like grinders.

Zelda made a chuckling sound. "Next time, listen to Mother. Strange things happened to all of us while you were in sleepy-bye land." A number of red lights on the combat readiness board began changing to green. "Knew it wouldn't take too much longer. Tell you what, why don't you suit up and go outside and watch while I take care of junior back there. You aren't going to believe what you're about to see, but hang with it. I'll explain everything when you get back. In the meantime I'll keep an eye on you."

Kurt made a dash for his space armor and wriggled into it. "I'm not running out on you, baby, but nothing seems to be working on this tub. If one of the other scouts is close enough, I may be able to raise him on my helmet phone and get him here soon enough to do us some good. But what about you?"

"Oh," said Zelda casually, "if worse comes to worst, I can always run away. We now have feet. Thirty on each side."

Kurt just snorted as he undogged the inner air-lock hatch.

Once outside he did the biggest and fastest double take in the history of man.

The scout did have feet. Lots of feet. And other things.

To begin with, though her general contours were the same, she'd grown from forty meters in length to two hundred. Her torp tubes had quadrupled in size and were many times more numerous. Between them, streamlined turrets housed wicked-looking devices whose purpose he didn't understand. One of them suddenly swiveled, pointed at a spot somewhat behind him, and spat an incandescent beam. He spun just in time to see something that looked like a ten-ton crocodile collapse into a molten puddle.

"Told you I'd keep an eye on you," said a cheerful voice in his helmet phone. "All central connections completed themselves while you were on your way out. Now we have teeth."

"So has our friend back there. Check aft!" The whatever-it-was was determinedly gnawing away on the rear tubes.

"He's just gumming. Our new hide makes the old one look like the skin of a jellyfish. Watch me nail him. But snap on your sun filter first. Otherwise you'll blind yourself."

Obediently Kurt pressed his polarizing stud. One of the scout's rear turrets swung around and buzzsaw vibration ran through the ground as a purple beam no thicker than a pencil slashed the attacker into piano-sized chunks. Then the reason for the scout's new pedal extremities became apparent as the ship quickly ran around in a circle. Reaching what was left of her attacker, she extended a wedge-shaped head from a depression in her bow and began to feed.

"Just the mass we needed," said Zelda. A tentacle suddenly emerged from a hidden port, circled Kurt's waist, and pulled him inside the ship. "Welcome aboard your new command. And now do you want to hear what's happened to us?"

When she finished, Kurt didn't comment. He couldn't. His vocal chords weren't working.

A shave, a shower, a steak, and three cups of coffee later, he gave a contented burp.

"Let's go find some worms and try out our new stuff," Zelda suggested.

"While I get fogged?"

"You won't. Wait and see."

Kurt shrugged dubiously and once again punched in the lifting sequence. This time when he pressed the activator stud the ship went shrieking up through the atmosphere. Gog, busily laying another egg, paid no attention to her strange offspring. Kurt paid attention to her, though.

Once out of the sheltering cloud cover, his detectors picked up three Kierian ships in stratospheric flight. They seemed to be systematically quartering the sun side of the planet in a deliberate search pattern. Then, as if they had detected one of the hidden scouts, they went into a steep purposeful dive. Concerns for his own safety suddenly were flushed away by the apparent threat to a defenseless ship from his flight. Kurt raced toward the alien ships under emergency thrust. The G needle climbed to twenty, but instead of the acceleration hammering him into organic pulp, it only pushed him back in his seat slightly.

The Kierians pulled up and turned to meet him. In spite of the size of the strange ship that was hurtling toward them, they didn't seem concerned. There was no reason why they should be. Their foggers could hammer a pilot unconscious long before he could pose a real threat.

Kurt felt a slight vibration run through the scout as an enemy beam caught him, but he didn't black out.

"Get the laser on the one that just hit you," Zelda suggested. "It has some of the new stuff hooked into it." Kurt did, and a bolt of raging energy raced back along the path of the fogger beam and converted the first attacker into a ball of ionized gas.

"Try torps on the other two."

"They never work. The Kierians warp out before they get within range."

"Want to bet? Give a try."

"What's to lose?" said Kurt. "Fire three and seven." He felt the shudder of the torpedoes leaving the ship, but their tracks didn't appear on his firing scope. "Where'd they go?"

"Subspace. Watch what happens to the worms when they flick out."

Suddenly the two dots that marked the enemy vanished in an actinic burst.

"Wow!" said Kurt in an awe-stricken voice, "we something, we is! But why didn't that fogger knock me out? New kind of shield?"

"Nope, new kind of pilot. The ship wasn't the only thing that was changed. And that ain't all. You've got all kinds of new equipment inside your head you don't know about yet."

"Such as?"

"For one thing," she said, "once you learn how to use it, you'll find that your brain can operate at almost 90 percent efficiency instead of its old 10. And that ain't all; your memory bank has twice the storage of a standard ship computer and you can calculate four times as fast. But don't get uppity, buster. You haven't learned to handle it yet. It's going to take months to get you up to full potential. In the meantime I'll babysit as usual."

Kurt had a sudden impulse to count fingers and toes to see if he still had the right number.

"My face didn't look any different when I shaved. Am I still human?"

"Of course," Zelda said soothingly. "You're just a better one, that's all. When the ship fertilized that egg, its cytoplasm went to work incorporating the best elements of both parent strains. Our own equipment was improved and the mother's was added to it. There was no way of sorting you out from the other ship components, and you were improved too. So relax."

Kurt tilted back his seat and stared thoughtfully at the ceiling for a long moment. "Well," he said at last, "best we go round up the rest of the flight."

"What about the Kierian mother ship?"

"We're still not tough enough to tackle something that big."

"But that thing down there was still laying eggs when we pulled out. If the whole flight. . . ." Her voice trailed off suggestively.

Kurt sat bolt upright in his seat, his face suddenly split with a wide grin.

"Bird leader to fledglings. You can come out from under them there rocks, children. Coast is clear and Daddy is about to take you on an egg hunt."

A babble of confused voices came from the communication panel speaker.

"One at a time!"

"What about those foggers?"

Kurt chuckled. "Tell them the facts of life, Zelda."

"The facts are," she said, her voice flat and impersonal, "that before too long you early birds are going to be able to get the worms before the worms get you."

Major Kurt Dixon, one-time sergeant in the 427th Light Maintenance Battalion of the Imperial Space Marines, grinned happily as he looked out at the spreading cloud of space debris that was all that was left of the Kierian mother ship. Then he punched the stud that sent a communication beam hurtling through hyperspace to Imperial Headquarters. "Commander Krogson, please, Dixon calling."

"One second, Major."

The Inspector General's granite features appeared on Kurt's communication screen. "Where the hell have you been?"

"Clobbering Kierians," Kurt said smugly, "but before we get into that, I'd like to have you relay a few impolite words to the egghead who put together the talking machine I have for a control computer."

"Oh, sorry about that, Kurt. You see, it was designed with Osaki in mind, and he does have a rather odd taste in women. When you get back, we'll remove the old personality implant and substitute one that's tailored to your specifications."

Kurt shook his head. "No, thanks. The old girl and I have been through some rather tight spots together, and even though she is a pain in the neck at times, I'd sort of like to keep her around just as she is.'' He reached over and gave an affectionate pat to the squat computer that was bolted to the deck beside him.

"That's nice,'' Krogson said, "but what's going on out there? What was that about clobbering Kierians?''

"They're finished. Kaput. Thanks to Zelda.''

"Who?''

"My computer.''

"What happened?''

Kurt gave a lazy grin. "Well, to begin with, I got laid.''

Afterword: The Wizard
and the Plumber

BRIAN W. ALDISS

This is going to be a tribute to the man whom I consider the finest artist ever to paint an SF cover, but there is an argument to undergo first. An argument about a Wizard and a Plumber.

Writing this, I have just returned from a mammoth event, a five-week-long science fiction occasion, which must have broken some sort of record. And not only an endurance record. For the occasion was not held in Los Angeles, or Tokyo, or Rio de Janeiro, or Trieste, or Copenhagen, or London, or one of those cities where they are traditionally kind to fantasy and science fiction. It was held in Sunderland, England.

Sunderland is not exactly one of Britain's foremost cities. Shipbuilding goes on there, and that is about all that the rest of the country knows; but Sunderland is currently celebrating 1300 years of existence with what it calls the Wearmouth 1300 Festival, the Wear being the local river. A monastery was founded there in 674 A.D.; the parish church still stands on the site. It seems to me a fine piece of madness, not to mention an indication of faith in the next 1300 years, to commemorate the centenary with a science fiction festival, which was christened "Beyond This Horizon" (Robert Heinlein please note).

The success of the event owed much to the director of the Arts Centre in Sunderland, Christopher Carrell. Among his many ambitious effects may be mentioned a superb catalogue and a glossy anthology of science fiction and fact which will undoubtedly be a collector's item (collectors interested should write, not to me, but

231

to Mr. Carrell at the Arts Centre, 17 Grange Terrace, Sunderland).

Among many thought-provoking items in the anthology is an article by Mark Adlard in which he seeks to establish an "Other Tradition" in SF. This he defines somewhat negatively as men who wrote science fiction but worked completely outside the pulp tradition. He includes in it authors like H. G. Wells, Jules Verne, and Olaf Stapledon.

His thesis is that these men chose SF as a medium in which they could say something which they wanted to say and which they thought was desperately important. Any SF hardware in their stories is incidental, and subordinate to their theme. Whereas, in pulp science fiction, "the mind-boggling ideas for which it is famous often do no more than explain the hardware."

What I would particularly like to draw attention to is a quotation Adlard uses from one of C. S. Lewis's essays in Lewis's posthumous volume *Of Other Worlds*. In this essay, Lewis says, "If some fatal progress of applied science ever enables us in fact to reach the Moon, that real journey will not at all satisfy the impulse which we now seek to gratify by writing such stories." He is making a plea for the imagination.

Adlard has evidently been brooding over this quotation for some while. He produced it in a recent issue of the British Science Fiction Association journal *Vector*, placing it there in striking juxtaposition to a quotation from Isaac Asimov, speaking in the James Gunn filmed interview. Asimov says, "The SF written in the '40s became fact in the '60s. When Armstrong stepped onto the Moon, it was justification of the work done by the writers in John Campbell's stable."

My personal feeling is that anyone (especially an author) who can believe either part of this proposition is self-deluded, and that in several directions—toward his own importance as a writer, toward the effectiveness of science fiction as a sort of glorified blueprint of the immediate future, and toward the nature of the kinds of experience which fiction (we'll clearly have to leave the word "literature" out of this) can provide. But my intention here is merely to discuss these conflicting points of view—the Wizard's and the Plumber's viewpoint—and indicate what sparks fly when they come together.

Deeply as I disagree with the Plumber, I also have reservations about the Wizard. In this disguise, as C. S. Lewis, he was deeply experienced in theological argument, and we can catch a whiff of rather stagnant Holy water in that phrase about the "fatal progress of applied science"—since, after all, one of the applications of science was to erode the foundations of Mother Church. But what the Wizard goes on to say becomes even more interesting: "No man would find an abiding strangeness on the Moon unless he were the sort of man who could find it in his own back garden. 'He who would bring home the wealth of the Indies must carry the wealth of the Indies with him.' "

This is acceptable. I have never got over the abiding strangeness of Earth, wherever I happen to be; even Southmoor, the village in which I live, continually interests and astounds me. So I suspect that the Wizard was being myopic in condemning actual lunar voyages. Apart from all the Plumber's reasons for getting to the Moon, which are of an economico-technico-politico sort of nature, there is a thunderingly good Wizard's reason for getting there. Many of us will then be able to look into the black lunar sky and realize just how abiding strange Earth is—to say nothing of how abiding strange we are, with our obscure sculptures of veiled bone and obsolescing animal claws at our fingertips.

Another factor we shouldn't forget is that the Wizard and the Plumber may seem like genuine opponents when one is standing in his pentagon and the other in his shower, or whatever these fabulous creatures stand in when on duty; but at other times they have interests in common. Among these interests is a concern to tell a tale.

You will recall that the article from which the C. S. Lewis quotations are taken is entitled "On Stories." It is a celebration of the pleasure and art of telling tales, the ordering of a series of imaginary events. The Wizard, whose business lies in spellbinding, has many stories to tell. The Plumber, whose business is strictly functional, also has stories to tell. So they are much alike in this respect.

And unlike in other respects. The Wizard, in telling his tale, will be careful to transport us to a different world or a different time. The Plumber may do that as well. But their intentions will be different. The intention of the Wizard is merely to keep us spell-bound; and, to this end, he will be sparing of his excitements and effects, in order to sustain what Lewis calls "a hushing spell on the imagination."

The Plumber makes the Wizard seem a very simple fellow. The Plumber works much harder. The Plumber, after all, labors at earning his living, and often makes a virtuous show of doing so, whereas the Wizard seems to have access to hidden gold. Because of this, the Plumber works twice as hard at holding his audience; he probably writes twice as much; he probably speaks twice as loudly, sweats twice as much, and fawns twice as hard on his readers. And what does he do in his stories? Why, he perpetually keeps up a series of excitements and narrow escapes, jokes, diversions, amazements, in order to weld the reader's gaze to his page.

Lewis, in his old-fashioned intellectual way, is skeptical about this expenditure of energy. He says, "In inferior romances, such as the American magazines of 'scientifiction' supply [Lewis was writing in 1947, but even so the use of the Gernsbackian term dates him—this was before he had a regular subscription to *F &SF*], we often come across a really suggestive idea. But the author has no expedient for keeping the story on the move except that of putting his hero into violent danger."

Lewis's theory is that in Romances, and he includes science fiction and fantasy in the category, we do not read because of the excitement; we read for the atmosphere. If we read only for excitement, then *kinds* of danger cannot be important, only the *amount* of danger. SF is frequently exciting, but what matters to us is that the fate which is about to overtake our central character is *not* a shot from a forty-five, or a broken heart, or a stampede of buffalo, but a—well, it could be a hitherto unheard-of disease, or a new mental illness, or a malignant life form, or the fact that the planet is about to blow up under him. The danger is there, but we require that it be a fantastic danger. This is what distinguishes us as science fiction readers. We may think that excitement and suspense are all-important, but what really nourishes us is giantism, otherness, the desolation of space, the anomia of a parking lot, etc. Almost an abstract of danger, you might say.

Much admiration and sympathy goes to the Plumber. We see how hard he works to entertain us; we appreciate how many marvels he parades before our very eyes; we understand how anxious he is to keep our attention and our custom. But perhaps we also vaguely comprehend that his means are in conflict with his ends, that his spells are ruined by his hyperthyroid activity.

The Plumber, whoever he may be, is often a clever man and understands the perils of his own situation; accordingly, he has devised a number of diversions which distract the attention. One of these is to claim that, since what he writes is not entirely successful as fiction, it is something more than fiction. He will say that it is designed to educate the young. Or to embody the myths of our day. Or to encourage would-be scientists. Or to predict what will really happen in the future.

It's hard luck on the Plumber, but fiction has to be judged as fiction or it's nothing. Even the Wizard has trouble enough when it comes to writing science fiction. Both of them dream up beautiful titles which by themselves take you halfway to some hitherto unimagined experience—"The Well at the World's End" (Lewis's example), "The Last Spaceship," "We All Died at Breakaway Station," "Deathworld," "The Left Hand of Darkness," "The Paradox Men," "The Terminal Beach," "Palos of the Dog Star," "The Naked Sun," "Beyond This Horizon"—but then they are faced with having to produce a whole book which lives up to (or survives) the promise of the title. It's a well-nigh impossible task, even for a Wizard who knows what he's doing. "Can a man write a story on Atlantis—or is it better to leave the word to work on its own?"

Which takes us back to the Sunderland Arts Festival.

There I met a man—and the man's work, which was more important—whose stories seem to combine good plumbing with skilled wizardry. Well, they really are not stories. They are paintings. Well, not paintings either, according to his rigorous definition. They are cover illustrations.

The man is Karel Thole. This was his first major exhibition in Britain or the United States, although his name is already well known through the work he has produced for Don Wollheim at Ace and DAW Books.

Mr. Thole was born in Holland, where he did poster work and book illustration. He moved to Milan in 1958, because it is the center of Italian publishing and from there, for Mondadori and other publishers, he has produced a steady stream of covers for science fiction novels.

What I admire about Thole as a man is that he is that rare thing, a Wizard masquerading as a Plumber, whereas there are numbers of Plumbers masquerading as Wizards. But I want to talk about his paintings, both for their own sake and because the subject of SF art has hitherto been missing from this annual column on which I perch like St. Stylites.

Let me show you just a few of the pictures in the Thole gallery.

A svelte woman standing before a strange round window; until we realize that it is an iris, we do not see that she is caught in an eye.

A man who opens the flesh of his face like the pages of a book to show us his teeth and the fissures behind: by way of illustration for Frank Belnap Long's *Lest Earth Be Conquered*.

A car with bumpers uncurled like mammoth horns, spearing a man with them on top of a pile of bodies.

Supernatural cities burning like torches on tall rock islands set in a somber lake.

A parched man, cracking as he leans to lick the parched ground: by way of illustration to J. G. Ballard's *The Drought*.

A superb domed city which represents Edmond Hamilton's *City at the World's End*.

One of the most enchanting pictures: a contented cat, with a grand old robot sitting in a wheelchair, amid a snowy landscape: by way of illustration to Robert Heinlein's *Door into Summer*.

A man in a lounge suit confronting, or possibly conducting, a herd of tyrannosaurs which stands smilingly around him.

A beautiful sleeping head with long trailing hair. Men stand on the coasts of a great sea of blood, looking across at it: by way of illustration to Howard Fast's *The General Zapped an Angel*.

Dozens of other pictures, with land battleships, machines like towns, piebald centaurs, women of rock and flesh, deserts, planets, calm faces and paranoid imagery. Here are Visconti's isolations, Goddard's amalgamations. Nipples become worlds, worlds eyeballs, eyeballs dung-beetles.

These descriptions suggest a strong horrific element in the Tholean landscape, and it certainly is there; but the delicacy of the coloring—and most of the paintings glow with light—provides a paradoxical light-heartedness to counterbalance the horror.

There are reminders of some of Thole's compatriots: Paul Delvaux, Magritte, and possibly Escher. But the organization of space, generally within a circular frame, is individual. A Thole is unmistakable a Thole; and whereas other cover artists follow trends, Thole originates them. His scenes have an ambiguity which none can rival. My favorites among SF artists include the great Paul, Dold, Powers, Emsh, Timmins, Orban, Frazetta, Schoenherr, and the delightful Japanese artist, Hiroshi Manabe, while Britain is now rich in SF artists, from established names like Eddie Jones and Josh Kirby, to newer ones like Chris Foss, Bob Habberfield, Andrew Stevenson, and Bruce Pennington. But Thole offers something unique—an enigmatic world in which the viewer's imagination is stimulated rather than bludgeoned.

That is the Wizard at work.

Yet Karel Thole insists he is a Plumber. He is by no means the first cover artist to work hard for his bread (though happily he earns a commendably large loaf). Characteristically, he never reads the novel he has to illustrate; his job, he says, is to sell it and, to that end, his publishers supply him with a short synopsis of subjects

—possibly sixteen lines, maybe less. From this synopsis he works, sitting down in the morning and completing the painting that day. Such is the pressure of work that he can rarely correct, rarely scrap and start again.

This is the Plumber at work.

Thole's work method fascinates me. At present I am writing a number of short stories on related themes (generally about art machines, as it happens), using a much looser technique than hitherto. I jot down a number of topics or phrases at random on a sheet of paper one day, and on the next day will sit down and free-associate a story from them. Sometimes the story seems to be startling and successful. This method is close to the Thole method, except that I am programming myself—and, I admit, I go back and do a lot of rewriting.

In Thole's work lies that "abiding strangeness" of which Lewis spoke. His superb visual sense carries him beyond the need of spurious excitements; he presents us with enigmas that are their own mysterious explanation, and there has never been another SF artist like him—a surrealist, not a mere illustrator.

Confronted with the array of his paintings at Sunderland, I thought again of Lewis's remark about the sort of SF writer who "has no expedient for keeping the story on the move except that of putting his hero into violent danger," and it occurred to me that most SF illustrators (Timmins was a notable exception) have used that same expedient to greater or lesser degree. The people in the Tholean landscape, however, are not in danger, or only rarely; they live among monsters and catastrophes; they undergo all kinds of alienation; but they remain untouched and undaunted. They are under an enchantment.

Something much more miraculous and interesting than mere danger has happened to them.

So—another Wizard is at work. This Wizard works like a Plumber. The old SF sweatshop suits his temperament, and for that we must be thankful. We are lucky that we have such a man around to illuminate our manuscripts.